DEPENDENTS

THE MENDING WAR CYCLE

BOOK ONE

DEPENDENTS

E. J. PENINGER

DEEPCALLS
PUBLISHING

This is a work of fiction. Names, characters, places, and incidents either are the product of the author's imagination or are used fictitiously. Any resemblance to actual persons, living or dead, events, or locales is entirely coincidental.

ebook - 978-1-7360129-3-2
paperback - 978-1-7360129-4-9

Cover Design:
Kirk DouPonce, DogEared Design dogeareddesign.com

Interior Design:
ProofYourBook.com

For Ernest, who taught our fathers
to anchor their souls.

SKAARAN

Contents

*Every day. Every day it's new. Every day
nothing changes. Every day I can't stop it.*

*The early morning mist in the Lupinwood
rises from the thick undergrowth.*

*I slow my breathing so my heart doesn't beat so loudly in
my ears. The cold air makes a thousand needles in my lungs.*

Be present. Focus. Listen.

*They are anywhere. They are everywhere. They killed
your father. They are animals. They have no soul.*

*There! Fifty paces northeast. Movement at the base
of a hawthorn. My men look to me. I give the silent
signal. We close in stealth. They take support positions
to prevent escape. One less Greefadth to harass my
outpost. He was foolish to venture this close to Rorgus.*

I draw the killing breath.

My father's dagger is thirsty.

Hesitation is my undoing.

The stroke is deft.

It is done.

The body folds neatly before me.

Not a Greefadth.

Not a son of magic at all.

A son of man.

Mine.

My only son.

My Titus.

Son of my youth.

Son of my love.

Son of my heart.

Darkness takes my mind.

And with it, madness.

1

The Errand

Kam woke in a sweat, panting. He sat up, rubbed his eyes, and reached for his tunic. Slipping it over his head, he felt his wife's gentle hand on his back.

"Titus?" her voice came softly to him.

"Always."

"It's been fifteen years, my darling," she said. "I thought I had lost you both that day. We must not build a house in that darkness. You were given back to me. Is that not reason enough to be glad?"

"It is," Kam said, as he finished dressing. Laurl's constant reminders were bittersweet drops of hope.

"Kiss me before you go," Laurl said. She thrust her arms outward, commanding his embrace. "I'll have breakfast ready when you've finished the morning's chores."

He pulled her out of bed and took her in his arms. Her embrace did much to quiet his mind every morning.

She somehow managed to put his ghost back in its box once again. Kam resolved to not be troubled as he pulled on his cloak and made for the door. Opening it, he found his farm blanketed with snow. The trees that his grandfather planted pointed their crooked fingers to the sky. Winter duties on the farm were not as tedious as the other seasons, and Kam made quick work of feeding stock and mucking stalls. Walking back to his dwelling, he glimpsed the yew grove in the northern part of his property. The snow-covered mounds there were a precious sight. The smell of baking cakes charged at him as he opened the door. Laurl had made him a plate of dried fruit and cheese and venison jerky. She was brewing tea.

"I've filled your horn with ale so you don't waste our money at the tavern when you go into town today." She was smirking.

"Money at the tavern is seldom wasted!" Kam said. "You know I like to listen to the travelers' stories of the Wilds. It reminds me that there is still life beyond the Wall. Besides, we had a good crop this year. We can afford simple pleasures."

Laurl heaved a sigh.

"Praius was asking to see you today," she said over her shoulder.

Kam felt a dark cloud descend on his spirit. His wife's mention of the Sage was unnerving.

"I won't have time," he said. "I've got to see the smith and the wainwright. Maughlin wanted to speak to me this afternoon about opening up some new fields along our border and moving a fence or two for the crop rotation. I'm very busy today, Laurl. Today is not a good day for Praius."

"With you, no day is a good day for Praius," she answered. "I told him you'd come by. Don't make me a liar for the sake of your pride. Please honor me in this."

"It's not right that you take liberties above your station with the Sage," Kam said. "He's odd. Everyone in Edraeth thinks so. No one goes out of their way to talk to him. Why do you feel the need to be so familiar? Do you know how many people look at me strangely? I've heard the rumors and whispers about you! About our family! Of all the things I adore about you, this is not one of them."

"I was leaving some of this year's harvest on his stoop as a token of thanks and he opened the door and spoke to me!" Laurl said in an exasperated tone. "How easily you forget that he helped us know where and when to plant this year! The least you could do is just go see him. I'm through with this discussion. I demand your honor in this matter. I do not withhold honor from you when you demand it. I belong to you, and you to me. Keep the peace in our home."

"I hate when you bring honor into it," Kam said grudgingly. "This case is not severe enough for all that. I will go see the old fool. I would ask you to not abuse the honor between us in such a way."

Laurl softened. "Please don't say he's a fool. He helped me when you were gone those two years and everyone took you for dead. He said it was very important."

She drew near and spoke low in his ear. "I am sorry for abusing honor between us. Now eat. There is a long day ahead of you."

Very little else was spoken at breakfast. Kam was tender toward his wife and spoke of the business of the farm when he did speak. After finishing breakfast, he walked over to the hearth and stirred the embers before placing a few logs on the fire. He returned to the table to kiss Laurl goodbye, and then made his way out the door.

Walking to the barn, Kam whistled an old tune his father taught him as a boy. He opened the barn door and approached his scythes hanging on the wall. Taking the longest one, he slung its strap over his shoulder and began the trip southeast toward the little town of Edraeth.

The golden orb of the sun grew in the sky above Kam as the town came into view. The familiar grey buildings of Edraeth clustered in rows upon the snowy back of a wide knoll, like protrusions on the spine of some great white and brown beast. *First things first*, he thought, *the smith will want his money*. The dense snow shifted beneath his boots. For a moment, the crunching brought a smile to his face.

Kam loved the winter, especially the snow. It caused his mind to hope that somehow life could carry on differently. Surroundings smelled cleaner, looked brighter. *The problem with snow*, he mused, *is that it never goes long unmolested*. His boots began to encounter brown slush as he entered Edraeth's outskirts. *The problem with snow,* he concluded, *is people*. He laughed so loudly at this cynical thought that he startled the smith's son.

"Apologies, Roen! I was lost in thought about the snow," Kam boomed.

"It... it is forgiven, sir," Roen stammered. He ceased his wood chopping long enough to peek up through his short, dark bangs at Kam in bewilderment. He straightened himself gradually and dusted flakes off his wool coat.

"Won't you come in, sir?" the boy motioned to Kam.

They tramped from snowy dirt onto reddish wood flooring, well-polished by years of busy feet. The thick walls bristled with metalworking tools and equipment. Every intimidating piece seemed to know its place. Near the forge, an enduring anvil stood resolutely in the center of the workshop.

"Is there something you needed, sir?" Roen spoke quietly.

"Where is your father?" Kam rumbled, following

Roen. "I am here to make good on my debt for him repairing my plow. I also need him to sharpen this scythe."

"My father is still on Pilgrimage to the Capital, sir," Roen said, taking the scythe and setting it in a corner. "I don't know when he will return, especially in light of this adverse weather." Kam noticed a wince from the boy.

Pilgrimage, ha! Plundering of our resources by the High Council... Poor lad. He's terrified of me. "It doesn't matter," Kam said, "Here are the fluerons that I owe your father— twenty, if I remember correctly. Now, make the mark! I'll have no smith's son making a thief out of me!"

Roen pivoted to his left, drew his father's signet from a wall drawer with his deft fingers, and traditionally sealed the agreement papers. A sideways grin tugged at his lips. Kam bid the young man good-day and departed, humming. On his way out, Kam thought he heard the boy chuckle.

Just outside the smithy, the wind picked up unexpectedly, wisps of air tugging at Kam's wool pants. His strange mood was blown away by it, and his attention now returned to his beloved Laurl's charge: *"Don't make me a liar for the sake of your pride!"*

Kam despised Praius.

He despised everything the Sage represented. Trudging down the main road, he was more than once tempted to turn in somewhere, anywhere. Here, the tanner's shop beckoned. There, the cobbler's seemed a haven. He could give ample reason for turning in. More than one errand needed tending to in Edraeth. *"Don't make me a liar for the sake of your pride!"* She always knew just what to say.

After a visit to the wainwright to commission a new cart, Kam found himself at the Sage's door at last. Winter nipped and clawed at his body, but the warmth emanating from this particular home felt sickening. To accept the invitation, even for physical comfort, seemed wrong to him. He rapped on the vertical planks weakly and wondered at his uncharacteristic state. *Perhaps the Sage is at the Kirk with the Elders, engaging in discussion of some useless philosophy to manipulate the affections of men,* Kam mused caustically. *Perhaps he is on Pilgrimage, will encounter thieves or beasts, and the town will finally be rid of him. Perhaps...*

"Come."

The dreaded utterance permeated the door and rang heavily in Kam's skull. He shivered slightly.

Crestfallen, Kam lifted the latch. The smells of earth, hearth, and pipe greeted him. If not for the gross fact that this dwelling housed the Sage, the place would be peace itself! It took a moment for Kam's eyes to adjust to the dimly lit room. Three tallow candles sputtered atop an intricately carved table. Sitting on it were books, both new and ancient. Some were weathered, while others were furry with dust, like little gray animals.

Kam had always wondered why the Sage had no

windows in his home. *What an odd little man!* Seldom was he seen in town. Villagers spoke about him only in whispers and rumors. Why Praius could not send word to him through an Acolyte or an Elder baffled Kam.

Time slowed to a crawl. With every silent second, Kam's anxiety roiled like the stormy sea. The frustrated man was a pillar rooted to the crimson rug. The strained atmosphere tightened its claws of unrest around his torso.

"Your barns are full, Kam? You are well?" Praius' tone was one of genuine interest and concern.

Kam turned for the first time to search the eyes of the speaker. The Sage sat in a fur-draped, wooden chair slightly pulled away from the book-laden table. His gentle, gray eyebrows rose in anticipation, revealing sky blue eyes. Taupe robes obscured Praius' outline, but Kam could tell that the Sage's stature did not come near his own.

"I am well, Keires," Kam managed. The title, *Keires*, was one that was inherited, and in Kam's opinion, unearned. He loathed the custom of giving such eminence to Praius.

"Your Laurl is a wise woman, farmer. Though she is wretched, as we all are, she employs kindness and frugality well."

"She *is* a gift, Keires. I am not learned in the ways of logic, but that much I know." Kam's deep voice resonated with more confidence in the room. He glimpsed the fireplace. The golden embers shifted, as if giving an ear to the conversation.

The Sage chuckled richly, and for a moment Kam could discern that Praius was just a man, even as his wife had said. It seemed right and acceptable to him that the Sage would praise his wife, for in many ways the statement complemented Kam's good sense to choose her. His temper toward the old man softened.

"Why do you hate me, Kam, as your fathers did?"

Caught off guard, Kam's answer was half-hearted at best. He fumbled slightly. "I...I do not hate you, Keires, I...I just don't understand all the inner workings of the council of Elders, and their dealings with you." Kam felt sick from the thinness of his ruse. He despised flattery and hypocrisy. *Why can't I ever just say what I want to say?* His chest tightened.

"You are kind," said Praius, slowly chewing on the words before releasing them, "However, you are a kind liar. Your father raised you to neglect the Ancient Wisdom, as his father did before him. You are proud. You are foolish. You desire isolation, independence. What you desire, however honest as it is, is an impossibility, *especially now*."

"Especially...now, Keires?" Kam stammered as his inner yearnings were exposed and thrown into a scorching light. *Independence.* He attempted to regain his protection after having it torn away. "I don't know what you mean. I have always been kind. I have always given tribute." He could sense an unfamiliar knot of anxiety rising in his throat. "All I ask of the Elders in return is peace. All I have ever

9

desired," he mocked, "is a simple life with my wife and stock. I am a good citizen of this country! I abide by the laws and give liberally to all who ask." He repeated his first argument: "I don't know what you mean."

A fire blazed suddenly within the eyes of the elderly man. A fire that seemed to be Praius' life source.

"The Oracle has called your name."

Kam flinched involuntarily. His fingers clenched into fists. Nails digging into his palms, he instantly became numb.

"There is a Vessel," Praius continued, "A Vessel given to the Oracle by His Father for the healing of all Skaaran. The Oracle is both vexed and saddened by the current state of the sons of men and of magic. This Rending must stop. The Innerlands and the Outerlands must come together. The Oracle seeks to make a Mending War upon all the land and would use the house of Hearthstone in the endeavor. You will walk through the Harrows to His Sanctum. You will retrieve this Vessel. You are the one chosen to escort me to..."

"The Oracle is not real!" Kam's slashing outburst stole his breath for a moment, and he realized that he had been holding it. Furiously, he dragged air into his starved lungs. Expelling pent-up rage, his plowman's arms waved about with conviction. "The Oracle is nothing more than a child's story! Praius, we both know that He is simply a creation of the Elders to breed superstition among the people for the purpose of control! The people respond to the story of the Oracle out of fear. *That* is how the Elders rule! No one can give reports of the Oracle-"

"I know that is what your father has raised you to believe all your life," answered the Sage calmly with even words, "but truth is truth, whether you affirm it or not."

Wrenching his gaze away and turning his back on the old man, Kam stared into the fire. "Where, then, are the witnesses?" Kam countered. "Where are the reports? No one has seen or spoken to the Oracle in my father's, or even grandfather's lifetime! Your Oracle has been silent for hundreds of years." Kam faced the Sage again, "And now you, mighty Praius, are supposing me to believe that He has spoken? Now? After hundreds of years? After dozens of generations? And to *whom* has He spoken? *Whom* has He called? Me? I have heard nothing! None of it is real!"

"The Oracle is the only truth in this world," chanted the Sage with intensity, "The Oracle speaks the Ancient Wisdom. The Oracle-"

"Save your rites and rituals for one who fears and believes, Praius! I'll have none of your sorcery!" Kam bellowed, his own shouts haunting the air.

"It is more than ritual," the Sage continued, unmoved. His tone rose to a climax as he shook his head. "The Oracle merely speaks, and things come to be. You *will* find yourself before Him. When you do, you will desire what He desires. The Ancient Wisdom speaks of the Oracle's beauty. The Song speaks of a Vessel of Power given to the

Oracle by His father. The time has come for you to retrieve this gift for the mending of the sons of magic and men. Then, you will come to me and give report. You will witness all these things yourself because He has called your name."

Kam gnashed his teeth at the Sage. "Never," Kam spit out, "I will *never* take part in such folly. May the superstition you breed turn to dust with you!"

With that cursing, he uprooted himself from the crimson rug, turned on one leather-clad foot, and clomped back toward the fateful doorway. Anger swelled with every heavy heartbeat. Bloodless fingers trembled on the latch. Kam forced away his scowl before risking a spectacle. He moved the door slowly; its hinges clamored. The whole departure seemed to pass in slow motion until the hollow sound of the closing door met Kam's ears; the frozen wind groped again at his clothes, and he stood in the moist dirt. He ground his right foot into the snowy soil.

"Curse that man!" He raged under his breath. "Curse the Elders! Curse the acolytes! Curse the Oracle...and curse my wife for sending me on such an errand! All I want is that which is mine. I am a peace-loving man. I am a good man, a law-abiding man! I work all day and strive with no one. I have no reason to be troubled by these..."

"Kam Hearthstone."

Kam suddenly looked up to see a man in dark armor draped in a heavy cloak. The wind whipped around them both and drove snow from the trees to their feet. The man was smoking a long, clay pipe that stuck out from a mass of beard that crept up almost to his eyes. The eyes were dark and reflected the bowl's embers when took a long draw. The man blew a cloud of smoke.

"You are Hearthstone, are you not?"

"A little far from the Capital, aren't you?" Kam asked, noticing the man's regalia. "Listen friend, I need to be on my way home to my wife. I have just received some very disturbing news."

"Seems to be the day for that," the man answered. "I am Skotos, Captain of the Shadow Guard of Skaaroth. I have been sent from the Capital city with a grave report. Starsgol has again come to Skaaran. He prowls the Daritundii plains north of Kofthus. Our sentinels on the Northern Wall between Soneluu and Vinnaes have spied many grey riders on blood-red horses prowling for weeks. From the northern reaches of the Lupinwood to Setertund, they fly the flags of abomination. It's almost like they lay in wait for something. Our spies in Setertund have risked everything to bring us this report: The forces of Starsgol seek vengeance on the house of Hearthstone for defeats suffered in the past age."

"Starsgol is dead," Kam said. "The ancestor whose name I bear made certain of that. Or have you not heard the legend? My family has been used time and time again to the point of being used up. My father served the High Council in your last great Rending War. *I* served *my* time, both in Skaaroth and at Rorgus! What more does your High Council want?"

"Nothing, my lord," Skotos said, bowing slightly. "We wish you only to be on your guard against this new threat."

Kam took a few steps to leave but heard the Captain speak again.

"There is just one more thing. A token."

Kam turned on his heels in anger but was arrested by the sight before him. Skotos was holding out Kam's father's dagger.

"Intricately ornate isn't it?" the Captain admired. "Xander Hearthstone's prize. I've only heard tales of its beauty."

"Where did you get that?" Kam asked in horror. He felt the ghost coming out of its box.

"A young man gave it to me when he heard I was coming here. Told me to deliver it only to you. He was on his way to Rorgus."

Skotos placed the dagger in Kam's open hand.

"This dagger is cursed." Kam's nerves were on the edge of breaking. "The young man. How did he come by this? What does he look like? What is his name?"

"Can't be more than twenty-five summers," Skotos replied. "A little more than a horse's shoulder high, raven black hair, deep blue eyes. Said he's always had it. Called himself Titus."

2

The Song

*T*he Oracle. Starsgol's return. Xander's dagger. Kam was reeling when he came to the fork in the road. *The solstice is just days away. How could I leave Laurl? This can't be true!* He turned right and made for the dwelling that was planted in the middle of an apple grove. *Maughlin will have answers. He will help me make sense of this.* Kam spied his neighbor through the window. Tapping on it, Kam saw Maughlin turn around suddenly and gesture for him to enter.

"Good evening, friend!" Maughlin said as Kam found a stool.

"Good evening, uncle." Kam said.

"Well now, something must be amiss," Maughlin

said, chuckling. "You only call me that when you are out of sorts."

"A Shadow Guardsman from Skaaroth has come to Edraeth, Maughlin." Kam watched the old man's brow wrinkle. "He brings word from spies in Setertund that Starsgol roams the northern plains beyond the Wall."

"Are you sure this Guardsman comes from the Capital?"

"He was in full regalia," Kam said. "I didn't check his signet. I'm not very familiar with the Shadow Guard. The troop was just being formed and trained when I left for my time in Rorgus. What do you know of them, uncle?"

"Not much," said Maughlin. "They're assigned to deal with threats from the Underlands." Noticing Kam's ale-horn, Maughlin brought him a mug. "How can Starsgol roam the Daritundii plains? He's dead."

"Tell that to the Guardsman." Kam said, pouring the ale. "There is something more, Maughlin. I..." Kam didn't even want to finish his sentence. "I went to see Praius today."

The dwelling erupted in deep, rich laughter.

"Why would you go see the Keires? Are you well?" Maughlin asked. "Come here son, let me see if you have a fever!"

"This is no joke, Maughlin." Kam finished the ale in his horn. "Laurl made me go. She was relentless, so I went. He told me the Oracle has chosen me to retrieve some Vessel of Power."

"Enough!" Maughlin suddenly looked concerned. "This conversation must not continue here. Your wife must be a part of it. Not another word, Kam. Let us go to her."

Kam felt himself being escorted very quickly out of Maughlin's dwelling and down the road to Hearthstone land. The afternoon sun was carving its path toward the small mountains that made the western boundary when Kam's home came into view. Laurl was standing in the doorway. Kam's mood toward her was a wash of emotion. *Oh, that woman!* When they drew closer, Laurl ran to meet them across the frigid expanse in bare feet. Kam threw his arms out as Laurl leapt into them. She covered him in kisses. Maughlin laughed.

"Oh, love," Laurl said, "I know you've had a hard day. Thank you for seeing Praius. You must tell me all about the news! What was it? What did he say?"

"Inside, inside!" Kam said. "You act like you haven't seen me in a year!"

Kam carried Laurl as he loved to do, and when they at last were all inside, he set her down so he could tend the fire. Laurl brewed a pot of tea. She served her guest and her beloved and sat down to listen. Kam spent the better part of an hour telling of all the day's events. He did his best to remember all the details of the conversation with the Sage. He hung his head a little in shame when he spoke of his reaction to the Oracle's call, but Kam kept nothing hidden concerning the conversation.

"What does it all mean, Maughlin?" Laurl asked.

"Well…" Maughlin began. "I don't believe there is any coincidence in the two different pieces of news. If Starsgol has indeed returned, you will need the Oracle's help. It doesn't matter what you believe at this point, Kam. If what this warrior from Skaaroth says is true, nothing will stop Starsgol. Not the Wall, not the garrison. Nothing. All of Edraeth is in danger as long as you are here. We will go to the Kirk tomorrow morning and speak with the Elders."

"I can't believe you are taking these sprite's stories so seriously, Maughlin! The sons of magic are diminished. They have been through plagues and wars and huntings." Kam said. "They are on the verge of extinction, and you think we are the ones in danger?"

"We will talk to the Elders in the morning." Maughlin said again, handing his cup to Luarl. "I will meet you at the fork. Get some rest, Son."

Kam stood and embraced his oldest friend. He knew that when Maughlin said something twice, that was the end of a matter. His thoughts turned to the dagger. *I can't trouble Laurl with this now.* Kam watched Laurl walk Maughlin to the door and bid him farewell. *I'll have opportunity to speak with Maughlin soon enough…* As she barred the door, he heard her speak.

"I can only imagine what you're feeling, Kam. You know you can always share your heart with me."

"I don't know what to share, Laurl. I honestly don't know what to think of all this. You know I don't believe in much of what you do. You love the old ways, the traditions that Praius holds to so tightly. You sing the songs, you keep the feasts. That's not my way. I was the truest believer until the day we lost..." Kam had to swallow a feeling he tried to kill every day: his guilt. "If ever I lost you..." Kam saw tears blooming in her eyes. "This whole day has been too much for me."

"Then Maughlin is right." Laurl said, wiping her eyes. "You should get some rest. Here," she handed him a bowl. "I have your favorite stew prepared. Eat all of it."

With that, Laurl sat down on the floor at his feet and began to mend some torn garments. The gesture of respect was not lost on Kam. *Such a strong woman. Yet she employs her strength to care for me.*

For as much as he suffered throughout the day, Kam tasted the joys of home and love with every bite. The woman at his feet worked so hard to preserve his sanity on a daily basis. With all her faults, she was his truest love.

"Laurl?"

"Yes, husband."

"Why do you take such great pains to love me so?"

She was silent for many moments and just stared into the fire. At last she turned to look up at him and smiled.

"Because I live for adventure."

"You mock me!" Kam chided. "My question was serious, Laurl!"

"So was my answer, Kam." Laurl said. "Now, to bed. I'll be in shortly."

Kam gave her the empty bowl and one more kiss on the cheek before making his way to their bed. As he lay facing the small light of the fire, he watched Laurl cleaning until he could no longer keep his eyes open. He fell asleep to her humming an old tune.

"Kam!" a woman's voice cried out in the darkness. "Kam Hearthstone! Help! We need help here!"

"Where are you?" Kam cried back.

"Here! Please hurry! He is wounded!" came the voice again.

"I can't see anything!" Kam answered. "Do you have light with you? A torch? Anything?"

From the voice in the distance a song rang out, and a light shone forth. The song danced with Kam's being like the very elements themselves. Storming, burning, and crashing with one another in a structured tempo and melody; the verses were contained in perfect order. Intonations both ancient and cosmic sang and percussed, dashed and frolicked. Mystery lived in it, like the trackless oceans and starry infinitudes, the rushing rivers and steadfast rocks: all the wild things surmounting mortal comprehension or control. It was very far away, but Kam found the song useful to get his bearings. He began to run toward the light, but just as he made some progress, the song stopped and the darkness returned.

"Sing again!" Kam called out through the darkness, which seemed even darker now. He ached to know the song, indeed, to sing it. But the enchanted music did not return.

"Sing again!" Kam shouted. "I need the light to help you! Sing out! Send the light again!"

"Kam!" the voice came. This time it sounded more familiar. "Kam!"

"Kam! Wake up!"

Kam opened his eyes to find Laurl shaking him. Dawn was creeping into the room. He was soaked with sweat.

"Are you all right, love?" Laurl asked. "You're feverish! I have been trying to wake you for quite some time now. You woke me with your shouting."

"I…" Kam had to grasp his surroundings. "The darkness was so deep, Laurl. Like the thickest cloak. There was trouble. A woman cried out for help, but I couldn't find her. Someone was hurt. They knew I was there and were calling for me."

"It was only a dream, Kam. Everything is all right."

"There was something more, Laurl." Kam said, trying to draw deep breaths. "There was a *song*. It sent out *light*. I can't begin to describe it, but it was full of both desperation and hope all at once. It felt like all the elements of nature were at war within me. Have you ever heard of such a thing?"

Laurl suddenly had a faraway look.

"*The Song.*" She whispered.

"Which one?"

She did not answer, but remained transfixed.

"Which song are you talking about, Laurl?" Kam repeated. "Laurl! Can you hear me?"

Kam tried to shake his wife out of the trance with no success. Being no stranger to these fits, Kam quickly dressed himself and made long strides to Maughlin's. Halfway there, he broke into a run as the morning light was growing. Taking yesterday's track, he made good time through the packed snow. Reaching the front door, Kam did not even knock. He threw the door open with great commotion.

"Maughlin!" Kam called out. "Maughlin! Wake up! Laurl has gone again. Maughlin!"

"Here. I'm here, son." Maughlin said, working to rouse himself. "What do you mean, she's gone?"

"I don't know, Maughlin." Kam said. "Wherever she *goes* at the feasts, or when we talk of her people for a long time, or the old songs. I don't know where she goes! I can normally bring her back, but this morning is different."

"Well, where is she now?" Maughlin asked.

"Home."

Maughlin rose from his bed fully clothed. Kam smiled

and shook his head at his eccentric friend. He watched the old man walk to the full log mantelpiece and pick up a small chest. Opening it quickly to check the contents and shutting it again, Maughlin tucked it under his arm and gestured for them to leave. They followed the well-packed track back to the Hearthstones' dwelling and quickly went inside. Finding Laurl where Kam left her, Maughlin pointed to the kitchen.

"Stoke the fire and boil some water, Kam."

Kam set to work while Maughlin took some of the herbs from the chest and measured them out into Laurl's big mortar. Kam watched as Maughlin carefully ground the mixture into a powder. Finding a large bowl, Maughlin combined the boiling water with the powder. He held the mixture up to Laurl's nose so the pungent steam filled the air all around her. She blinked several times and looked directly at Maughlin.

"Welcome back," Maughlin said, handing her the bowl. "You should drink some. It will give you clarity of mind."

Laurl looked around the room. Kam saw embarrassment light upon her face.

"How long this time?" she asked.

"Only a few minutes," Kam said. "What was it this time? Where did you go?"

"Hard to describe... It was like the dawning of the world. So much light."

"Which song did you hear, Laurl?" Maughlin asked.

"I didn't know it." Laurl said. "I've never heard it before. It was frightening, actually. Maughlin, we've sung hundreds here at home and at the feasts. But this one..."

"What was frightening?" Kam asked, hoping for understanding. "Was it dark? Was the sound dark?"

"Not at all..." Laurl said, still half-way dreaming. "It was bright. It was so bright, Kam. Brighter than the sun. Beyond its radiance. It threatened to consume everything..."

"That's enough, Laurl," said Maughlin. "Drink the rest of my tonic. Think no more of it for now. You must stay here. Kam and I are going to the Kirk to seek out the Elders' counsel. Do as I say now. Have a care for yourself."

"Of course, Maughlin," she answered. "I will await your return."

3

The Verdict

Kam's feet set him on the snowy track to Edraeth for a second day, and he nearly flew over the road. This was not his unwilling plod of yesterday. Maughlin kept pace, and Kam wondered how he must look being so driven by *barbarian superstitions*. Little was said between them on the road. Kam more than once glanced at Maughlin. The older man's expression of severity did nothing to ease Kam's mind concerning the day's business ahead.

"I wish my father were here with us," Kam said after they had walked a while.

"As much as I miss him, he would have tried to talk us out of consulting with the Elders," said Maughlin. "Especially with half of them gone to Skaaroth on Pilgrimage."

"In all my days I have never understood why we send a

quarter of our resources with half of our Elders every year to Skaaroth, Maughlin."

"It is a tribute, son. The Capital is limited in what it can produce. There are many people there. We show our unity as Innerlanders in caring for our leaders and their people. We have more than enough provision left over."

"It's a waste."

"Rotting food is a waste, Kam. Full bellies are a joy both to the giver and the gainer of them. The Ancient Wisdom says..."

"That's for Ancient Wisdom!" Kam said, spitting on the ground. "Out of love for me, uncle, please do not speak of it!"

"It is out of love for you that I *do*, son."

Choosing not to continue the conversation further, Kam put his head down and trudged on. He didn't look up again until they passed the tanner's shop on the out-skirts of town. Kam spotted the twisting spire of the Kirk. In the east, it climbed up like a corkscrewing horn of a beast, imposing itself on the skyline. He tried to set his mind to the meeting ahead but could not escape the dream from the night before.

The song. The words. The light.

The sounds.

Branded in his mind as with a hot iron, there was no escaping them now. The two men slowed to a walk, and then a measured stroll. *Where do I even begin with the*

Elders? Kam mused. *How will I keep my temper if they ask about the Oracle? How will they not think me entirely, hopelessly mad? Hearthstone is a stoic name, a skeptic name. We do not subscribe to giants' fables and sprites' stories.*

At that moment, the sky loosed a thunderclap that shook Kam from his musings. He looked up only to see frigid raindrops starting to fall in sheets. The Kirk loomed just ahead. Maughlin motioned for them to run.

The now soaked companions arrived at the etched marble stoop of the Kirk. The white stone with its black veins glistened as if lacquered. Kam's boots ascended its three graven steps, and he groped for recollections of the Kirk—a place he did not frequent. Between these portentous walls where voices echoed like ghostly whispers, he had stood. He had come here many years ago as a child... just after the Rending War—when Maughlin had led him here to lay his father to rest...

Lions and winged beasts romped motionlessly across the risers of the stairs, staring bleakly back at Kam with sullen eyes. Some uniquely skilled artist had rendered them almost cognizant, even critical of the happenings in their surroundings. He stood in the shelter of the stoop for a moment and studied them.

Vaulting to the sky, the convex front wall of the Kirk dwarfed the men. Kam grunted unconsciously, for the great cedar door now rose before him. Its intricacy immersed his focus. Carvings of entwined leaves and vines played diagonally across the redwood door. A plain brass knocker nestled in its center. Resting his forearm upon it, Kam felt the door budge inwards, without even a telltale complaint from its hinges. They ventured a few steps into the empty, circular vestibule. The round foyer abutted another section on their left—a black, burrowing stone hall. To their right, the main chamber with its carven ceiling loomed past open doors. Inside sputtered a solitary candle upon a lonely footstool. Kam inhaled deeply, smelling the dank air. Dripping leaks from the roof tapped a resonating cadence in tiny, widespread puddles. For the slightest of moments he thought he recognized the rhythm from his dream.

The Song.

Shutting out all other perception, he focused on the familiar pattern of the falling water droplets, utterly engrossed. From a distant corner of the chamber that the light did not illuminate, a cryptic voice sounded forth.

"Welcome, Maughlin Ravenhill. We see you have Kam Hearthstone with you. Please wait where you are until the Council is assembled."

A large bell soon rang out several times between the intermittent peals of thunder. *Funny,* Kam mused. *I always mocked the bell ringing to convene this useless Council. Now look at me: a beggar in a fool's court.*

The time seemed to pass so slowly that Kam turned to walk outside.

"Call me when they're all here, uncle."

"Don't be foolish, Kam!" Maughlin said. "Turning your back on the Elders is not a good start to seeking their help."

Heaving a sigh, Kam turned again and assumed a more respectful posture. He resigned himself to wait. The bell rung out again, and Kam knew then that all the Elders were not yet in the Kirk.

"May I at least sit down, Maughlin? Is *that* disrespectful? There's no telling how long it will take these old men to get out of bed and make their way through this cloudburst! Honestly, can't we just come back?"

"We can *not* come back," Maughlin said, never taking his eyes off the front of the hall. "I think you may sit down. The Elders know what you think of them. Their expectations aren't that high when it comes to you." Kam noticed Maughlin smirking.

He found a dry spot and sat down. Being dependent upon a nonsensical form of government stirred up great irritation within him, and the longer he loitered against the wall, the more irritated he became. He felt like a youth again, enlisted in the martial school in Skaaroth, waiting for the master to begin class. He picked up random scattered pieces of straw and broke them into smaller bits to pass the time. Coming to the end of his patience, Kam heard the great door open suddenly. He looked up and saw Praius enter with two other Elders. Behind them was Skotos, the mysterious Captain of the Shadow Guard.

That figures. They must have taken conference before the meeting. No telling what ploys will emerge in the coming hour...

A single peal from the Kirk's intimidating bell rang out in announcement of the Council's convening, and Kam stood to walk forward with Maughlin. Reaching the middle of the great hall, the two stopped and stood attentively. Kam did his best to muster respect for the moment.

"Maughlin Ravenhill, you are a most welcome sight to this Council. Your wisdom and kindness have aided us in years past, and we thank the Oracle in advance for any words you would offer concerning this newest challenge that faces our little town."

Kam could not see the face of the speaker. The Council chairs formed a semicircle, and the middlemost chairs stood in shadow against the far wall. There were a few candles on tall stands scattered throughout the part of the room where the Elders sat, but these offered little help when it came to judging the facial expressions of the speaker.

"Sirs, please," Kam spoke out of turn. "I was visited in a dream last night by something that I would seek your counsel on..."

"We have order here, young Hearthstone!" the voice interrupted. "You will speak when we give you permission.

For now, we yield to Skotos of Skaaroth, Captain of the Shadow Guard: honored guest, and harbinger of dread tidings. Captain, you may begin."

"Thank you, my lord," Skotos said, stepping forward to stand between the Council and Kam. "A new threat from the Underlands has emerged. Starsgol, Execration of the Ruined Lands, has returned to seek the overthrow of the Oracle. He has been breathing threats against the Innerlands for weeks now in the open plains of the Daritundii. Our spies' reports confirm that grey riders fly the flags of abomination in their prowlings. They drive their blood-red horses beyond the point of madness. Ever their horns cry out in the deep night from the northern reaches of the Lupinwood to Setertund. We have even had some sightings along the Rending Wall as far south as Darmesh."

Skotos took measured paces as he continued.

"Before the Rending War, Starsgol's movement was shrouded by deception and misinformation. This current campaign is brazen and rash. Our sources think he has acquired something of the Oracle's. We fear the Vessel has fallen into the Enemy's hands."

"Not likely, my lords." Praius was quick to interject. "I spoke to the Oracle myself two days ago, and He assures me the Vessel is still within His possession. He does wish to lend His aid against this threat but desires to give the

Vessel to the one for whom it is destined. He has named Kam Hearthstone and issued a call."

"And has young Hearthstone responded to the call?" the spokesman for the Elders asked.

Heaving a sigh, Praius answered: "He has refused it. I have sought the Oracle for a replacement but have been met with silence. Until I hear otherwise, Kam is the one chosen."

"My lords, may I speak?" Kam asked, surprising even himself with his civility. "It unnerves me to hear this type of talk. Starsgol is dead. The Oracle has been silent for generations. Why would the Oracle call and choose someone who doesn't even believe in Him or fear His Name?"

"Because that is what the Oracle does!" a girl's voice rang out in the darkness. "If you would care to take five moments to listen to the Ancient Wisdom, you would know that."

"Fidaelii, that's enough now," Praius said, looking behind him. Addressing the Council, Praius changed his tone. "My lords, forgive my Acolyte. She is zealous for the Oracle's fame. Unfortunately, sometimes her zeal is unbecoming." Turning to Kam, he continued. "The girl is right though, Hearthstone. The Oracle's ways are beyond our understanding. He has called you. Whether you or I, or anyone else in this room agrees with His choice does not matter. The laws of our town state that you must answer that call. Just as pressing, this threat from Starsgol *must* be subdued. Your mother's ancestor was chosen. He was used in a mighty way in his generation. Do not besmirch that name now by cowering on your land. We are dependent upon your obedience to the Oracle's command."

"Cowering!" Kam raged. "Cowering! Who was made Lord High Arbiter by the High Council in Skaaroth for the purpose of purging the Outerlands of the sons of magic? Who led campaign after campaign into the Wilds when every other man in this town became fat from the increase of my lands? Cowering. How dare you? You who have yet to walk beyond the Wall! Cowering? You who have yet to endure the loss I live with every moment! Cowering! Were my father's sword at my side, you would see how much of a coward I am. Trouble me no more with your fool's speech, Praius."

Kam barely noticed Maughlin's strong arms restraining him from assaulting the Keires. The room was silent for several moments. The only sounds that reverberated off the high stone walls were those of Kam's labored breathing and Maughlin's calming whispers.

Kam wanted to leave that place more than he wanted to live. Yet his marrows insisted that the Elders held some keys to understanding the dream, the Sage's words, and the Oracle's call. He held nothing in common with these people. At once his father's voice rang out in his mind: *"The elders are very useful for gathering information concerning the inner workings of a man, Kam. Use them to your advantage. Garner what you may from them but keep them at the end of your arm in trust and philosophy. They are bound to barbarian superstition and tradition. Not all of their ways of discerning are backward, but the fiction they subscribe to can be pervasive. Guard yourself well if ever you find yourself among them.*" So lost in this memory, Kam hardly noticed the next words of the Council—

"The trouble, young Hearthstone, is you," the spokesman said. "Your outburst with the Keires is most unsettling. We have order here, Kam: order and decency given by the Oracle to our fathers, passed down for generations. Your grandfather was once a member of this Council, and your father served us faithfully. Despite their private passions and opinions, they were never so mastered by their tempers to the point of displaying such discourtesy as you have presented lately. We will give you one last chance to answer: Do you stand in open rebellion to the Oracle's call given to you by Praius? What say you to these charges, young man?"

The word *charges* struck at Kam and brought to him a sobering revelation. He stood unlearned in laws concerning the Keires! *Are these civil charges, or criminal?* He looked at Maughlin for answers but the old man just continued to stare straight ahead. To make any progress in moving closer to discovering the secrets of his dream, Kam realized he must now assume another posture.

For reasons still beyond his reckoning, he advanced

a few paces into the chamber and into the light of the candle. His knees pressed wearily against the coarse stone, Kam lowered his head before he spoke.

"Most gracious, noble sirs," Kam replied, his words pleasantly deliberate and evenly paced, "I am, as my father before me, servant to the will of the Elders. My loss of temper and undisciplined passions burst forth as from a child. I am at your mercies." At this point, the man who knelt became prostrate. His forehead dipped pitifully in a puddle of water. "I beg forgiveness of this court and of the Keires." He hoped his words resounded more sincerely than the angry pulse of his heart. He sought answers alone; this display was employed to achieve that end. Hearing nothing but hesitant mumblings at the other end of the Kirk, Kam surreptitiously lifted his downturned eyes as far as they could stretch without raising his head. Making out only gloom and a few insignificant words like "father" and "pathway", Kam sighed. Foreign to him, one other word repeated in his head, sounding something like "*Ekkleon...*"

"Young man, there is something you must know," said the voice from the darkness. "We have been given the task by Praius, and ultimately by the Oracle himself, to govern the affairs of this little village. There are Elders elsewhere throughout the Innerlands, and you may go to them if you seek appeal. You will not likely find an ally in your plight elsewhere. Our verdict for you is thus: The Oracle's Call is absolute. His command supersedes every written law. You will seek out the Oracle's Sanctum and retrieve for us His Vessel as proof of your quest's completion."

Kam heard a shuffle of movement around him and found himself being helped back onto his feet by Praius and a young girl. *The Acolyte that reprimanded me.* As he stood, the voice continued.

"Praius and Fidaelii will accompany you to the pathway through the Harrows and beyond. Praius will be your best connection to the Oracle in the Wilds, and Fidaelii has served him all her life. You will be in good hands and will represent Edraeth well in this quest."

"Sirs," Maughlin interrupted. "Kam cannot go back into the Wilds alone. The Outerlands hold ghosts for him. There is an oath I swore to his dying father that binds me to him in this undertaking. I respectfully ask permission to go as well."

"So be it, Maughlin Ravenhill."

"I am indeed thankful for Maughlin's help," said Kam. "But to command that I take this child and the Keires into the Wilds beyond the Wall is folly. I've lost so many strong warriors to the Lupinwood and the northern plains that it is an everlasting sorrow. I cannot guarantee their safety."

"That much is wholly understood," said the spokesman of the Elders. "We however must submit our judgment to Praius. If his command is that he and the girl accompany you, that is the final word."

"I understand the risk, Kam," said Praius. "I was once a child of the Wilds. For many years I walked her paths, ate her food, attended to the sons of magic. I know many roads to the Sanctum. All will be well if we hold on to hope."

"And what of the child?" Kam asked. Addressing her directly, he said, "Have you been beyond the Wall, girl? Are you ready to meet a most certain and gruesome death?"

Kam watched her raise her eyes to pierce his. There was a strength there that he found rare, even among men from his past garrison.

"I will do whatever is asked of me."

"So be it!" the Elder's voice rang through the hall. "Make your preparations tonight. Gather your *rememberings*. Prepare yourselves for the Wilds. You have a Day's Grace to make ready. You all leave in the morning."

4

The Rememberings

Kam's limited knowledge of the law worked about in his mind: *What will be required of me from the Sage? What are rememberings...*

The man's feet dragged on the cold road.

Kam made his way from the Kirk to the west side of Edraeth, toward the river. A familiar banging echoed between the homes—the mallets rapping on the doors, nailing up some declaration. "No doubt the Council's judgment concerning me."

"Take heart, son."

Maughlin's voice was always a comfort. Kam stilled his thoughts for a moment. He purposed to try to gain some wisdom from his oldest friend.

"What does it all mean, Maughlin? This quest? The Day's Grace? Rememberings?"

For a heartbeat Maughlin uttered nothing. He stood erect in the dirt and spoke slowly, measuring his words.

"The Day's Grace... speaks of a change: a change in your citizenry, Kam, a change in your station...a change in your very life. You will never again be able to carry on as you did. You are... marked. Your life, like it or not, is now a thing totally set apart."

"But why must..." Kam tried to interrupt.

"You see it now as an inconvenience; you see it as a chore. The truth, however, is that you must now set your face as flint to the task before you—or perish. To waste the Day you've been given would be like resigning to die. My counsel to you, Kam, is this: gather things to yourself that remind you of your life. Don't waste your time with trinkets, mind you, but tools that will help you remember. They are a maddening thing, the Wilds. You of all people know this. The Outerlands will try to make you *forget* your old life, more than is your natural tendency to do. What you must do—more than eat, more than drink, or sleep, or fight, is *remember*. Remember who you were, who you are. Meditate on who you might become."

Kam watched Maughlin make great strides to him and intensify his tone. He knew that his old friend was digging deep from his soul by the look in his eyes. He'd seen it before.

"Food and clothing are important," Maughlin said. "Fire and daggers protect. But you must root out knowledge about yourself, discover what you've never known. Some men fear the Day's Grace and bury the truth deep under distraction to try to stay safe. You must instead open yourself up to it. Nothing becomes more maddening to a man than fighting the truth. It seems the most dangerous thing to give in to, but there is nothing safer. It seems the pinnacle of weakness to yield to it, but nothing can be stronger. When you forget, *remember* this one thing: the Ancient Wisdom remains. Our feelings, our hearts may fail. Our motives may crumble. But knowledge of the truth is a weight in the soul that anchors all things. We drift, Kam. As men, we naturally drift. We no sooner settle into a pattern than we find that pattern was inconsistency. And we are content to do so. I tell you this, nephew: your father, for all his valor, was a drifter. He *died* drifting. *You* have a chance to be different. You have a chance to anchor your soul. It is worth the danger, Kam. It truly is."

"And this Oracle will help me find the anchor?"

"He *is* the anchor, son."

"Why do you believe the Oracle is real, Maughlin? My father would tell me stories of great men and gods who performed deeds of valor and warred with one another in the heavens. He told me of Zeus and Hera, of Achilles and Jason and Hercules. Tales that thrilled my young life

41

and made me desire to be great. Isn't the Oracle just a tale like that?"

Maughlin smiled more deeply than Kam had ever seen.

"Many years ago, there was an orphan boy who was lost in the Aeries. His father and mother were killed in a Maisorvantii attack. They were seeking a new home here in Skaaran. They were strangers to this land, sojourners from across the sea. The boy was alone. He was cold, hungry, and miserable and lonely from the loss of his family. His father had hidden him when the great noise of Maisor wings rose on the winds. After two days of wandering, the boy was found by a man who carried provisions with him. The man took the boy back to his dwelling. It was a humble dwelling surrounded by a lush vineyard. There, the boy learned a great many things.

The most beautiful things that he learned were the songs that the man would sing. Some songs were practical. Their purpose was to help remember medicine or mathematics or history. But others... Other songs would cause things to happen: Protection. Light. Fierce fire. Magic. The man became a second father to the boy. He raised him as his own and withheld nothing from him. As the boy grew, he desired to share all he knew with everyone. The boy couldn't imagine such wonderful beauty being kept to one's self. With the man's blessing, the boy left the heights and came to the lowlands to teach the songs to others..."

"I've heard this tale before, Maughlin," Kam said. "Laurl has told it hundreds of times. It is the legend of the giving of the Brothers, the Sages. What does this tale have to do with the question I've asked you?"

Maughlin drew a deep breath.

"I am the boy who was lost in the Aeries."

"Maughlin, what you say is impossible. The Brothers have walked Skaaran for more than five hundred years. How can you be the boy of the legend?"

"There are explanations that will come in time, Kam. For now, you must keep this knowledge to yourself at all cost. No one must know my connection to the Sages or the Oracle. I tell you only that your faith in this quest will be strengthened. You will meet the Oracle because that is His desire. It was His desire to find me. Take courage, Kam. I will lend you all the aid I can. Speak nothing to Praius or Fidaelii or anyone else we meet on the Road. Promise me."

"You have my confidence, Maughlin."

"Good."

Kam didn't know whether to be comforted or disturbed. *Is Maughlin mad? He cannot be almost a full age of men old! What son of man can live hundreds of years and not die? What is happening? Everything is coming undone! Starsgol threatens at the Wall. My oldest friend is losing his mind, and I can't tell anyone.*

Kam was plunged into a sea of memories. *The Wilds.*

Kam saw himself as a child accompanying his father's troop on their occasional peacetime patrols. The glint of Xander Hearthstone's eyes seared Kam's conscience. Even now he could see their silver-blue gaze. Never before had his father even *dreamed* of braving the Harrows to wend the pathway. *The dead walk the Harrows...The dead... my Titus...*

"Uncle..."

"What is it, Kam?"

"I've been hiding something in my heart and mind and could not even tell Laurl what it is..."

"Don't carry needless burdens, Kam," Maughlin said. "You were just given trust by me. Return it now."

"You'll think me crazy," said Kam.

Maughlin chuckled. "I think there is more than enough room for that now in our friendship. I've just told you I'm hundreds of years old."

Kam reached in his satchel and pulled Xander's dagger out. He took Maughlin's hand and placed the dagger in his palm. He watched Maughlin's face turn white.

"How..." Maughlin stammered. "Where... I... I don't understand."

"The Shadow Guardsman gave it to me," said Kam. "The moment I left Praius' house, he was there waiting. Maughlin, you know this weapon better than I. You knew my father better than I. Is it really his? My memories are blurred by the madness and I fear that I am easily

44

manipulated. I've examined it as thoroughly as I could. Is it a fake?"

"What was said when Skotos gave it to you?" Maughlin asked. "Try your best to remember everything."

"He said a young man in Skaaroth gave it to him to deliver to me," Kam said. "No older than twenty-five... Raven black hair, blue eyes... No taller than a war-horse's shoulder."

Maughlin was studying the ornate scabbard and handle.

"Maughlin"

"Hmmm?"

"Did you hear what I said?"

"Yes."

"Skotos gave the name of the young man to me."

Before Kam could say the name, Maughlin held up one hand to silence him.

"It's not possible, son. Your boy is under the stones in your Yew grove next to your father. I was there. We all were. Praius and I were with Laurl almost every day for the first year when you were given up for dead."

"But what if it *was* possible Maughlin?" Kam pleaded. "My dream was possible! Your story is possible! Gods below, I'll even venture to say this call from the Oracle is possible if you will at least give me the slightest sliver of hope that my boy is alive again! I have to know!"

"I fear that there are too many coincidences colliding around you in the last day, Kam," Maughlin answered.

Handing the dagger back to Kam, his voice took a more hushed tone. "Keep this to yourself for now. You were wise not to trouble Laurl or reveal it to the Elders. Only you, I, and Skotos know of its existence. That is enough."

The old man's face remained in deep, troubled thought.

"I have money enough to provide for you before we return to Laurl. Come, son, let's see the merchants."

Maughlin's reaction shook Kam momentarily.

"Thank you, uncle." Kam embraced him.

As they made their way through the shops, Kam's mind became full of tales. Tales of Trampers, Lupines, Squallors, and Greefadths festered among the people of Rorgus, Kofthus, and Darmesh who journeyed to Edraeth to buy and trade for grain. Many stories were spun in the alehouse on a long winter's night—stories of experience and valor required for surviving an encounter out in the Wilds. Of late, all the tales from Rorgus revolved around the dragon peoples from the south. *The Maisorvantii...* The lands beyond Rorgus were peopled by tribes hostile to Kam's way of life—as well as to the Elders' "law."

Yet...somehow, amid the fray, I will find this "Path Way"? There exists, in the midst of unspeakable peril, a Being that cares for every detail of Edraeth? This assumption of the Elders *most* alarmed him, among others. The looming question gnawed at him. *If the Oracle is indeed real, why is He not active here among the people that speak of Him and adhere closely to His commandments?* It seemed to him that darkness lurked in these thoughts, and so he forced the enigma to leave his head.

Maughlin's generosity humbled Kam. As he watched Maughlin settle debts in every shop, he remembered the high praise that always came from his father's and grandfather's mouths concerning Maughlin and his family. They had been neighbors in the vale all of Kam's life. Some of his favorite moments growing up had been Maughlin's stories. Stories of adventures alongside Xander, of Kam's grandfather as an elder and the founding of the town, of the lean years with the crops...these were stories Kam begged time and again from Maughlin.

As the two made their way from merchant to merchant procuring supplies, Kam once again voiced his thanks to Maughlin.

"I'm glad you are coming with me into the Outerlands, Maughlin."

"I'm glad the Council gave me blessing. They know of the high regard in which I hold you. They know of my love for your father."

Kam clasped him on the shoulder. The two talked all the way to Kam's dwelling, where the smoke rose from the welcoming dinner fire that was blazing inside. As Kam opened the solid door, the song that was his wife's voice rose on the air to greet them. She embraced Kam and met his gaze with loving eyes. Knowing he would have a lot of answers to give, Kam poured Maughlin and himself a mug of mead and sat down at the table.

Kam studied the tiny cracks of the mug folded within his hands. His stare wandered to Maughlin, who sat to his right, swimming in thought. The old man still looked distracted, his hands folded on Kam's oak table where the three rested. His wrinkles pinched together between his brows. With a twinkle, his silver eyes flicked over to meet Kam's. Maughlin's mere glance beckoned Kam back to the discussion at hand.

How Kam longed to share the Day's Grace with Laurl! Yet everything came only in pieces. He scoured the maze of his mind for scraps of an explanation to fit together. The fire of his discussion about the dagger had disintegrated some of these fragments while a sudden wind of doubt scattered others outside the door of his mind. Unfortunately, the myriad of questions posed by his bride did nothing to aid his attempts at clarity that evening.

"What am I to do while you are away, Kam? Haven't you spent enough time beyond Rorgus? Why would the Oracle have you return to some of the darkest days of our life together?"

Fixed in his chair, Kam wrung his hands under the table. He groped for words. *Should I tell her why I'm really going? Should I tell her about the dagger? About Titus?* Kam opened his mouth to give an answer.

"Come now, Laurl!" cried Maughlin, gripping his

empty cup, "Let him alone for an hour or two. The best thing for him to do now is pack a satchel of rememberings."

"Rememberings? What could those be?" Laurl's voice faltered, her lips pursing. Maughlin pondered. "Well... Rememberings can be anything provoking a memory. They will be the most important objects for Kam to carry on his journey to the Oracle."

"What if Kam doesn't find Him?" Laurl threw up her hand, her tone rising to an impassioned crescendo. "Maughlin, help me to understand. What is the truth in this matter?"

As they continued speaking, a memory and a purpose captivated Kam's mind. It ambushed his thoughts. He leaned over to interrupt Maughlin and whispered something in his ear. Maughlin shook his head negatively.

"Uncle, please."

"What is it?" Laurl asked.

"Excuse me, Laurl. I must retrieve something for your husband," Maughlin said with a concerned look. "I will return shortly."

After Maughlin closed the door behind him, Kam spoke.

"Laurl, I need to go to the grove."

"Kam, I don't understand any of this."

"Maughlin has urged me to take this day to remember. A lot of who I am is in the yew grove."

Chair scraping across the dirt floor, he arose. Kam

walked to his wife and kissed her forehead before turning to the door, leaving the enticing scents of dinner behind. As he entered the wet blackness, the moon bathed him in grey. Owls perched nearby like watchmen. The mood of their murmurs drew his gaze outward. Nothing but darkness could be discerned. Fetching a carven torch, he struck it aflame.

Kam ambled down the rain-softened lane from his cottage. The moist ground held a welcomed embrace to his bare feet. Once he found the tallest walnut tree, he leaned against it. His eyes roamed up its high boughs, which stretched for the clouds. Their lofty shelter soothed him.

Closing his eyes, he tried to still his mind. On Laurl alone could he meditate. He envisioned her dancing and, oh, how she loved his music. Seeing her smile in his mind, her laughter serenaded the evening. Kam relived her kisses in the moonlight. He recalled her dreams of hearth and home and her adoration of the colors of harvest. Laurl's courage in their quarrels warmed him. Through even the difficult times, his love and respect for her increased. He imagined all that could be...

Most vividly, he remembered the wind playing with Laurl's wavy, raven-black hair in the summer sun. A sigh of pleasure escaped his lips. As he often did when matters were well between them, Kam desired to feel her silk curls slowly running through his rugged palms. Whenever he tramped home, he searched for her shimmering head atop their cottage's knoll. Each time he returned to her, her tresses danced blithely as she greeted him. Laurl's locks crowned her in pure glory.

The man under the tree grinned and pushed away from its craggy bark. Kam stared into the cloudy gloom, where his barn sat: a black square, the surrounding mountains a bumpy black line on the horizon. Images from past and present and imaginations of the future danced within his crowded mind. Like prime kindling, the pictures and memories roared up into a bonfire. The moon mounted the clouds above his fields as he walked toward the northern end of his land. Rich blue cloaked the low rises and dips. *The Song and the light.*

Upon entering an intricate grove of yew trees, he passed through the opening of the most treasured plot on his farm. Craggy branches bowed to the ground, forming an arched forest hall. He leaned against the massive trunk of the middlemost yew, firmly planting the dying torch beside it in the dirt. Just inside the thicket, he knelt, as was custom, to respect the fathers and mothers resting there. Examining their green-carpeted burial mounds, he noted the unique arrangements of limestones on top, designating generations. Each of them spoke the life's message of the one resting beneath.

Kam stood up.

He had not often visited the grove since his father's passing. Calmly circling around, he placed his hand on several of the burial mounds. His thoughts wandered to his youth and memories of his parents washed over him. When he rounded his mother's resting place, another smaller rise of grass summoned his gaze. He pressed his tensed fist to his forehead, calming his fervor. He knelt and placed his right hand on the mound.

"Good evening, Titus. Are you resting well, son?"

Kam choked back a strong inclination to weep. He fought the memories that assaulted the fortress of his mind. The mist of that morning. The smell of the Lupinwood. The words of his patrol... *Enough!*

Then, his eyes focused outwards. Slowly, Kam stood up and he approached his father's burying-place.

"Good evening, Father. I..." No words came for Kam.

"I... I must go back to the Outerlands, Father. After all that you've done. After all that I've done..." he gazed at his son's grave. "Maughlin says that this whole ordeal is both real and necessary. I'm sorry. I'm so sorry I must go back. But this will be the last time, I swear it." Kam knelt and kissed the ground covering his father. He walked to where his mother lay and knelt and kissed the soft grass there. Lastly, he walked the short distance to the smallest mound of the three. Lying down on the wet grass next to the mound, he placed his hand on the middle polished stone. He felt the engraved name there: *Titus*.

"Farewell, son. I go to gain peace for us all."

Kam rose, retrieved the extinguished torch, and made

his way back to his dwelling. His heart ached with gladness when he spied the glow of their fire. Laurl was boiling meat in a pot while wrapping dried fruits in crinkly parchment. Healthy aromas greeted Kam as his wife faithfully prepared food for his Road.

The opened door revealed Maughlin waiting in his chair at the table, an ornate chest was before him. Without a word, Kam walked to the table and opened the chest. Xander's light armor and his sword, his *kopis,* were expertly packed inside. Kam drew the kopis from its resting place and unsheathed it. Sheathing it again, he returned the deadly instrument back to the chest. *I have to tell her about the dagger and Titus. I can't leave without her knowing at least why...* He pulled the dagger from his satchel once again. Maughlin's eyes grew wide as he shook his head *no.*

"You need sleep, love," Laurl murmured over her shoulder. "There's no telling how much rest you will find in the Wilds..." Laurl turned, and her eyes fell on Kam's hands and what they gripped. Her lips separated in a silent gasp. Then they closed stiffly, and her complexion turned ghostly white. The woman's kind face twisted almost beyond recognition. She took the dagger from him.

"Kam, where did you get this?" She spoke as if it were a dying breath.

Kam was a stone, unable to move or speak.

"This... is... not possible." Laurl could not seem to

find the words. "Kam, you would seek to undo years of happiness which I have tirelessly worked to instill in you! Xander's ghost *must* stay locked away from this family, Kam! He is not welcome here!"

Laurl threw the dagger on the floor and hid her face, a piteous wail escaped through her hands.

Kam rushed to his beloved and took her in his arms.

"Maughlin instructed me to pack things that will aid me in remembering who I *had* been. My love," Kam sighed, placing his rough cheek against her soft one, "there are happy things I will take with me, but life is not all happiness. The river's rocks are smooth because they have been beaten by it. Sometimes our lives are beaten by sorrow. We can't blot out the world we know, Laurl. We can't live in a dream. *If* the Oracle is real, and *if* He is who everyone says He is, He will have answers. You need answers. I go to ask questions for you. This will help me remember." Laurl's tense posture loosened.

Kam went on to explain the story of meeting Skotos and his claims of the dagger's source.

Her hands were shaking, but Laurl found a way to retrieve the dagger from the floor. She handed it back to him and gently closed Kam's fingers over its hilt. She gave a wary peek at Maughlin, who was listening intently.

Kam drank in her beauty.

One tear came to her eye. Her brow quivered. Kam took in her emotions. His own tears warned him of their coming, and Laurl gently brushed the streak away. Overwhelmed, Kam fixed his gaze on his father's dagger. He barely noticed Laurl leaving him for the kitchen. He only looked up when he heard a squeal of grief from her.

All but the last of her gleaming curls lay in her open hand. A kitchen blade was gripped in the other. Frantic, he lunged to stop her.

"No!" Laurl pierced the silence. "No!" She severed the last strands of hair and held the mass up to his eyes. She settled herself with one deep breath.

"No. If you are determined to take *that* thing with you, you *will* take some happiness with you as well! You will take part of *me* with you!"

Before Kam could form an argument, she bound her thick locks together with one brown section of twine. She garnished it with one of her ribbons and placed it in his other hand.

"Put my hair in your satchel and think of me. Think of me when despair comes. Think of me in the darkness. Think of me in the Outerlands. Remember *me*." Her eyes blazed with passion.

"Oh, love."

A wave of ardor Kam had experienced while courting Laurl had crept into him. "I do not need this to think of you, but I will keep it always." Then were his tears unleashed, coursing shamelessly down his cheeks. Through them, he watched Laurl's hand rush to her mouth.

She flew into his arms.

After what seemed like years, Laurl pulled away from her husband's fond embrace and gave him a stern look.

She whispered, "Now, go, my husband. I have much work to do yet. You will find some bread and meat in the larder. Eat your fill and take your rest. I'll wake you at first light." Kam studied her silhouette. Her shorn hair stuck out like a forlorn, little mane on her head.

"Yes, love."

5

The Road to Rorgus

"Come! The Council will set us late on the road with their parting ceremony."

Maughlin's words seemed to swim in a sea of a million thoughts. Kam just stared at his now far-off dwelling. Laurl was in the doorway, her hand raised in parting. Kam could hear just a few notes of an old song she sang as a blessing for his journey. Then, as if desire from his heart commanded the wind itself, a breeze carried the last lines to him with great strength.

For though the Way in which you walk
There many dangers be
Just one moment there, and love
Will bring you back to me
Will bring you back to me

Dependents

Maughlin pressed the handle of Xander's sword, his *kopis*, into Kam's open hand. The younger man grunted, still fixed in the vision of his watching wife. His tears of last evening were held prisoner. Kam knew they would not be freed for many weeks to come. Turning at last, he made a few steps down the road toward the fork.

Every step burned. He could not fathom how his legs carried him forward. He forced himself to follow Maughlin. Hoisting his pack, he gazed backwards one last time, pausing on the drying road. Only a dab of black and a green speck of a dress remained of Laurl. Raising the polished sword in hand to her, a silent goodbye formed on his lips. After a moment, she turned and closed the door. Kam fixed his cottage, framed by his grandfather's trees upon its round rise, within his mind. *Clang!* Kam sheathed Xander's kopis as he started forward again.

The mountains vaulted to the heavens on their right, and ahead just to their left the Kirk's spire waited amid the grey roofs. Kam's feet numbed. The walk to Edraeth whizzed by in a blur. In what seemed like an instant, they stood before the Kirk. Maughlin tapped the brass knocker of the intricate red door. They waited some minutes. The carved creatures lurking on the step faces leered at him again. He leered back at them, and this time their glares appeared to weaken. The door squeaked. As the steward admitted them, Kam almost felt curious about the future. He sensed a new determination in himself.

The Council was convened. Kam's vision followed the ascending ceiling as they passed into the main chamber. Eight half-awake Council members stood facing them in a semicircle. A few inquisitive villagers loitered along the walls, including Roen, the smith's son. Kam averted his gaze and focused on the Sage who stood to their left at the head of the gathering. Praius had not changed. He did not glare at Kam or show any hatred whatsoever.

They met this last time with the Council to receive any final instructions. Praius began to offer his blessings for their journey. Fidaelii, the young Acolyte who was so vocal at the trial, stood attending the Keires. A shining, metallic cloak adorned her shoulders and billowed richly around her diminutive form. Kam couldn't help but be captivated by its ornate nature. As everyone settled, Kam examined her cloak.

Silver gilding curled throughout the bright garment bathed in blue. The crest of the town, a large tree swathed in flames, embellished its back. Fidaelii shifted, and the tree's leaves seemed to blow in a breeze. Cradling the tree, the outlines of two unstrung bows glinted green. From the tree flowed a river, and the silver water wrapped around both sides of the cloak. By her small boots the river ended in deltas sparkling on the cloak's corners.

As the Sage continued his prayer and blessing, Kam studied her face. The girl could not be more than twelve or thirteen summers old, yet as Kam looked at her, he saw a riddle wrapped in a mystery. Her long neck sprung from the cloak like a quail flushed from the bush. It tripped into a soft chin, which melted into some very rosy cheeks. This ever-present blush peeked out from behind raven-black hair that draped it like splendid, curly banners. Kam noticed the girl fidgeting.

Embarrassed for his absent-minded staring, he looked away. The concern for her care burdened him now more than ever. *They are all the more foolish for ordering this young girl to go with me into the Outerlands. She won't make it back, especially with such a cloak to mark her as an easy target...* This uncomfortable thought held him captive. Everything else that was said was lost upon him. The Sage's lips were moving, but Kam did not hear. Every gesture of the Keires, every warning sounded by the Council did not matter. He sneered to himself, his heavy brow creasing.

Then Skotos stepped forward and addressed the assembly.

"Revered Elders, Skaaroth does not wish for Edraeth to bear this burden alone. I have sent word to the Capital of my intent to journey with Kam and his company through the Harrows. As needed as I may be in Skaaroth, this quest will be instrumental in preserving our way of life. If we fail now, much may be undone from our past efforts to subdue the Sons of Magic beyond the Wall. If Starsgol is allowed to gather their tribes to himself, unimaginable evils may befall us. Therefore, I feel it is my duty to lay my hand to this task—with your permission."

"We welcome any help you may give, Skotos," came the reply.

Very few words after were spoken, and suddenly everyone was exiting the Kirk. Kam started and once again followed Maughlin. Out of the corner of his eye, Kam watched Fidaelii shoulder her petite pack. It did not mask the obscene brilliance of her apparel. Kam quietly fumed, sidling closer to Maughlin. "Could the Council be more foolish in how they dress her? Her cloak draws every eye!"

To Kam's further annoyance, Maughlin only stopped and sighed, "Ask the Council."

Kam did so with as much feigned grace as possible. One member, a grey-haired man with blurry eyes, rasped an answer. "The Oracle will approve of our young acolyte. We desire to please the Oracle with a worthy representation."

Flummoxed, Kam could only nod and politely thank the Council for their assistance. Troubling thoughts continued to gnaw at him as they departed Edraeth. Ten feet set their prints in the eastern road. Grey huts immediately transitioned into bushy plains. Stands of evergreen trees smattered the wide, brown landscape. The five traveled abreast when they could, Fidaelii in the middle.

Silence drenched the travelers. It pushed them forward. Absence of conversation piqued Kam's pace. His ear caught Maughlin's steady steps and the Acolyte's tiny padding. She would occasionally ask Praius a question, and he would reply. Once or twice, Kam glanced behind him to see Skotos bringing up the rear. Edraeth dwindled until it looked like scattered fragments on the horizon. Nothing but the drab expanse and tall shrubs greeted their vision, but this aspect roused thoughts of destination. The village soon disappeared completely from view. The purr of a familiar river met them. Its shallow ravine dropped on their left alongside the road. Kam spoke.

"The easiest way to Rorgus is southeast, following my river," he said. "Wouldn't you agree, Uncle?"

"Mmm," Maughlin nodded, searching for a path down to the bank. "It's the best way to keep safe from marauders, to be sure."

"Marauders?" the girl's eyes opened wide. "I was under the impression that the garrison at Rorgus patrolled the roads around our town."

"The garrison is... depleted of late, child." Skotos said, not wanting to get into details. "We are best served by not relying on them for safety."

"The Elders do not tell you every bit of news, eh, girl?" Kam smirked.

"The Elders do what they deem best!" Fidaelii gaped at Kam, hurt by the man's sneer, "And, I have a name. You would do well to use it. It may help you remember why we're going! Fidaelii means..."

"I know what it means, girl!" Kam snuffed. "The

Elders are cruel indeed in their judgments. They think I go on a quest for faith. They send with me a child that reminds me constantly of their thoughts and intents. I should just throw you in the river now and be rid of you. I could simply give report that you were set upon by a beast in the night. Or a sneaking Outerlander caught you." He let himself rant. Maughlin kept silent. "Or perhaps something worse: a sprite or giant or some other devilry found you out in the night, and that was your end. It gives room for wild speculation, especially with that cloak of yours shining like a beacon. Who knows? Whatever happens to you, there will be no extra care showed from me. You may put that down."

"Have a care, young Hearthstone," Praius said. "There are many valuable assets that Fidaelii possesses. Her place in this company is no coincidence. Once we pass the Gap..."

"Have a care for yourself, old fool!" Kam snapped back. "Oracle or no, you are all going to be in my domain soon. Make no mistake, all of you! *I* am the leader of this company. *I* will make whatever decisions need to be made on this journey. If I am to endure days and weeks away from my wife, I will have as much peace as possible." Turning again to face Fidaelii and Praius, he continued:

"Don't presume that I will have a care for either of you."

At that, the girl began to weep. Praius tried to comfort her.

63

Kam quickened his tramping, moving ahead of them.

"Hearthstone!" Skotos called after him. "Was all that necessary? We have a long Road, Kam! We must work together."

But Kam continued his quickened pace. He descended into the small ravine ahead of them and stepped onto a riverside path. Mud squished under his boots, and the kopis swinging at his left hip caught his attention. With a rasp that tickled his mind, Kam drew the weapon. Satisfaction shuddered through his right hand.

Both Praius and Maughlin could be heard trying to comfort Fidaelii with kind words, but she sobbed inconsolably. At times she cried so loudly that Kam heard nothing else.

Though her whimpering grated his patience to shreds, Kam kept close to the company. In this fashion he continued on, and the landscape did not alter. Monotony crept in. *When will the night come? This ravine is endless...*

"Why did you deal so harshly with the girl?"

Kam had not noticed the Shadow Guardsman catching up to him.

"I'm angry about her being here with us."

"She's here through no fault of her own. She attends the Keires."

"It's the height of folly, Skotos," Kam said. "These woods aren't even safe! Neither one of us can guarantee her return to Edraeth. Do you deny that?"

"Of course not," the Captain replied. "That still fails to justify you terrorizing her. If she is to die, let her face it on her terms. There will be enough terror from outside of this company. Another foolish outburst like that, and she'll have a defender in me."

"Fine, Captain. I'll not offend your sense of barbarian honor again."

"Don't be a fool, Kam!" Skotos said, grabbing Kam's shoulder to stop him. Kam wheeled around. Skotos continued. "This isn't a game! I don't know what scars you bear in your soul, but none in this company would have you come to harm. We would bear you to the Sanctum over our corpses if need be. We are for you! We will all perish if you don't start believing that."

I go only to find the truth concerning the dagger, Kam thought. *I go for Laurl. I go for myself.*

Kam looked over Skotos' shoulder to see the rest of the company standing behind the captain. All eyes seemed to be full of genuine concern. Kam tore his cloak from Skotos' hand. Turning east once more, Kam trudged until the sun was well at his back. Dusk was creeping over the tops of the trees when Kam came to a halt. He thrust his foot into the sand for balance.

Moonlight transformed the brown sand to crystal powder. Then it revealed something more. A narrow passage yawned from the ravine wall to Kam's right. He turned, eyebrows up. Slinking between root fingers that stuck out of the passage sides, he discovered an entwined alcove. The tree belonging to the roots soared above. Its tendrils encased the quaint hollow. Removing his boot, Kam wiggled his sweaty toes, feeling the dry grit. *Good... dry ground for pitching tents.* His pack hit the earth, his hands brushed the root-roof, and he grunted, stretching. Fingers rummaging, Kam drew out a hefty, woven fabric bundle. By the time he assembled his short shelter, footsteps sounded. He froze, peering out from his hole.

Four silhouettes picked their way toward him. Hunched shoulders overshadowed a shiny figure. Staring into the faint moon glow, he sighed. *Praius and Fidaelii.* Close behind, Skotos and Maughlin were enjoying a quiet conversation.

"Hullo, lad!" Maughlin said in a hushed tone.

"Hello—" Kam's breath caught.

"So, you have found us a camping place?"

Kam nodded in the dark. Maughlin patted his shoulder. Fidaelii sighed with a whimper. "Shhhh, girl!" Kam hushed.

"Let me set up your shelter, Fidaelii." Maughlin gestured for the acolyte to enter Kam's hideout.

"Thank you," she squeaked.

As Skotos and Maughlin set to hanging shelters, Kam just shook his head at the prospect of survival beyond the Wall at Rorgus. A full day's walk awaited them tomorrow before they would see the outpost.

6

Losing and Finding

Sunlight cracked through the root web. Dust crumbled onto Fidaelii's nose. Her head stuck halfway out of the cloth shelter. She sneezed and jumped up. Kam's head suddenly poked up, a white bump on the top of his tent. "Why don't you just wake the whole forest?"

The girl slid out of her cocoon, smiling at the bars of light above. Maughlin emerged slowly but surely. Skotos was already awake, speaking with Fidaelii's master. The company ate quickly after packing their shelters.

As they departed, Kam struck out ahead again. *I wish he wouldn't move out so far,* Fidaelii thought.

A thin, green-hooded tree gave momentary shade: the first of the thick forest ahead. A canopy of evergreen needles completely sheltered the river, which meandered straight into the trees. The water rushed in the same direction they hiked, and they found their legs racing it. *The river cheers us on,* she thought. After what seemed like hours, Fidaelii saw Kam backtrack toward the company. She glanced down to see sunlight dancing on the top of the water, which drew her eyes to her own adornment. *My cloak! I hope the Oracle likes it...*

She looked up to see Kam raising his hand as a signal. When he did, a blackbird flew between his ear and his elbow. *Whoosh.* A little riot of wind assaulted her left ear. A strained groan broke through the ravine's silence. Kam's eyes flew wide. Fidaelii quickly turned to her left when she realized the groan came from her master. A black something sprouted from Praius' belly. Bright red immediately soaked his torn tunic. *An arrow!* Before Fidaelii could react, Maughlin and Skotos had their arms around Praius. They were taking the Sage to a nearby stand of rocks. Fidaelii hardly noticed Kam gathering her into his arms as he ran to follow them. He dashed forward to help Maughlin behind the stone shield. Kam's eyes blazed with zeal while the older eyes locked on Fidaelii.

"Oh, my master!" Fidaelii cried. "Oh, my father! Tell me what to sing! Tell me how to help you!"

"What color is the blood, my daughter?"

"It's black, Father," she wept, "with a bit of dark green..."

"No song will help me, sweet one." Praius' breathing was labored. "The wound is mortal."

"No!" she cried. "There must be a song! There's a song for everything."

"Peace, now, child. There is little time. Listen carefully: when you get to Rorgus, you must seek out my brother Lucian. He is to take my place in the company. He... He will know... what needs to be... done.... Beyond the Blades... Make for the Gap... the Gap of..."

Praius' eyes took a faraway look, and Fidaelii knew he had died. She lay her head on his chest and released great sobs. She had little time to weep, however, before a wonder presented itself. Praius' body wavered a moment. Then, its substance began to ripple. A humming surrounded the company, and his body began dissolving slowly. Praius' body became a blue mist, picked up by the wind and driven away. A cry erupted from Fidaelii's mouth that frightened even her. She stood straight up heedless of the danger and shouted through the forest.

"Cowards! You've killed one of the Brothers! You've robbed Skaaran of one of its richest treasures. Why? Why would you be so foolish? Come now and be cursed!"

"You're a long way from home, little girl!" a deep voice called back. "We spied your cloak. It will fetch a good price! What other treasures do you have there with you?"

"Your evil deeds will not keep us from the Oracle!"

"The Oracle? I didn't know people still believed in those sprite stories!"

Fidaelii heard laughter echo through the air.

"We will be happy to speed you on to Him, girl! Hathlos! Shoot her!"

Fidaelii winced. But no arrow came.

"Put away that stupid cloak!" Kam said, pulling her down.

"I wish to face them!"

"You'll be shot like Praius. These marauders care less for you than I do. This is work for butchers, not bards."

Kam nodded to Skotos, who took a deep breath. Before Fidaelii could say another word, the captains leapt over the rocks and into the river with a war cry. They found two separate trees to shield them and let loose a barrage of taunts and jeers.

"Hathlos! Let fly!" came the voice again. But whoever Hathlos was did not shoot. Fidaelii mustered enough courage to peek over the rocks. Marauders were emerging from the trees on either side of the river. She counted nine, and her hope for the quest began to dwindle. Their weapons were crude and cruel. Their stature was as varied as the weapons they carried. Two of them were very short and broad for men, and Fidaelii thought for a second that she spied *tails*. They were barely clothed, with only loincloths for cover. They carried pickaxes and small hammers. *Greefadths! What are Sons of Magic doing inside the Wall? We are in grave danger.* Skotos' next call to Kam confirmed her thoughts.

"Mind the Greefadths!"

"I know what to do!" she heard Kam call back as he plunged himself into them. They were quite close to the stand of rocks, and Fidaelii could see that Kam had both his sword and dagger drawn. The weapons were magnificent, like works of art, and Kam was quite the artist. Against the strength of the Greefadth blows, Kam would deftly maneuver and use momentum as an ally. Immediately, he threw one to the ground and plunged Xander's dagger into its neck. Gurgling a death throe, the Greefadth wrapped strong arms around Kam and trapped him.

"Skotos! He's shifting!"

But Skotos had problems of his own. He had dispatched the other Greefadth by running him through. His sword arm was locked in the now stone grip of the dead shape-shifter. Fidaelii watched in horror as Maughlin jumped over the rocks to try to free Kam. The other seven marauders were walking slowly toward her three companions. Maughlin pulled desperately at the arms of the dead Greefadth, but they held fast.

"Take my sword, Uncle!" Kam said as Skotos attempted to pull away from the heavy Greefadth arms binding his sword arm.

Maughlin did and stood to face their imminent doom.

"Filthy things, Greefadths," said the leader of the bandits as they approached. "But really handy in a pinch. Even in their death, they can guarantee at least one kill."

The man looked to be a Son of Magic himself. He was almost eight feet tall and wielded a warhammer six-feet long. The others looked like Sons of Men and stood waiting for their next command.

"Why would a son of the mountain maraud inside the Wall?" Maughlin asked, buying time.

"Times are hard, old man. The Maisorvantii have moved into the Eastern Streotas and roam throughout the Aeries. The Lupines grow again in number in the eastern wood. Innerlanders are... easier to do away with. I'm neither quick nor sly. But I am strong—as you will soon find out."

The Warhammer raised his weapon to the sky. Fidaelii watched Maughlin ready himself. At that moment, a flock of blackbirds flew in among the bandits. *The archer!* Four bandits fell as arrows found vital marks. The hammer struck the ground, missing its intended target. Maughlin made use of the distraction. As the warhammer turned to prepare for the next strike, another giant rushed in from the woods. This son of the mountain was smaller than the warhammer and looked younger. He carried a staff the size of a small tree. The young giant knocked over two of his allies to stand in defense of Maughlin. The archer appeared out of a thicket of brambles to the left of the fray. He quickly notched two more arrows and dispatched the two bandits that were trying to stand back up.

"Treachery!" said the Warhammer. "Hathlos! Why

would you do this?" Turning to the smaller giant before him, the bandit king issued commands: "Hadros! Stand aside, boy."

"There is evil in this!" the archer called out. "Skaaran was given three Brothers, and I have just killed one. May the Oracle forgive me! I knew this Way was cursed."

The archer loves the Oracle! Fidaelii thought. *There is hope.*

"Cursed? Ha! If you call riches a curse, maybe you should find another occupation. Come to your senses, man." He then addressed the other giant standing before him. "Hadros! Move! Let me finish my work."

"You should listen to my father, madman. Stop this! No more bloodshed."

But the warhammer did not stop. He raised his weapon again. As quickly as he did, Hathlos shot him in the neck with a thick bolt. Hadros used his staff to block the falling blow of the hammer. It splintered and knocked Hadros back. The leader of the bandits staggered forward and was hit by two more arrows. Hadros rushed him. The boy pushed him backward until he fell. Once his former leader was dispatched, Hadros quickly claimed the hammer for himself.

The remaining two bandits stood ready to attack. Skotos had managed to free himself from his snare and was working desperately with Maughlin to free Kam. In spite of the danger, Fidaelii climbed over the rocks to help. She came at last to where Kam lay trapped. Hathlos and Hadros stood between them and the marauders. Fidaelii took hold of one of the Greefadth's stone arms. Humming a tune Praius taught her, Fidaelii watched the arm glow and grow soft again. Kam pushed the arm away. They all stood to face the two bandits, who were now hopelessly outnumbered. Seeing the futility of their cause, the bandits fled, shrieking curses.

Before Fidaelii could thank their new companions, something moved in her periphery. She turned just to see Skotos fall face first into the river. Kam and Maughlin rushed to pull him out. They carried him to the riverbank and laid him down.

"Why?" Fidaelii shouted at Hathlos.

"This is not my doing!" the archer said.

"There," Maughlin said, examining Skotos' shoulder. "That Greefadth bit him. See the teeth marks?"

The archer knelt down next to them and drew a file of salve from his leather satchel.

"Hadros, build a fire," Hathlos said. "Quickly now, boy; do as I say!"

Boy? Fidaelii marveled at the speed with which the "boy" called Hadros built the fire. Hadros ripped dead roots and mosses from the ravine walls and piled them together. The flint was dwarfed in his massive palm as he struck it, lighting a blaze on his first strike.

Fidaelii watched the archer, who moistened his fingers

with the salve. *He knows some of the old songs... that medicine will surely help.* It struck Fidaelii that the archer was not much younger than Maughlin. Fidaelii gasped when Hathlos ripped open Skotos' tunic. The wound looked angry. His skin was already turning green with a fever. As the archer smeared the salve onto the laceration, Skotos tensed, flattening against the rock. Two deep puncture wounds were bleeding steadily.

"The fire is strong enough, father," said Hadros. "I'll get the iron."

"No time for that, son," said the archer, "take this and throw it in the coals." Pulling out a fishing weight, he tossed it to Hadros, who snatched it from the air. Hadros planted it at the center of the blaze. Turning to Kam, the archer said, "Tell me, stranger—what is your name?"

"Kam."

"Your family name. What is it?" Hathlos asked again, reaching for an iron gauntlet. Fitting it firmly over his hand, he snatched the glowing metal orb from the fire. "Sit him up."

Before Kam could push Skotos straight up, Hathlos had seared the front two punctures. Without a moment to lose, Hathlos then seared the wounds in the back. Ripping up a stretch of canvas and coating it with sticky salve, Hathlos dressed the wound and bound it tightly. Skotos hardly moved through the whole ordeal.

"Go now, Hadros, get the horses," Hathlos ordered. "It

seems some will have new riders tonight." As Hadros disappeared down the path, Hathlos faced Kam, one jagged brow arched. "Well, young man, your family name."

Kam spoke nothing.

"It has been long indeed since I've witnessed such a display of skill with a blade, Kam. What business takes you to the outpost of Rorgus?"

"My own business, old man. Why did you help us? Why are you so bothered about the death of our Keires?" Kam asked while Fidaelii silently examined the shoulder bandage.

"I was taught the Ancient Wisdom in my youth." Hathlos climbed atop the rock where Skotos was leaning. He sat cross-legged and cocked his head to watch for his son's return with the horses. "I had no intention of slaying one of the Brothers. You must know this." Fidaelii saw deep sorrow cover the man's face. "You come from Edraeth, yes? You dispatched those Greefadths too quickly to just be any Innerlander. I have not seen such talent with a kopis in many years. Long ago, a captain whom I served in the garrison possessed such skill. Watching you almost brought me back to the Rending War. My captain had raven black hair, like yours. He lived in Edraeth, just down your road. He was a mighty man. His name was Xander Hearthstone. Did you know him?"

"Most of us have the black hair in Edraeth, old man,"

Kam said, kicking sand. "The War of Rending ended before I was seven years old. I don't remember much of it."

"Sir, please." Fidaelii said, addressing Hathlos. "If it is true that you were once in the garrison, why do you now maraud? Do you not hold to the code of the garrison? I thought they were defenders of the innocent." She saw Kam frown.

"Most of the men still alive who served with Hearthstone are now bandits," Hathlos replied. He looked down, but no grimace twisted his face. "After the War, the Council at Rorgus excommunicated us from the garrison when the new order in Skaaroth came to power. According to them, we did not act in a way that brought honor to Rorgus during the Rending War. Stripped of our titles and lands, we turned to the only thing we could do to feed our families. In truth, the High Council made us what we are."

"No man can give or take honor," Kam said. "You gave yours away when you turned to thievery. The Council did not take it from you. You could have sought appeal in Edraeth or Kofthus or any other town."

"Hadros comes." Hathlos pointed behind them. The boy was crossing the river, leading six black stallions.

"As penance for my tragic mistake," said Hathlos, "we will speed you on. You will not like Rorgus, I think." Fidaelii noticed a sad smile tugging at his lips. "But if your Road takes you there, we will journey with you." He slipped down from his perch on top of the rock to help the others secure their packs to one of the largest steeds.

Fidaelii's thoughts flew to Praius, and she was suddenly overcome. The prospect of her own death had crowded out any opportunity to mourn the loss of her adoptive father. She took the neck of her horse and wept. The horse bowed slightly in sympathy. It tried to nuzzle her. She stroked his great mane. *Oh, friend. If you only knew how lost we were right now. My father is gone. He was our greatest hope in finding the Sanctum. We must pray his brother at Rorgus will know the Way.*

Fidaelii felt strong hands on her shoulders. *Maughlin Ravenhill.* She faced his comforting smile. *All is not lost.* He nodded and looked down at his cupped hands. She placed her small left foot in them and mounted her steed.

Kam and Hadros slowly hefted Skotos atop a large stallion. Kam then clambered up behind the captain and secured him for the ride ahead. Hadros chuckled when his father mounted up nimbly. They climbed the steep bank. Back on the road, they all made as much haste as Skotos could stand on to Rorgus, hoof-prints dotting the dirt.

Nightfall advanced. Underneath the forest canopy, shadows lengthened. Then suddenly the trees melted into wasteland. Fidaelii's eyes wandered along the ground. A thin shadow reached greedily toward her. Rather, several stretched shadows with round caps. Pikes lined the path just outside the darkening wood. Her horse nickered, a grating sigh. Fidaelii looked up. The company neared the Outpost gates. The foreboding pikes hemmed them in on the road for at least a mile up to the city entrance. Fidaelii shrank back. Deathly shapes were mounted on them. Severed heads watched with eyeless, maimed faces from atop the pikes.

"So this is your first visit to Rorgus, eh, child?" Hathlos rumbled into the dusk. "Half of these heads were of my company. Look long and hard at the thanks you will get for your service in the garrison!" Turning to Kam, he asked, "What do you think of your business here now?"

"I think many of my questions will be answered before I go into the Outerlands." Kam leaned forward to examine Skotos, who slept.

"Well, don't stake your life on that," Hathlos replied. "The Elders in Rorgus are of a different breed than those of Edraeth. They are less concerned with means than they are ends. They are far more... practical."

The black and menacing portcullis appeared first. Its thick, tar coating glowed in the moonlight. Grey, crumbling bricks gripped the sharp steel.

As they neared the gate, a horn groaned a low, long, and sorrowful note. Teetering between hope and despair, the horn's cry suited the place that now loomed before Fidaelii. The Maisorvantii had built Rorgus as an outpost to their lands ages ago. Dominating the entire horizon and stretching as far as the eye could see, a wall of stone stood. The Maisors used it to rend the most fertile parts of Skaaran from the barren in ages past. The Rending Wall now embraced the Innerlanders' domain and guarded it from the Wilds. Seeing the Wall for the first time, Fidaelii could think of nothing but the old songs of history that Praius taught her: songs of the Elder Races of the Sons of Magic; of the dragon peoples to the south that once roamed all of Skaaran; of the great hunt that diminished the Eagloni; of the Lupines and Greefadths; of the Vulkeeri and the Daritundi; of the wretched races underground. Forced to behold one of the subjects of these songs held her in a trance.

Rorgus was one with the Rending Wall. Some of its buildings extended into the Innerland borders, but its bulk was contained within a widened portion of the Wall. Towers, halls, and fields were contained in its immense thickness. The Wall's colossal height utterly dwarfed them, stretching to the heavens. Like the other outposts of Kofthus, Darmesh and Hopfmoon, Rorgus was indispensable in coordinating attacks on the Outerlands. Now, all such violence had long ceased after the War of Rending. Rorgus endured like an old dog with soft teeth: its bark was much worse than its bite. *I hope I find Keires Lucian soon...* Fidaelii tried to remember all of Praius' parting words.

*Screeeeeeee...*the portcullis cracked open its maw to spit out a group of five mounted soldiers. The man at the head of the column glinted in the setting sunlight, encased in brilliant silver armor. Drapery and golden fittings dressed his sleek, silver-grey horse. *How out of place that leader is...coming from such a rubbish heap as Rorgus,* Fidaelii thought. Shadows obscured the four other men on skinny horses. The leader addressed their guide.

"What gift is this, Hathlos? Have you come to offer yourself for my highest pike in front of the gate? No chase this day, I see."

"Sadly, no, Captain Tulpos," Hathlos said, a gleam in his eye. "I am merely paying penance. We set out to get a cloak and were robbed of seven men."

The Captain turned and examined Fidaelii and her cloak. He smirked. "What are you doing out here, child?"

Fidaelii perked up, speaking her first in hours. "Sir, please," she breathed, "my master was Praius, gifted Brother to all of Skaaran. He was slain on the road here. We were to walk the PathWay with the one whom the Oracle has called. That is the will of the Council of Edraeth." Steadfastly she kept her eyes on the Captain, testing his reception of her answer.

The sunny day that was the Captain's face was washed away in an icy rain. His pointy nose wrinkled under the visor of his bright helmet. "Then you will need to give report to the Elders," he said. "Come with me."

Then, he locked eyes with Hathlos. "*All* of you."

7

The Gates of Folly

The huge, scattered nest of stone dominated Kam's vision. In the dark, shadows cloaked the walls. Near the ground these shadows melted from black into dark grey, like roots of the night sky. The city's stony gloom overwhelmed his eyesight. The Rending Wall snaked outward to each side and beyond. Its ramparts and the walkway topping it extended farther than sight allowed. The Wall endowed Rorgus with a massive ruse. *If the Sons of Magic only knew how feeble we were here...* His horse grunted underneath him and the still-sleeping Skotos slumped over the horse's mane. Their group trotted below the thick rock arch that barely held onto the raised portcullis. The gate's black teeth poked out from its ceiling lair. Cracks spider-webbed through the arch above. It occurred to Kam that he and his companions were at its mercy. At any moment it appeared the stone could crumble and crush them.

Captain Tulpos led them down unpolished streets. Every detail of his armor glowed in the torchlight. Brilliant, golden curly etching entwined his shoulder pieces next to a flawless breastplate. Swathing him and his steed was red silk, richness in the midst of neglect and decline. The four attendants of the captain were encased in dilapidated metal. Kam could even see cracks in their armor. Here a dent from a war-hammer, there a gaping hole from an axe. *How absurd.* But Kam refused to dwell on the Captain's flamboyant display amid his troops' brokenness.

Approaching the great hall of Rorgus, Kam's mind ran back and forth in time. He was no stranger to the Outpost, even though it had been well over fifteen years since his last passing through. Now, all the buildings were failing. Roofs rotted into gaping black holes and windows were dusty, black mouths. Rorgus reeked of poverty and despair.

Through the gloom, dirty tradesmen shouted out their last advertisements of the day in throaty yells while mangy dogs snarled over scraps down an alley. There were no children. Not even a scolding mother could be heard calling her little ones to dinner. An absence of family life darkened this vicinity. No smells of comfort greeted them. A sickness loitered in the air of the stone-paved courtyard as they reached it—a sickness of the soul. The horses clopped toward a huge circular building of grey bricks. *The entrance to the Great Hall.* A few guards argued loudly atop the sad structure. *Laughable,* Kam thought. As they reached the hall's black metal gates, two guards opened them outward. The company entered a dingy, dim atrium. The room was long and oval in shape. Balconies wrapped around its perimeter three stories high, supported by pillars of stone. Several men leaned over the railings, smoking pipes and casually watching the company. The cobblestone flooring continued within the atrium. Hooves sent a rancor of echoes up to the ceiling. Cobwebs veiled the support beams far above. A wooden fixture hanging from a rusty chain held several torches that sputtered oily smoke.

Suddenly they were halted by the captain. Skotos slid forward on the mighty steed he shared with Kam. Kam moved and readjusted his comrade on the saddle. Miraculously, Skotos slept on, unconscious of the broken city surrounding them all. Their polished host turned on his horse to Fidaelii.

"You will find provision just inside the iron doors yonder." Tulpos gestured straight ahead across the atrium. "As for lodging, you will find suitable quarters on the benches. I will send a page to see you are properly tended."

Why did he address the child? Kam thought. *I'm the reason we are in this hole.*

"Thank you, sir." Fidaelii replied. "But our friend Skotos here must visit your physician. As you can see, his shoulder requires attention." Kam noticed the girl graciously left out the reason for the wound.

Without a blink, Captain Tulpos stated, "Our physician is blind. He will welcome your eyes, young one."

"I intend to accompany him."

"He can be found in what we call the pit, just down those stairs there," he said, pointing to his left. Kam saw the shadowy staircase barred by another black metal gate. It delved to lower depths. "You!" Tulpos called to his largest man. "Lead the child and the injured man to Lucian."

Kam and Fidaelii swung off their horses. Kam touched Skotos' limply hanging hand. The guardsman sighed and roused himself. With Kam's help, Skotos slowly dismounted, and Fidaelii linked his uninjured arm in hers. The bandage was redder now. Kam could see it in the torchlight. He showed it to Fidaelii. "Take care, girl. He has lost more life-blood."

"Here, child," Maughlin said, taking Skotos' weight upon himself. "I'll help you with him. Those stairs look treacherous."

Fidaelii only answered him with a brief glance. She turned carefully. Led by the Captain's man, they moved down the tunneling stairway into "the pit," and its darkness slowly swallowed them. Her ever-glinting cloak was Kam's last glimpse.

Once they were gone, Tulpos dismounted. He eyed the remainder of the company. Turning his attention to Kam, he finally spoke.

"I will have my men ring the Council Bell. We will wait for our Elders to assemble in the hall, that we may discuss your...*situation*."

At that, the captain nodded to two of his remaining three men. They dashed up a side staircase that disappeared in the first balcony level. Tulpos and his last servant remained.

"Follow me." Tulpos motioned.

Kam looked at Hathlos and Hadros. Father and son nodded. Through the thick, iron doors they all marched, emerging in the empty banquet hall. This room was long and narrower than the atrium. Tattered banners of former garrisons hung from the walls. Rotting pillars of carved wood lined its length, and many old tables stood alongside them. Kam's eyes followed the rows to a fireplace hewn into the back wall. A gigantic bonfire roared there like a lonely beast in its cave. It spanned the entire wall, and its heat reached them from fifty paces. It took them a minute to walk down the aisle between the tables to sit near the fire. It was sweltering. Even so, a good sweat was welcome after the chilly evening winds.

All Kam's memories of this place seemed overtaken

by this ghostly shell. No longer was it full of coming and going, of song and laughter and reverie. The hour was late, and they were practically the only people in the huge place. The five men sat in silence as their stomachs rumbled. Kam stood and walked to the corner of the hall closest to the kitchen. Amused to find the mead barrel in the same place as he remembered, Kam grasped a flagon and filled it. Golden liquid filled the metal mug. Kam looked up from the flowing drink and noticed Tulpos scrutinizing him.

"You seem to have a familiarity with our hall, sir," Captain Tulpos noted, breaking the silence.

The fire shifted and snapped.

"This place looks anything *but* familiar, *sir*," Kam replied nonchalantly.

Bong... ...bong. A low, deep bell tolled through the building. *The Council Bell.* Kam marked it. *The Elders assemble.* Speaking again to Tulpos, Kam continued his response. "The hall I knew had songs and tales and games and camaraderie. I've seen more life on the rack than in this room."

"Truth, sir," Tulpos replied. "Since the Rending War, we here at the outpost have had to make more and more accommodations to the Sons of Magic in the Outerlands. The necessity of survival has greatly affected our Council's judgments."

"I would take great care as to how you use the word

'survival', friend." Kam retorted. "If this is surviving, I would have none of it."

Tulpos scratched his stubble as Kam sauntered back toward their table. "Since we are discussing words," Tulpos countered, "I would caution you to use them very little, if at all, once the Council assembles." He moved in closer to whisper. "You are not in Edraeth, man, and the games of the living days have long since passed."

Kam nodded where he stood, concentrating on his mead. Even the quality of the drink in his hand tasted compromised.

A bushy, grey figure resembling a man entered the hall from the kitchen. Standing only to the shoulder height of Kam, the hairy one had an odd lope. Wearing only a leather apron and a long brown tunic, he carried an iron pot and ladle.

"Finally, food," Hadros whispered to his father.

The cook approached them. The only noise he made was his banging on the pot with the ladle. Kam still stared into his flagon.

"Well, sit down, boy! Have some food!" The hairy figure rasped gruffly to Kam. The shout echoed. Hearthstone dragged out his stool. Before Kam could sit down, the cook dropped the pot on the table, snatched five of the dirty bowls that lay nearby and threw their contents out onto the floor. He then ladled some of whatever was bubbling in the pot into the bowls and placed them before the men at the table. Hadros grimaced.

"What's the matter, son?" the cook chuckled. "Haven't you ever had Medras stew?"

"Oh, I have, sir," young Hadros replied, transfixed by the greenish slop in his bowl that kept quivering long after it should have stilled. "Yet...I can't remember any stew from Medras actually moving..."

"Eh. You'll get used to it." The hairy cook hefted the stew pot, banging the ladle on it again. He disappeared into the kitchen. The five men began eating, but suddenly the cook was back in the hall, already in the corner where Kam had gotten his mead. His footsteps were soundless.

Hearthstone recognized something about this sneaky cook. This was no mere man. Coarse fur completely covered him. A long tail with a barb emerged from the bottom of the cook's tunic! Kam could spy only three large toes on each foot that moved deftly across the floor. Kam closed and rubbed his eyes, then opened them. *Yes.* Now, as the old cook was slinking back to them with a mead barrel, Kam could see that just beneath the old one's bushy, grey hair, two knobby horns, about an inch high, protruded from his skull.

"I never thought I would see the day when a Greefadth would be free to keep his head in Rorgus," Kam said, stabbing at his quivering stew.

"Funny thing, time," the Greefadth's gravelly voice

said. The creature placed flagons on the table. Tulpos and his last man took some of the mead. "It makes friends of enemies. Then," he stared far away, living a memory behind his eyes, "if you live long enough, the friends will find a way to become enemies again."

"You are old, Wall-Walker," Kam observed. "I thought your people did not live so long."

"A popular Innerland myth these days," he sighed. "Our people live much longer when we are not being hunted by madmen driven by superstition. Sadly, I loved power and prominence more than my home of Medras and tried to use the Innerlanders' quest for *purity* to serve my own means."

He leaned in to whisper in Kam's ear.

"That is why I am here...Hearthstone."

Kam sat up suddenly.

At once the old Greefadth wrapped Kam's wrist up with his tail and pinned it down on the table. Kam ground his teeth, struggling to put up a defense. *How does this Greefadth know me?* The other men stared, calm—except Hathlos. His eyes narrowed on Kam. Now they all knew that Kam was indeed the son of Xander Hearthstone. *Must I never keep my privacy? I am always being undermined.* But the old creature kept getting closer, breathing in Kam's ear.

"Oh, yes, I know you, boy. You have Xander Hearthstone's eyes, his voice. I was his scout. My name is

Grimmalt. I was a good traitor, to both my people and to him. This now is part of my penance. You may be able to hide from everyone else, Kam, but not from me."

With his free hand, Kam snatched Grimmalt's tail in the same vice grip he used earlier in the river. The creature's eyebrows knotted together and his forearms tensed. The old Greefadth took hold of Kam's wrist. Now Hadros' gaze locked on them. The young giant gripped the table, nervous. But Grimmalt concentrated on his words, squeezing Kam's wrist like a constricting snake.

"Xander told me much about you during our days in the War together. I only wonder how much you remember of me from your days as Lord High Arbiter here. Surely you can recall the summers you spent seeking out the Sons of Magic for *purging*. That is why you came here from Skaaroth, is it not? To carry out the High Council's will for all of the Outerlands? Dark days, terrible days those were. Days to steal the souls from men."

Now! Kam stood up quickly, wrenching the old Greefadth out of his way. He hissed, "Quiet, cur! Shut your mouth!"

The ranting creature did not obey. "Hearthstone!" he was seething now, "I must tell you—" Kam let his fist fly. It crashed against Grimmalt's yapping jaw with a *snap,* and the creature's head jerked sideways, hair draping over his face. The old creature rubbed his jaw, crouching down. In less than a moment, he launched himself into the air, tail whipping, ready to give Kam a welt for his rudeness. The bench screeched over the floor as Kam dove away from the table. An instant later Hathlos and Hadros narrowly escaped a slashing by Greefadth tail barbs. They dove with Kam, shouting with boyish glee.

I must not hurt this old creature too severely. I need informa... Kam barely had time to think. Grimmalt had mounted the bench and towered over him. The hairy silhouette was intimidating. Kam glanced at Tulpos and his man. Amusement sparked mischievous smiles on their faces. But Grimmalt seized Kam's distraction. Catapulting toward him, Grimmalt almost succeeded in flooring the taller man. *This one is bold!* Kam intercepted the flying Greefadth. With two strong hands he caught the barrel-chested torso. The creature's hands were loose, though. Kam had just enough time to glimpse Grimmalt forming rock-hard fists. He pounded Kam's left temple.

"Ugh!" Kam used the Greefadth's momentum, whirling himself around with his writhing, beating cargo in tow. The fire roared in their faces. A mortal thought blazed through Kam. *Burn, Wall-Walker!* He hurtled Grimmalt toward the jaws of the fire. The other men gasped. The stocky body flew toward the greedy conflagration. The Greefadth's fur began shifting shape! Kam watched in frustration. In a heartbeat, the Son of Magic's hair morphed into a leathery coat all over his body. Crashing into the glowing embers on the edge, the old one grunted. He bounced straight back out, stood again to face Kam and cackled. Kam sent him a determined glare. *I'll give this devil something to laugh about!* Before Kam could grab the creature again, however, Grimmalt bounded away. Down the aisle between tables he skipped, leathery flesh smoking, giving an occasional glance over his shoulder. Grimmalt drifted to his right where an arched door yawned from the wall between two tables. Without another sound, he had disappeared.

Kam turned away and trudged to the hearth, rubbing his throbbing temple. *That creature must have hardened his fists into stone!* He stared into the fire, kicking the scattered embers back. As the glowing pieces rejoined the blaze, visions of dwellings burning and Outerlanders screaming rushed back into Kam's mind. These visions swarmed like night terrors, specters haunting him, robbing him of the thing that he battled to find: peace. Indeed, Kam's days at Rorgus *had* steeped him in unbridled violence. He had led many to sacrifice themselves for the High Council's calls for "purity." All these thoughts were interrupted by Tulpos' voice echoing through the bare hall.

"Hearthstone? Kam Hearthstone?" Tulpos gave salute. "My Lord, but you are no ghost. All of Skaaroth thought you dead! That is the report we received over fifteen years ago. I was sent to Rorgus to replace you as Arbiter in the East when word came of the tragedy…"

"Hold your tongue, snake, if you value unstained

armor!" Kam whirled away from the fire and closed the distance between them. His fingers grasped Xander's kopis and ripped it from its sheath. Whipping its point up to the Captain's neck, he continued his warning: "Keep your obeisance. That man is dead. Every breath I have drawn since my return from the Wilds has been a dying one." Kam applied more pressure with his sword, emphasizing his next words. A trickle of blood ran down Tulpos' neck. "If one more soul in this accursed place tries to raise the dead with their words, those words will be the last spoken!"

Tulpos raised his hands and stepped back from Kam's threatening metal point. He wiped his neck with a handkerchief. The small cut bled no longer. Yielding the hall with a slow bow, the Captain straightened again. He signaled his last man, and the two walked into the side archway without looking back. Kam watched them go. He sheathed Xander's blade. He sat back down on the bench next to Hadros. Noticing that Hathlos' wide eyes begged a question, Kam spoke.

"Well, Hathlos... Do you see little of Xander now, or much?"

8

Hidden Counsel

Kam touched his bruised temple again. He was being watched. A particularly familiar, unnerving feeling rushed through him. He twisted on the bench.

Black and grey eyes bored into his.

The Greefadth stared at Kam from a few paces away. Without a telltale whisper, he had returned.

"Come, unexpected guests." The Son of Magic chewed on his words. "The Elders convene. They will hear words concerning your journey."

The Greefadth vanished back through the mouth of the side archway. Kam snatched his mead and downed the last sip. Hadros scooped up his last bite of Medras stew and stifled a burp. Hathlos looked up at his gigantic son, a grin gracing his wizened mouth. The three men pushed away from the table and followed the Greefadth into another room.

Kam took in the high ceiling of the crescent-shaped Council hall...and the old Greefadth walking quite close to the Council table. Horror clawed at Kam. The creature sat down on the Elder's chair far to the right.

Kam and his three companions had entered from the arch in the center of the crescent's flat side. Like a crescent, the room was wider than it was deep, and in front of them a rounded window of thick glass covered the entire curved portion of the moon shape. Overgrown gardens could be spotted through the panes. In the distance, a high grey wall, crumbling in areas, rose where the unkempt lawns ended. Kam's focus returned indoors. The Council table stretched wide, nearly spanning to the crescent point on either side of the room. Immediately past the worn table, just enough space remained to walk between it and the window. A mere three high-backed chairs accompanied the long, low ironwood table, one at each lonely head and one in the middle on the window side. Kam also noticed many of the same chairs pushed up against the walls next to them.

"Three Elders?" Kam asked. He strode toward the old Greefadth, "And *you* are one of them?"

"Do your eyes not see the desolation of this place, lad?" He asked. "We have only just enough to maintain a Council. You will find no *luxuries* here."

Just then, Fidaelii stepped into the room, leading the blind physician, only as tall as she. Maughlin walked in behind them. The slightly hunched, little man spoke through a thick, white beard. His voice was thin, yet rang clear in the Council room. "Well, my Sons, whoever dressed your friend's wound in the woods has done it before. Skotos required just a few stitches more. He must be still for the next day or two. He sleeps now in my ward." Then, turning aside to Fidaelii, he motioned, "The one on the left, my dear, take me to that one."

Kam stared in disbelief. The girl led this blind physician slowly to the far-left Elder's chair.

"Good! We are all here, then," boomed Captain Tulpos, twisting into a wry smile. *We?* Kam nearly flinched. *A Council of incompetents!* He wanted to roar and rage. Yet he was still as Tulpos made his way to the middle chair and sat down. Promptly the Captain addressed Fidaelii, who stood at attendance by the physician. "Our Council will hear you now, young lady."

As Fidaelii began to tell all she was commanded by the Edraeth Elders, Kam felt a great uneasiness wash over him. This uneasiness grew *loud.* Once again, Kam's ears did not hear the Elders' words. Questions fired throughout the chasms of his thoughts. *Exactly what does the old Greefadth know of me? How does he know my father? Why can't I remember him from my time as Arbiter? That was a different lifetime. What does he know of the campaigns to purge the Daritundi plains of all Outlanders?*

The memories multiplied and compounded until they echoed like screaming madmen. The wailing, slashing, booming. So thick were these, he barely noticed he was being addressed.

"Fidaelii tells us of Praius' desire to accompany you to the Oracle's Sanctum."

Before Kam could reply, Hathlos nearly ran and knelt in front of him.

"My lords, I beg the mercy of this court for the murder of Praius. He fell at my hand alone. I was a fool to join myself to wicked men. I have disgraced my fathers and would give myself to the Oracle's will as penance."

"We will hear your case in a moment, Hathlos son of Katafygios," said the old, blind physician. "Well, Hearthstone?"

"It was Praius' wish, yes." Kam answered. "My lord, it was Hathlos that saved Skotos and us as well. All of our company would have fallen in the river without his intervention. You must weigh that in your decision concerning his future."

"Very well," the old blind physician concluded. "I must seek the Oracle in order to discern whether I should take my brother's place in your company, Hearthstone."

"You're... Lucian?" Kam could barely get the words out of his mouth.

"Yes."

"Don't bother asking, Keires," Kam said. "I thought it folly for Praius to come. The roads of the Innerlands aren't safe, and he received proof of the danger. Here we are on the doorstep of the Outerlands, and you would be double the fool. I doubt Praius even heard what he says he heard from the Oracle. I beg of you, Keires Lucian: make Fidaelii stay here and let Maughlin and me go on alone."

"Never have I heard such impudence!" Tulpos cried out. "A Brother sits before you, Kam Hearthstone, and you would dare..."

"I do dare it Captain! For the sake of the Innerlands, I dare it. Two Brothers now remain, if Iyoskothe is more than a fable. This quest is barely two steps old, and you would seek out whether I am to be an old blind man's walking stick?"

"Peace, friends!" Lucian said. "This day has been difficult. We should reconvene in the morning. Perhaps daylight will bring cooler heads and clearer vision. We should get some rest."

"Agreed," the Greefadth said. "Captain Tulpos, will you show our guests to their lodgings?"

"Of course," Tulpos said, still glaring at Kam.

"Captain," Lucian said, stealing Tulpos' gaze. "I will tend to Hearthstone. I must speak with him in private. Come here, Son. I need a *walking stick*."

Reluctantly, Kam approached Lucian's chair and

helped him up. Lucian directed Kam back into the feasting hall before speaking to him again.

"My brother Praius told me often of your contempt for the Ancient Wisdom. He told me you were hot tempered," the old man chuckled.

"Keires..."

"Let's dispense with the formalities, Hearthstone. You will call me Lucian. Do you remember how to find the stairs to the pit?"

"I served here for over five years, Lucian," said Kam. "I know where the pit is."

"Oh yes, I'd quite forgotten you were an Arbiter here."

"I've done my best to forget," Kam mumbled.

Kam helped Lucian down the stairs. Suddenly the air acquired a peaceful coolness. Yet comfortable warmth seeped into Kam's lungs. He could see that a light waited ahead. The stone steps veered to his left and began a spiral. One torch held onto the clean brick wall. The staircase curved onward. Periodically darkness would return, and the next torch would drive it away, illuminating Kam's path. He sensed they had traversed at least three stories. The spiral ended in a landing. The door to the infirmary lay just ahead, flanked by large torches. Kam and Lucian made their way through the door. Skotos was in a deep sleep on a bed to the right.

"There is a hatch in the far-left corner of the room, Kam," Lucian whispered. "That is where we must go.

It lies behind the great shelf of medicines. Do you see the shelf?"

"I do."

"Take us there, quietly."

Kam found the hatch. Opening it quietly took some doing. A ladder descended into unsearchable darkness.

"You go first, lad," Lucian whispered.

"What's down there?" Kam asked.

"No time." Lucian answered. "We must go now. The others wait for us."

For a reason Kam cannot give to this day, he started down the ladder. He made eight rungs when he heard Lucian's robes rustling above him. He counted nearly fifty rungs when the Sage whistled a few notes. A little yellow spark erupted, and then another, followed by a third. A high-pitched tone softly emanated from each spark, almost as if they were whistling back. They danced around Lucian's head, as if waiting for him to speak.

"Hello friends. Kam needs to see his feet, please."

Immediately the sparks floated down to the rungs where Kam's feet were resting. Kam continued his descent with the sparks keeping pace. At last they reached the bottom. Kam helped Lucian with the last few rungs. Once the Sage was on the ground, he began to sing.

Wisdom's house would be my home
I dare not venture out alone

But seek to know the answers there
When all is dark and hearts are stone
Hear me when I anxious call
Give a door where lies a wall
Be my help, Your vision share
Be my light, my eyes, my all

At this verse, a dim light appeared and began to brighten the space where they were standing. A wondrous scene appeared before Kam. No fewer than twelve massive stones stood before him. Fifteen feet thick at the base and rising at least thirty feet by Kam's estimation. They were pillars without a roof. Kam could hear water running down a stone wall in the distance. *The river?*

"Come. We must stand in the center of the light to see them," Lucian's voice now rang strong.

Kam led Lucian apprehensively into the center of the stones until they were bathed in bluish-white radiance. Three figures stood with them in conference. The one on their right was mighty. He was like an obsidian pillar of muscle with a golden scythe at his back and flames at his feet. On their left was a boy, not much older than Fidaelii. Standing directly in front of them was a man who looked to be Kam's age. He had matted light brown hair. He wore the clothes of a vagrant, and he was filthy. It was he who spoke first.

"A sad night, brothers. Praius has left the waking realm."

They all stood silent for some time, reflecting on the news. Then the man addressed the boy on Kam's left.

"Sokii, what news from Skaaroth? How sits the High Council?"

The boy stepped forward.

"Brothers: in my service to the High Council of Skaaroth I have seen and heard a great many things. None of those things have concerned me more than now. Starsgol's influence has grown these past ten years. The songs have changed. Not much, mind you, but enough to convince the majority that Starsgol is the true Oracle. The High Council has forgotten their verse. They have allowed the servants of Starsgol to teach them another one. There are rumors that Starsgol himself walks the halls of the Kirk in Skaaroth. These are dread times, Brothers. The High Council would go again to war. The village councils are, for the most part, opposed to it. However, we saw this same drama play out before the Rending War. There was talk of a verse in the Ancient Wisdom about purity that was perverted by the High Council. We all saw the ill effects of that desecration. And now they would engage in the folly of making war on the Oracle Himself, and on the Ancient Wisdom."

"Do we know their table of time?" the tall black warrior asked.

"Sadly, we do not," answered Sokii. "That is what concerns me the most. War could come before we are ready.

Iyoskothe, what news from the Streotas? How are things among the Greefadths?"

"The Council of Thieves still love the Oracle. Many of the younger ones are seeking new songs, but the Steward Mendlakk is still with us, it seems. If we lose Medras to Starsgol, we will have a difficult time convincing the Maisorvantii or the Vulkeeri to join us in the coming fight. The Greefadths are a necessary hinge for our campaign. We must find a way to unite the tribes again if we are to have victory."

"Agreed," spoke Lucian. "There is no time. We must speed Hearthstone on to the Oracle. There is one of the Shadow Guard in his company. What is his name, Kam?"

Startled upon being spoken to, Kam struggled to answer.

"Skotos... My lords, there is something more... when I first met Skotos, he brought me warning that Starsgol is prowling the Daritundii plains in the north. Is there merit to this warning?"

The dingy man turned to the large black warrior, "Iyoskothe?"

"I have not walked the plains in three years, my Lord. I will make my way south to validate the reports. What are your plans, Lucian?"

"With the Oracle's blessing, I will walk the Harrows with the company," said Lucian. "I have not returned to the Sanctum since we left it all those years ago. The child

Fidaelii will be better equipped to find it than me. My hearing is dulled from the years at Rorgus, I'm afraid. What are your plans, Sokii?"

"I see no choice but to gather with you all at the Oracle's Sanctum. There is no more reasoning with the High Council, despite all the village Councils' efforts. Will you take the Sea Road that leads through the desolation of the Aeries? The Maisorvantii have moved in there, but it may be the only way to make the Sanctum in good time. We could use all the help you could offer, Iyoskothe."

"I will see if Starsgol is indeed prowling the Daritundii and then make my way to you," replied the warrior. "If you dress as trappers you would stand a better chance with a Maisorvantii hunting party. They seem to be sympathetic to others trying to survive these hard times. No guarantees, of course."

"Of course," replied Lucian. "But having you with us would be a great comfort."

"Then all is settled if we are agreed," said Iyoskothe. "I will meet Lucian in the Lupinwood and then make my way to the Sea to give my aid. Lucian will have a task maintaining everyone's sanity in the Harrows. The dead do not go gently."

"All will be well," Lucian replied. "I have Fidaelii. She brings no ghosts."

"Farewell then, Brothers!" called Sokii. "We will see you on the Road."

"Aye! On the Road, then..." Kam heard Iyoskothe's voice faintly as the blue light began to dim. He didn't want to leave this place. There were so many questions that raced through his mind, but he could not piece any sense together. As the darkness returned, and Kam's eyes once again became familiar with it, he heard Lucian whistle. The three sparks returned and gave their light.

"Can you guide us back to the ladder, Son?"

"Yes, Keires," Kam replied. "I remember the way."

"Good," Lucian sighed. "Very good. I am weary Son, very weary. For more than five hundred years, we have been gifted to this land, to walk it and to work it. Now we must give what is left of it to another voice, another verse. The Oracle only knows what will become of Skaaran now, Kam. We have tried to make it a better world. Have we failed? Yes. Oh, in so many ways, yes. The War of Rending will be for what we are most remembered. We could not stop it. For all our strength we... it remains our greatest sorrow. And, yet, there is still hope. There is still... you."

Kam felt discouraged at Lucian's words. "Keires, if what was said is true... if Starsgol is more than a ghost story... and what is said about him is truth, then how can I..."

"Those who take Starsgol lightly do so at their own peril, Son," Lucian rasped. "When you walk the Harrows, you will gain a greater respect for him. We have worked against him these five hundred years with varied measures of success. But now he has focused on what the sons of

Skaaran believe they truly desire. Independence. His verses will deceive them into thinking they can actually attain it. These verses are sweet in the High Council's ears. They wish to live free from any consequence or regard for others. But when there is no provision for the helpless, hope for future generations is lost."

Kam soon found the ladder. As he helped Lucian up the first few rungs, a gnawing question escaped his lips.

"Lucian, who was that filthy man who stood with us in conference?"

Lucian sighed.

"That? That was the Oracle."

9

The Haunted Halls

"*K*am!" *a woman's voice cried out in the darkness. "Kam Hearthstone! Help! We need help here!"*

"Where are you?" Kam cried back.

"Here! Please hurry! He is wounded!" came the voice again.

"I can't see anything!" Kam answered. "Do you have light with you? A torch? Anything?"

From the voice in the distance, a song rang out, and a light shone forth. The song danced with Kam's being like the very elements themselves. Storming, burning, and crashing with one another in a structured tempo and melody; the verses were contained in perfect order. Intonations both ancient and cosmic sang and percussed, dashed and frolicked. Mystery lived in it, like the trackless oceans and starry infinitudes, the rushing rivers and steadfast rocks: all the wild things surpassing mortal comprehension or control. It was very far away, but Kam found it useful to get his bearings. He began to run toward the light, but just as he made some progress, the song stopped and the darkness returned.

"Sing again!" Kam called out through the darkness, which seemed even darker now. He ached to know the song... indeed, to sing it. But another song did not come.

"Sing again!" Kam shouted. "I need the light to help you! Sing out! Send the light again!"

Now the song rang out, and Kam began to run in the direction of the light. When the singer had to take breaths, the light would dim, but then it would resurge in brilliance when the singer started again. As Kam ran, the patch of light ahead grew nearer and nearer. He could make out two figures. A lady knelt cradling a young wounded child in her arms. On her shoulders she bore an enormous golden shield. She was singing the sweet Song amidst sobs that shook her body. Kam ran harder. He pulled his father's kopis and dagger from their sheaths. As he did, he heard the roars of a dread beast. At the sound of the first bellow, the lady looked up suddenly. Kam only had moments to mark her appearance as he ran by to take a defensive position.

"Laurl?"

She spoke to answer, and when she did, all was darkness.

"Kam, don't you remember me?"

The beast thundered again, and Kam felt the heat of a thousand furnaces.

"I need your help!" Kam cried out in the darkness. "I can't see to strike! Please! My lady! Sing again!"

But no song came. He was being shaken...

Kam awoke to the sight of Hathlos' concerned look.

"Thank the Oracle! I thought you would never come out of that dream. You've been screaming for half an hour." Kam tried to sit up but could only lean on an elbow. He could tell that great sorrow still hung upon Hathlos.

"Thank you for your kind words among the Council yesterday, Kam. I did not sleep last night. I don't deserve to live another day. I first met Praius in my youth..."

"My words were neither kind nor forced, friend," Kam said. "They were merely truth. Maughlin once told me that as men, we naturally drift. That is how you found yourself among the thieves. Everyone in this hall knows you saw the wrong. You corrected your course. I don't believe for one moment you killed the Keires in cold blood."

"But I did!" Hathlos countered. "And if the girl had not been so bold as to stand in the face of her own death and cry out about Praius, I would have killed the rest of you!"

"But you felt the conviction of your wrong, Hathlos. Sometimes it takes great sorrow to give light to what is right, and what is wrong. I will vouch for you at the Council this morning. You and your son found valor and honor in the river yesterday. You were both great champions. Nothing will happen to either of you while I draw breath."

Kam watched tears grow in Hathlos' eyes.

"Then I pledge my life to your quest, Hearthstone, as I pledged myself to your father in the Rending War. If I am spared ill judgment this day, every breath 'til my last will be in your service."

"I don't know how much I believe in my *quest,* Hathlos, but there will be right judgment today," Kam said. He stood and stretched. Kam walked to the window of his room and marked the sun. *Midmorning.* "Come, Hathlos, let's eat."

The two men made their way downstairs to the great feasting hall. The Elders were there, sitting at one of the long tables with the rest of Kam's company. Hadros looked up and saw his father approaching.

"Good morning, Father. How did you sleep?" Hathlos just shook his head.

"How is Skotos, Fidaelii?" Kam asked.

"His wounds are not so angry this morning. Lucian says he only needs one day more to rest."

"Very good," Kam replied. Turning to the Elders, he asked, "My lords, what is your judgment concerning Hathlos and Praius?"

"The bandits' actions in saving your company show the

true intent of their hearts," Lucian said. "Praius' death will not be held against Hathlos."

Kam turned to look at Hathlos, who was embracing his son.

"A right judgment," Kam said. "Since Skotos has made such a good recovery, we will leave tomorrow and make for the Eastern Verdant in the Lupinwood. The less time we spend in this ruin the better."

"Why would you go east to the sea road?" Tulpos asked. "You would fare better tracing a northern path just along the Wall and cross the Biting Fens. From there you could follow the Shifting Falls into the Blades to the Gap. It's not as treacherous."

"Every road in the Outerlands is treacherous," Kam answered. "The Lupinwood gives us cover to the Deltas. After we cross them, we are in the Aeries. I would much rather cross the Aeries than take my chances with the Blades...too many Greefadth patrols from Medras for my liking."

"The path through the Aeries is an easier one," Tulpos said. He stood and walked over to the old Greefadth. "But Grimmalt here knows every path through the Blades. He can keep you hidden."

"The Black Prince!" Fidaelii gasped.

The traitor! Kam was shocked. *This Greefadth is the root of hatred in me...*

"I have no need of treacherous leeches in my company,"

Kam said, looking directly at Grimmalt. "You were my father's scout in the War. You are the reason I hunted Greefadths when I served as an Arbiter. It was you who drove my hatred all those years. You should know that before I kill you."

Instead of anger and hatred in the Greefadth's face, Kam found a sea of remorse.

"You must do what you think is right, Hearthstone," Grimmalt said. "I have begged Iyoskothe for death every day since the failed plot for the throne. If he comes for me at your hand, I will not resist. If you let me live, I will strive to undo all I have done in my waking days in Skaaran. There is much danger beyond the Wall. I can help you..."

"Liar!" Kam said, unsheathing the kopis. Once again, Kam found Maughlin restraining him.

"Kam! Stop." But Kam did not stop. He pushed Maughlin away and walked toward Grimmalt, sword drawn. Suddenly the Acolyte stood before him, her eyes blazing.

"No, Kam! Not now. Too much blood has been shed already."

"Much more will be shed before you see your home again, Fidaelii, if ever you see it at all. This creature is the cause of my father's death. Now stand aside, girl. I have work to do."

Kam felt a strong hand in the crook of his left elbow. He heard Maughlin's voice yet again.

"Kam, walk with me."

Kam turned to see a more serious look in Maughlin's eyes than he had ever seen. His oldest friend motioned his head to the door of the great hall. "I would speak with you."

Never releasing Grimmalt from his gaze, Kam gave the final word.

"This isn't over."

Kam sheathed the kopis. He turned and walked toward the great door. One of Maughlin's big hands was on his right shoulder. He saw the other push the door, and the two walked into the courtyard. Kam was tired. He was hungry. Whatever Maughlin wished to talk about, Kam wanted nothing of it. They found the nearest massive staircase and climbed it. Soon the two men were walking slowly along the top of the Rending Wall.

"There are too many ghosts here, Uncle." Kam broke the silence. "Too many ghosts. These halls are haunted."

"A man's past is always haunted, Kam."

"Don't play the philosopher, Maughlin. Not now."

"What do you want me to say? Do you want help, or not?"

"Why is that murderer here, Maughlin? Why do they make provision for him? Don't they know what he did?"

"Grimmalt is a hero to the Innerlanders, Kam. He is responsible for Medras' fall in the Rending War. You have to remember that, Son. The High Council acquitted him of the charges concerning your father."

"And yet, for all our efforts, Medras was rebuilt. The Greefadths grow strong again," Kam said.

"Yes."

"As do all of the Sons of Magic."

"Yes."

"Give me one reason not to kill Grimmalt."

"No one else in your company knows the Blades as well as he."

"We're not going through the Blades, Maughlin! We will take the eastern Road to the great sea and north through the desolation of the Aeries."

"And if that Road fails?" Maughlin asked. "What if you have to cross part of the Daritundii plains and follow the Shifting Falls into the Blades as Tulpos said? Who else can keep you away from Medras and the patrols? If you have to walk the Road your father walked, who will guide you?"

At this Kam stopped walking. Maughlin stopped a few paces ahead of him, then turned to face Kam.

"Uncle, our company grows by the moment...." *Should I tell him of the Brothers' Council of last night?* "Lucian is determined to go. If Fidaelii is not prohibited, she walks my Road as well. Hathlos has sworn his life to my aid, and you know his son will accompany him. I was forced to take three travelers from Edraeth. Now you tell me I must add three more? Staying hidden is easier when there are fewer people in your company. If we dare to take Grimmalt, our number is eight. Not only will I have to concern myself with Sons of Magic from without, I will have to watch for threats from the treacherous Greefadth prince as well. You would have me walk the Road to the Sanctum with a knife in my back?"

"Do you think Starsgol will spare any resource to destroy you?"

Kam didn't answer. He stood like a stone, gazing over the expanse of the Lupinwood stretching out to the horizon. The morning sun was still burning the frost off the branches of thousands of trees. It hung just over the treetops. A chorus of birdsong sailed through the air. Kam faced northeast. He could barely make out the outlines of the massive pillars that marked the boundaries of the Eastern Verdant. Once again, Maughlin ventured to speak.

"Of every race in Skaaran, who better than a Greefadth to be your scout? Their sense of hearing and smell are unmatched. They are silent when moving. They can blend into their surroundings and be practically invisible."

"I can't believe what I'm hearing, Maughlin!" Kam cried out. "You helped bear Xander's body home from Rorgus in the War! You carried my father's corpse yourself. What has changed that you now would plead his murderer's case?"

"Much, Kam," Maughlin said. "Much has changed. I hated the War. I was one of the many who spoke against it before the High Council. They did not listen. Your father did not listen. How did Skaaran benefit? The Sons of Men now stand weakened as a tribe. How did Medras benefit? Grimmalt's father and elder brother were slain. They are now governed by lesser Greefadths while Grimmalt lives out his days in shameful exile. What can I say of the Maisorvantii? Of the Vulkeeri? Of the Daritundii? Of the Lupine peoples? By the Oracle, boy, don't you want a better world?"

"I want to be left alone! Why does it fall upon my house to solve all of Skaaran's problems?"

"The Oracle only knows, Son. We have to believe He has a plan for the mending of the tribes."

"We can only hope!" a voice called out from behind them. It was Skotos, who was making his way toward the two. "Forgive my intrusion. I wanted some fresh air, so I picked up some breakfast before coming out. Fidaelii told me you hadn't eaten yet, Kam. I have some bread and cheese here."

"Thank you, Captain," Kam said. "Maughlin is trying to convince me to allow Grimmalt to come with us into the Outerlands. What are your thoughts?"

"Grimmalt was a tremendous asset in the Rending War, from my study of history. He would make the perfect scout."

"See?" Maughlin said. "Grimmalt holds many surprises, Kam. Give him a chance to prove his worth. You may fall in desperate need of his skill before you reach the Sanctum."

"If he goes, it will be under protestation from me," Kam answered. "At the first sign of treachery, I *will* kill him."

"There will be no treachery, you'll see," Maughlin said.

"You are far too trusting, Uncle."

"And you trust far too little. Come, let's restock provisions."

As the three made preparations for the next day, new feelings of helplessness came upon Kam. The tide of his quest began its pull toward the Outerlands and he was not ready. Two of his company were incapable innocents. Two were newfound allies. One, his oldest friend. One an intrusion from the capital. One, the poison in his soul.

10

Into the Wilds

First light came, a wink of sunshine through a crack in the wall. Kam lay still, watching it emerge and following it now as it gleamed, for there had been no sleeping in the haunted halls of Rorgus. Turning to his side, he stirred the dust and it puffed into the air from the mess hall bench he sat atop. In fact, every surface was coated in dust. He sneezed. Hadros jolted awake. Next to Kam, the large boy's bedroll spread over two benches.

"Good morning, Kam."

"Hadros." Kam huffed, scrambling to his feet. He tugged his boots on and brushed himself off. Picking his way around Hathlos' empty bench, he snatched up his two satchels. He stuffed his bedroll inside the larger leather one. He felt around to find his most prized

Remembering: *Laurl's locks*. Quickly, he assembled the satchels in the manner he had invented so that, once attached by leather straps, they formed one pack. He slung it over his shoulders.

Once again, the black metal gates were opened for him, and he emerged in the courtyard. Three of Captain Tulpos' attendants were packing the last of the supplies on three horses for the party.

"Where are the horses for riding?" Kam called, "You'll have to get more."

"There will be no riders," an old voice cried out behind him. Kam turned and saw the old physician-Sage. Lucian stroked his beard. "We travel on foot. Besides, once we pass the Aeries Gate, we will have to turn them loose or kill them. By then, we will have used the supplies they carry. I won't be unnecessarily wasteful."

"As you wish, Keires Lucian," answered the oldest attendant.

It did not take long for the rest of the company to assemble. The eight made their way out of the great hall's shadow between rows of rotted dwellings and down the rough paving toward the east gate. Rorgus took people in and spit them back out by two gates. In the Innerland west was the black portcullis within the cracking stone arch by which the six had first entered. They would leave from the other. Sixteen boots and twelve hooves marched toward the east gate.

Beyond the gate before them spread a forested marvel. *The Lupinwood*. Rorgus terminated into rolling treeland, crowned by a scintillating belt of blue. *The Great Sea*. The Rending Wall's edge dropped off before them, a cliff. The isolation of the Outerlands from the Innerlands: *The making of purity*.

In front of the east gate opening into the Wilds, the cobblestones curved to either side to form the Wall walkways. Kam stepped outside the gate to study the ramparts' fortifications. Lichen covered the inmost layer of the gigantic stone bricks, most of which were cracking... slowly. The Wall was dying a gradual death on the inside. On the outside it was covered with new stone. Where the flawless rock met the ground, a deep moat fed by the Stone River extended past Rorgus' sides for a good day's ride along the Wall. The sturdy rock face stunned Kam. *It's even newer...stronger than before.*

"Kam! It's time." Maughlin called out.

Kam said nothing. He tramped back toward the sound of Maughlin's voice as the company made their way down the ramp to join him at the East Gate.

On this the fifth day of his journey, Hearthstone had seen his company grow to five, shrink to almost three, and grow again to eight, all against his will. *Am I the one going to see the Oracle, or is all of Skaaran going with me?*

"You know the way to the Eastern Verdant, bandit?"

Grimmalt barked to Hathlos. "You've been there before, no?"

"I've been there. You know that, old goat."

"Good. You and the large boy take the lead, then," he replied.

"Mmm."

Hathlos laid a hand on his son's shoulder. With Hadros he passed the others to come up alongside Kam. In the early morning light, Kam studied Hathlos. Long silver hair played about his high cheekbones. The tall archer wore a dark green cape over a sleeveless grey tunic. Arms like huge tree trunks melded into mighty hands. A weighty leather belt secured several daggers and a short sword, but these were outshone when Kam's eyes caught the glint of several dozen black bolts stuffed into two quivers, also attached to the belt. Like miniature, fletched spears, the black bolts loosed sinister gleams.

Beautiful instruments, Kam mused. *I'm glad for his company.*

Hathlos leaned close to Kam and said, "Have a care for Grimmalt, Son. At least I gave you the courtesy of shooting at your company from the front side."

Kam grunted in response and glanced over at the bushy Greefadth. The creature's lips twisted into a smirk. Kam growled to himself. He kept moving one foot in front of the other.

Soon the company left Rorgus behind. It was almost

a two full day's ride east-northeast to the Verdant, which meant it was three full days' journey on foot. The first day was spent along the eastern trade road that stretched from Rorgus to the Eastern Fork. The edges of the Lupinwood were populated with hemlock that had been taken by disease, so cover was sparse. Within the first mile, Lucian broke the tense silence.

"Do you play music, Fidaelii?"

"Yes, Keires. What would you like me to play?" she offered.

"*The Breaking of Time* would be wonderful to hear, if you can," he replied.

Fidaelii walked to one of the horses and retrieved a lute from a satchel. After tuning it, she began singing. The air all around Kam became sweet and thick, the way his home smelled when Laurl was making sugar cakes. Fidaelii's voice was sweet and soft:

"I walked once with You, in the soft verdant way
In the garden of dreams, where our loves ever played.
There all that would be, that we ever would need
Blossomed and bloomed in perpetual day.
The lark and the swan and the birds in their flight
Gave voice to the morn and their song to the night.
And every ear ope'd to their glorious line.
And every heart swayed to left and the right.
The wolf and the bear and the cats in their den;

They all frolicked and played in the wood and the fen.
As they sang their own verse and remembered their line,
You gathered them all in the heart of the glen.
And with every note, every rhythm and rhyme,
The song grew and grew with every new chime
'Til with a great shout all the stars bowed their light
And every voice stilled at the breaking of Time."

When she finished, every mouth was agape. Kam had hardly noticed that everyone had stopped walking to hear the song. He watched the Sage and the Acolyte gazing deeply into each other's eyes. Kam looked up. All around the company, a crystalline dome had appeared. The dome had a yellow-green hue. He followed the shape of the dome downward until Lucian appeared before him.

"That was wondrous, young one," Lucian said tenderly, "Thank you. Our first day among the Sons of Magic will be one of safety."

"We should take to the riverbank that runs parallel to the trade road as soon as the wood thickens," Kam said. "I don't want to take unnecessary chances."

"There is no need," Lucian replied, "Fidaelii's song has hidden us from every eye. I have given my voice to hers, and we are protected."

"Don't be a fool!" Kam said. "We are in the open. We must..."

"Are we in the open?" Lucian asked. "Walk beyond the dome. See for yourself."

Kam approached the dome wall. He could see through it perfectly well. He placed his right hand on it, and it quivered slightly. He pulled his hand away, and the quivering stopped. He looked back at Lucian and Fidaelii.

"Go on!" Fidaelii said. "It's all right."

Kam took a deep breath, and quickly stepped through the dome wall. A rush of warmth washed over him, followed by the cool of the morning. He turned around and saw nothing but the road. Flanking it were the failing hemlocks. *If I hadn't just been with the company, I would swear I was alone...* He stepped back in the direction of the dome.

Nothing.

He took three more big strides back to where he knew his company was waiting.

No warmth.

No company.

"Lucian!" Kam called. "Fidaelii!"

Suddenly, the warmth rushed over him again. Kam found himself back inside the dome. Fidaelii was giggling.

"Well?" She said, trying to calm down.

"It's unbelievable," Kam said. "Where was that when we came under attack on the way to Rorgus?"

"I'm only an Acolyte, Kam. I can't initiate magic yet. I'm completely dependent on the Brothers' will. Praius

didn't see fit to utilize my voice on the road to Rorgus."
Fidaelii was gazing in wonder all around them at the
dome. "I've never sung that song in power before, only
in lessons. Is it really difficult to see us from the outside?"

"Impossible," answered Kam. "Lucian, why couldn't I
get back in?"

"Fidaelii controls the dome," Lucian said. "She hides who
she wants to hide. Those inside the dome are both in Skaaran,
and not in Skaaran. We are realm-walking right now."

"So a Maisor or a Lupine could be standing right next
to me and not see me?" Kam asked.

"They could be occupying the same space as you in
Skaaran and not see you," Lucian said. "It's a complex song."

"Why don't we just realm-walk all the way to the
Sanctum?" Hathlos asked.

"Because it would kill Fidaelii. I can't ask more than
a day for now. We may not even get that. We should get
going," Lucian pointed up the road.

"Lead on, Archer," said Fidaelii. She placed her small
hand on his mighty shoulder. Kam saw her smile at him.
"Don't worry. I won't let you leave the dome."

Hathlos and Hadros led the company, followed closely
by Grimmalt. Fidaelii, Skotos, and Lucian were close
behind. Kam walked in the rear with Maughlin and the
pack horses. Many miles passed beneath them, and still
the wonder from the song refused to leave. The air stayed
thick and sweet and warm. The song lingered in the walls

of the dome. It was faint, but Fidaelii's voice was still in it. Kam could swear that the tones colored the dome and made it pulse slightly. Just before noon, several healthy, thick, green branches crossed through the dome just above the company. The diseased hemlocks had melted away. Kam could see all manner of evergreen trees crowding each other in every direction. *Here begins the heart of the Lupinwood.*

Kam barely had time to form the thought before a great cry rose up. It came from their right. Hathlos motioned for all to stop. Thunder echoed through the wood. After it, more cries. The sky broke out in great laughter. *Maisorvantii!* Ahead on the road, five Lupines came screaming onto the road from the midst of the thick trees. Their coarse brown fur was soaked with morning dew from the bottom branches of the evergreens. Two of them were amazingly on fire, catching dead brush as they ran. One paused for a moment on the road. He rose up on two legs and sniffed the air in the direction of the company. Thunder broke out again, followed by the laughter. The trees just behind the Lupine were suddenly ablaze. The creature snarled at the fire and sounded a warning cry of the impending Maisor danger. Its gaze was drawn upward. Kam followed it. Three great silver Maisorvantii raced overhead. The wings of the Maisors were majestic to behold, and they cut through the air like the sharpest swords dancing. The sun reflected from the scales on their silvery breasts like a thousand mirrors. The dragon people seemed to be playing a game with the Lupines. Before the Lupine on the road could move, two Maisorvantii had landed. Both stood well over eight-feet tall.

Elder Race, Kam thought. *Argyros. Why are they not in Reesliks?*

The larger Maisor took hold of the Lupine at its scruff as if picking up a sack of feed.

"Hello, mongrel," he said. "Did we have the pleasure of your company in the Verdant last night? Several fruit trees were struck with disease this morning."

The Lupine snapped its jaws at the arm of the Maisor to no avail. He then sounded a cry for help.

"Oh yes. Call them," The silver maisor chuckled. "Let them all come to see Arete'! I have gifts."

Arete' threw the Lupine to the other Maisor, which made Kam tremble slightly. *That's no small Lupine. He must weigh at least 350 pounds.* The Maisor caught the creature effortlessly. He threw it to the ground and pinned its neck with his large talons.

A great rustling came from the company's left. As expected, the four Lupines returned for their companion. Two were badly singed on their hindquarters. They were at a full run and turned directly toward the company. Kam drew his kopis. Hathlos notched a black bolt. Maughlin drew a sword.

"Lucian..." Fidaelii said. "Will it hold?"

"Be at peace, daughter. You must trust the writer of the song."

The Lupines ran through the midst of the company in retreat. It took everything within Kam not to strike. A bolt of intense white heat came down among them. Fidaelii jumped. The dome flickered. Lucian took her hand, and the dome became firm again. Behind them came a Lupine's pitiful cry. The Maisor had ended its life. The two Maisorvantii on the road joined their brother in the air to pursue the fleeing creatures. When the noise of the hunt had diminished, Kam looked to Fidaelii. She was leaning on Maughlin.

"Are you all right?"

"I'm so tired, Kam," she said. "I didn't think it would be this heavy."

"There is a place to camp in just a few hours. Do you think you can make it?"

"Yes. Let's be going."

The company started off again. Hadros helped Maughlin with Fidaelii. By the time they made camp, she could barely walk. The dome by now had almost completely diminished. The company left the trade road at Kam's direction and walked north almost half a mile into the thick of the wood.

"There is no clearing for shelters," Skotos said.

"We tie the horses here," Kam said. "Camp is yet a mile away. We turn northeast from here. Gather your provisions."

After the mile northeast, no clearing presented itself.

"Well?" Skotos asked.

"We'll sleep in the trees," Kam said. "Find thick enough branches and latch yourselves on. Eat your food and get some rest. Tomorrow we will reach the Verdant, if we're still alive. Once we break camp tomorrow, I'm not stopping until we do. We'll go on through the night if necessary. I'm taking the first watch."

Kam helped Fidaelii up into a large joint where two branches sprung forth.

"Thank... you..." she muttered. "Kam... I'm sorry for letting the dome flicker back on the road."

"Shhhhh," he said as he secured her latch. "You did well. Sleep now. I've put food in your pack if you wake in the night. Be sure you eat it. We have a long road tomorrow."

As the company made their way up into the trees for the night, Kam climbed Fidaelii's tree until most of the large branches were below him. He found a suitable branch from which to keep watch. The food and drink were refreshing after the ordeal with the Maisorvantii. Kam looked down at Fidaelii, now soundly asleep. The song from the dome would not leave him.

And with every note, every rhythm and rhyme
The song grew and grew with every new chime
'Til with a great shout all the stars bowed their light
And every voice stilled at the breaking of Time.

11

The Lupinwood

"*S*ing again!" Kam shouted. "I need the light to help you!
Sing out! Send the light again!"

Now the song rang out, and Kam began to run in the
direction of the light. When the singer had to take breaths,
the light would dim, but then it would resurge in brilliance
when the singer started again. As Kam ran, the patch of
light ahead grew nearer and nearer. He could make out two
figures. A lady knelt cradling a young wounded child in her
arms. On her shoulders she bore an enormous golden shield.
She was singing the sweet Song amidst sobs that shook her
body. Kam ran harder. He pulled his father's kopis and
dagger from their sheaths. As he did, he heard the roars of a
dread beast. At the sound of the first bellow, the lady looked

up suddenly. Kam only had moments to mark her appearance as he ran by to take a defensive position.

"Laurl?"

She spoke to answer, and when she did, all was darkness.

"Kam, don't you remember me?"

The beast thundered again, and Kam felt the heat of a thousand furnaces.

"I need your help!" Kam cried out in the darkness. "I can't see to strike! Please! My lady! Sing again!"

Thunderous bellows mingled with evil laughter echoed all around him. The heat increased, and Kam felt hot breath upon his face.

"Sing, lady, or we perish!"

Fire erupted before him. The sun itself could not have made for a more terrifying assault. It gave faint light but not the light Kam was looking for. He heard a rustling at his back. In a moment, the woman was standing beside him. She held the glorious shield before them both. Both of them crouched behind it to be spared the blast. When it came, they were pushed back several feet. Kam put his left hand on the shield's grip to steady it. It was blazingly hot. He removed his hand in an instant.

Awestruck, he beheld the woman. She held the shield with both hands, unwavering. The look in her eyes was one of vengeance. She sang again:

The night is long,

Longer still before the dawn,
But dawn must come,
And all that hides must now be drawn...

Light rippled from her hands into the shield's grip. It spread to the edges and began to quench the flames on the other side. Her song continued:

Drawn out to give account
Of all the deeds done in the dark
Of men and beast and demon-spawn
To the One who keeps all time...

The shield now glowed with a golden fire. It wasn't clumsy or reckless like the fire that had just been hurled at them. The great shield glowed like heated crystal.

"Come, Champion!" she called. "We strike!"

Kam tried to lift his kopis but found that he could not. He was falling...

The man woke with a start. Kam had rolled halfway off of his branch. His latching was the only thing that kept him from falling out of the tree. The first signs of the dawn had fought their way into the early morning sky. Kam clambered back onto his branch above Fidaelii. He looked down. She was still sleeping. After stretching, Kam packed his satchel and began a careful descent. Upon reaching the bottom, he was met by Skotos.

"Last watch uneventful?" Kam asked.

"As uneventful as the Lupinwood can be," Skotos smirked. "Should we let them sleep?"

"No. Wake them. I'm going to get the horses."

Skotos nodded. Kam watched for a moment as Skotos made his way up Hathlos' tree. In the slowly growing light, Kam turned southwest. The frost from the evergreen branches brushed against his face. He was so lost in thought that he almost missed the left bend back to the small clearing where the horses were tied. Was Laurl dream-walking to him? Was she trying to warn him of the Road ahead? *Was it her in the dream? The woman bore a resemblance, but her voice was different... It all happened so fast! The beast's fire was so powerful.*

A Lupine cry sounded out. Kam approached the small clearing silently. The smell of death spoke great disappointment to him. To Kam's horror, a pack of seven Lupines were enjoying the company's horses for breakfast. The creatures fought over the carcasses with extreme malice. *They'll be looking for more food. Better move the company toward the Verdant right away.* Kam inched away slowly until he was sure to be out of earshot of the pack. He walked briskly back to camp, careful not to break a sweat or give a tell-tale scent.

Upon reaching the camp, Kam found everyone but Fidaelii awake and packing. Kam climbed the tree and quickly roused her.

"Up, girl. Up! Unless you want to wait here for Lupines to eat you."

"Lupines!" Hathlos called up. "Close?"

"Close enough," Kam said as he descended. "A pack of seven has made quick work of our horses. We will leave for the Verdant now. Right now."

"Give a moment for Fidaelii to pack," Hadros said.

"We leave now, boy. Skotos! Maughlin! Take Grimmalt and scout ahead. Continue northeast. The bandits and I will bring Lucian and Fidaelii as soon as possible. Double back in an hour if you aren't met by danger."

Skotos gave a nod of agreement, and the three soon disappeared into the thickness of the forest. Kam made sure the rest of the Company was not far behind although the going was slower with Lucian and the girl. With yesterday's events still fresh in his mind, Kam moved to the rear guard position. He sent Hathlos and Hadros to walk the point. *If the Lupines catch us, I may be able to hold them until Hathlos gets the Sage and the Acolyte to safety...*

They moved through the thickness as quickly as Fidaelii could lead Lucian. Kam was surprised when the first hour passed and the company reunited with the returning scouts. He was most glad to see Maughlin. Kam motioned for Grimmalt to take the point from Hathlos. Skotos and Maughlin were to strengthen the rear with him. The frozen morning began to melt in a wash of warm air carried on by a westward wind.

"The Great Sea!" Maughlin ventured a whisper. "She brings her blessings through the Wood."

Lupine exultation rang out a few miles behind them.

"And a curse!" Kam cried out. "They have our scent! This wind will serve to uncover us completely. We have to make a stand."

"No." Skotos insisted. "The Verdant isn't far now. There is sanctuary there. The Lupines fear the Maisorvantii. I will delay them. You should have enough time to make the Verdant. Kam, continue beyond the Verdant to the Road along the Sea. Do not turn west to the Daritundii. Doom awaits you there."

"Don't be a fool, Skotos!" Kam said. "Your death won't buy us enough time to make the Verdant. There must be another way."

"Not enough time? Don't underestimate the Capital's Shadow Guard. If the Lupines catch us, there will be no one left to retrieve the Vessel. The Oracle's Call is yours to answer. Yours *alone*, Kam. Enough talk. My Road ends here in the Lupinwood. I am at peace. Farewell, son of Xander."

With those words, Skotos fell behind. Kam watched him slow to a walk and draw his weapons. Kam fought turning back with every breath. It was true. The Verdant was within reach by nightfall. Skotos might delay the hunting pack. The Lupines may become satiated with his bloodshed. It seemed injustice to sacrifice the captain. Kam wanted to send Grimmalt back instead.

The traitor.

The murderer.

"Kam!" It was Fidaelii. "Come on!"

He caught them. He hadn't noticed just how far behind he had fallen. Kam gave Maughlin a nod toward the girl, and Maughlin responded, taking her arm in a run. Kam took up Lucian's arm. The two ran faster. The four of them were right on the heels of Hathlos and Hadros, who were themselves close behind Grimmalt. Every now and then, the Greefadth turned to look behind. Kam noticed his nostrils flared, drinking in every scent of the Wood. The scout's lope was an incredible pace, and it took all of Kam's strength to keep up. He knew Lucian and Fidaelii were exhausted, but he drove them all the harder toward the Verdant. *I will reward my captain's sacrifice.* Fidaelii's pace slowed. The moment it did, Grimmalt stopped and turned.

"The Lupines!" Kam said.

"Are not in pursuit." Grimmalt answered.

"Are you certain?" Kam asked. "We are still a half day from the Verdant."

"The winds came around to the south in the midst of our flight." Grimmalt said. "Our scent has been lost to them. Do you doubt it?"

"I doubt *you*."

"I will gladly take the rear guard," Grimmalt said.

"Too late for that, usurper."

"Where is Skotos?" Hathlos asked.

Kam just shook his head.

"By the Ancient Wisdom, why?" Fidaelii wept. Lucian put his arms around her to give comfort.

"I can remember a time when the Lupine peoples walked in the daylight among the Sons of Magic." Lucian said. "No more. Starsgol has made them into wildlings. They only thirst for death."

"We mourn for the captain at the Verdant if we reach it tonight." Kam said. "Enough rest. We run again. Honor Skotos with your flight."

The rest of the day rushed by in a blur for Kam. Only twice more did they briefly stop because of noise ahead on the Road. The threat of the Lupines never returned, however. Soon, seabird song met their ears, and Kam knew they would reach the Verdant before nightfall. Every muscle ached. Breath seemed impossible to catch. A clearing ahead. *Beyond that, the long slope running to the Verdant by the Sea.* From the top of the hill, Kam surveyed the Eastern Verdant. High stone walls set the ancient garden apart from the surrounding landscape. In relief on the walls was carved the history of ages past. Inside, a myriad of fruit trees and rich, succulent crops grew in the midst of the harshest of winters.

"It's a wonder, no?" Hathlos said. "The Eagloni have

left Skaaran eternal gifts in the Verdants. Think of the good they would do if the Elder Race were still here."

"We must approach carefully," warned Lucian. "The Maisors that tend this Verdant fear the Oracle, but they have little regard for Sons of Men."

The Company renewed their flight down into the valley. The wind once again shifted to the west, and the warmth from the Verdant rushed up to meet them. Carried joyously upon it were a thousand sweet smells. As they reached the floor of the valley, they were met with hundreds of summer insects. Bees made their rounds in the blooming clover. Kam felt like he was back inside Fidaelii's dome. Everything was so completely out of place for the season. Dragonflies darted about in the growing gloam. Kam slowed the company as they approached the intimidating walls. These made the Rending Wall look like a child's plaything. Unlike the Rending Wall, the Verdant walls were welcoming with openings on each of its four sides, no doors to keep visitors out.

"Built for the feeding of Skaaran by the Elder Race," Lucian continued. "The Eagloni were a beautiful people. They walked in light for three ages of men before the Maisorvantii took to hunting them. The Great Hunt is one of the Oracle's greatest sorrows."

"Where do we shelter, Lucian?" Kam asked.

"There are five great stone halls within the Verdant. Any of them will suit."

"And if we are met by Maisorvantii?"

"I will speak with them," Lucian said. "You will find fresh water within the walls as well as provisions for the Road ahead. Get all you require, but go quietly."

Kam felt the magic of ages past as he led his company to the opening in the western wall. Upon reaching it, the grass turned to a polished stone path that led straight to the center stone hall. On either side of the path were rows and rows of fruit trees surrounded by bushes and vegetables. They soon reached the center stone hall. Towering above them were gardens hanging on the walls for hundreds of feet. Water trickled down from an unseen source.

"Maisor craft," Hathlos whispered. "They pay homage to Eagloni ways."

"There is much that the Eagloni taught us," a deep voice echoed loudly through the Verdant. "We could have learned much more."

The company turned as one to see the terribly beautiful silver Maisorvantii. Standing at ten feet, he made even Hadros look small. His piercing blue eyes glowed in the darkness. So fixed was Kam in the depth of them, he found it difficult to move or speak. The Maisor continued to address them.

"Do not fear, little ones. You are all most welcome in my Verdant. Lucian Pharmakeos, too many summers have passed without our feasting together. We will feast tonight."

"Arete' Argyros!" Lucian said. The Keires walked to the great prince of the Maisorvantii and embraced him. "How I have longed to hear your voice again, my friend. How live your brothers?"

"As well as exiles can live, friend. Brukkheom the Supplanter still rules in Reesliks. He allows our tending the Verdants. He sees it as folly and has little regard for all the business of the nobler races. Brukkheom destroyed the Southern Verdant when he led the lesser tribes in our overthrow. He has not come to destroy the two remaining Verdants yet. He is more concerned with rebuilding the Aeries for his purposes, I should think. And your brothers, Lucian? How fares Iyoskothe?"

"Full of *thrilling* conversation, as always," Lucian said with a chuckle. "We were in conference not long ago. Iyoskothe should be coming from the Streotas by way of the Daritundii Plains."

"Evil prowls the Daritundii," said Arete'. "We have seen grey riders all along the northern reaches of the Lupinwood. Dozens of them. They drive blood-red horses to the point of breaking day and night. Underland flags are their standards. A great warrior in flaming black armor leads them. It chills my blood to think that Starsgol has returned, but it feels very similar to the days before the Rending War."

"Do not fear for Iyoskothe's safety, Arete'. He can remain unseen if he so desires."

"I pray you're right, little Brother," Arete' said. Calling out into the darkness, the silver prince continued: "Come! Argyrotu! Light the torches! Bring the food! We feast the Oracle's beauty!"

Hundreds of silver Maisorvantii descended from heights unseen into the Verdant. It was at this moment that Kam realized just how desperately his little company was in need of Arete's good graces. The Argyrotu made short work of preparing the feast. Torches were lit all over the Verdant by the fire from their mouths, and soon the whole of the great garden was aglow in the warmth of Maisorvantii hospitality.

12

The Eastern Verdant

As Arete' led Lucian away from the Company to have a moment alone, the silver prince's subjects set out enormous tables and chairs, rich linen cloths and bejeweled chargers and goblets. Kam watched as casks larger than shipping barrels were brought to the heads of the tables. Stringed instruments were being tuned to flutes and pipes. Drum skins were being stretched taut over great lengths of hollowed-out logs and tied. In the midst of the musicians, some daughters of Argyros were placing large crystals in jeweled mounts fashioned to hold them perfectly. Kam approached the beautiful Maisor maidens slowly. The crystals they held appeared to contain stars. Kam was held captive by their beauty. Every step inside the Verdant held for him the crafting of richer, deeper moments than any he'd ever known. *I am a child in this place. No soul in all of Skaaran would believe any tale I could give of this night.*

"Hail, son of man." Kam was caught off guard by the maiden's salute. Her voice was kind but grand. "By the Elder Race, I welcome you to our home. You have never seen an Astori? These are morning stars that were gifted to the Eagloni in ages past."

"Never before."

It was all Kam could muster.

After an awkward pause, the maiden continued: "These stones sing the old songs, some of the oldest heard in the waking realm. Iyoskothe gave them to us after the Great Hunt as a token of the Oracle's love and thanks for our attempts to save the Eagloni. These Astori originally belonged to them."

"I thought all the Maisorvantii hunted the Eagloni to extinction," Kam said. He expected a vengeful response. It did not come.

"The three noble tribes resisted the murmurings of genocide," replied the maiden. "Iyoskothe warned all the Maisorvantii of the curse that would follow such violence, but the ignoble tribes coveted the Aeries for their riches. Brukkheom spread the lies that Eagloni blood would make all Maisors noble. He told them that Eagloni blood would give them all hearts of fire. The Great Hunt that followed our civil war is a horrible stain on the soul of all of our peoples."

"Have you ever seen one?" Kam asked.

"An Eagloni?"

Kam nodded.

"Sadly, no," the maiden answered. "The last of them were slain when I was very young. The tales my father tells me are worth the full hours of the night. Perhaps we'll hear one!"

The High Council knows nothing of this history! There are Maisorvantii that follow the Oracle as well...

"What strange twists these are!" Arete's voice jolted Kam from his musings. "The house of Hearthstone to feast with a Maisor lord. Be at peace, young master. The noble races did not take part in the Rending War. I am sorry for the many losses of the Sons of Men at the hands of my lesser brothers, though. If your tribes had sought my counsel, they would have known the fruitlessness of a southern invasion."

"Your words are generous, great Prince," answered Kam. "but my father was a part of the northern campaign in the War of Rending."

"Ah! So his Road was through the Blades..." at this Arete' noticed Grimmalt. "And a son of Medras walks with you?"

"Not by my choice, sire," Kam said. "Lucian assures me that I have need of him."

"Then you should listen to our gifted brother. Lucian and his brothers have given light to many a dark path for nearly half an age. Our world would be dim without them and their songs. Look! Our tables are set, our fires are blazing. What now prevents the feast?"

"Only the songs, my Father," answered the maiden with the crystals.

"Then let them come," Arete' said with wild eyes.

With knowing nods, the musicians began to play a single note on their instruments. It softly droned for a few moments then grew gradually with intensity. As it did, the Astori began to hum. The star in each crystal swayed back and forth. Soon, each of the three crystal's stars carried a note. The musicians shifted from their droning to follow. The notes turned into a single melody, with the musicians still following. The motif soon developed into a round. As the round grew in complexity, a golden light came from the stars and spread throughout the festal tables. The light crowned each chair in shimmering essence. Arete' led Lucian to the place of honor at the head of the middlemost table. He then stood to Lucian's right and gestured for all to sit. As the song grew, Arete' took up the enormous cask of wine and made his rounds to fill the pitchers. Kam shook his head in wonder.

"Why does your prince serve the wine?" He asked a nearby Maisor. "Have you no servants?"

The Maisor smiled and shook his head.

"To serve your kin is the highest honor among us. Joy is richer after it is given. It returns with many friends back to your heart. Have you never heard the song?"

"What song?" Kam asked.

At this, the Maisor leapt up into the air, beat his strong wings a time or two, and landed among the musicians. He bellowed a quick run of notes that gave them a cue. They chased the melody and smiled. Then the Maisor sang words that Kam would never forget.

Joy returns with many friends
When she goes out hand in hand
With many a smile and servant's heart
To give her gifts to every part.

So take my hand and go with me
To know the depths of revelry.
We'll dance and sing in blinding light,
And drink and feast to slay the night.

The king of sprites knows not such mirth
As we know now throughout the earth.
For Joy is giv'n without a price,
And when she's giv'n, she's giv'n twice.

So take my hand and go with me
To know the depths of revelry.
We'll dance and sing in blinding light,
And drink and feast to slay the night.

Once there was a scowl or two
Joy chased him out, gave him his due.
She jumped and laughed and turned about,
And beat the little devil out.

So take my hand and go with me
To know the depths of revelry.
We'll dance and sing in blinding light,
And drink and feast to slay the night.

Wine is her friend, the fat pig, too.
The birdsong in the dusking hue,
The smell of pipe, the kiss of love.
The stars all singing up above.

So take my hand and go with me
To know the depths of revelry.
We'll dance and sing in blinding light,
And drink and feast to slay the night.

So take my hand and go with me
To know the depths of revelry.
We'll dance and sing in blinding light,
And drink and feast to slay the night.

The musicians continued the theme at a faster and faster rate. Kam was so fixed in the song itself that he did not notice the dozens of Maisors dancing. They made their circle all the way around the feasting tables. The singer took his place with them. Something in Kam wanted to dance, but the fear of making a spectacle of himself as well as the possibility of being crushed restrained him. His heart danced though. For the first time in many years, the teasing taste of joy skipped slightly within him. He glanced down the table at his little company. Grimmalt seemed to be transfixed in a memory. Fidaelii was laughing and clapping and singing all the words. Hathlos had his arm around his son. The two were nodding their heads to the rhythm. Kam looked back to the head of the table. Lucian sat still, soaking in the moment. Kam barely noticed Maughlin until he heard his oldest friend's whisper.

"The world…"

The music drowned out the words.

"What?" Kam shouted.

"The foundation of the world, boy!" Maughlin shouted back. "Pleasure and great joy! This is what the Mending War will look like when it's won. This is your task. Is it a worthy endeavor?"

Kam gave no answer. He thought of Praius and Skotos. In the midst of the songs and the dances and the revelries and the wine, firm questions still gnawed at him. Questions that held no answers. Questions about the Road ahead. Questions about Roads already travelled. Of unnecessary loss. Of hope deferred.

The Maisorvantii songs went long into the night. As the moon rose to its zenith, the songs became more and more gentle and subdued in nature. Kam took leave of his host and sought solitude. After the day's flight, he was exhausted. The food and wine served to strengthen his body, but his mind was as plagued as ever. *This fool's errand will end us all, even the girl. To seek out the Aeries' Gate now that bloodthirsty tribes of Maisorvantii have moved in there might not be the best way. But it must be better than the shifting Blades around Medras. Gods and demons! I just want to be with my beloved again. I just want to drink in the sight of her. Smell her hair. Her hair!* Kam reached into his satchel and pulled the sweetest gift from it. *Laurl...* He held her locks to his cheek and wept.

"You miss her."

The Acolyte.

"Why do you follow me, girl?"

"I want you to know you're not alone."

"I *want* to be alone!"

"No one wants to be alone, Kam," Fidaelii replied. "People are made for each other. That is why you cling so dearly to Laurl's gift there."

"Spare me the idle tripe. What do you know? What days have you lived, girl?"

"Lonely days. Days spent wondering about my mother, my father," said Fidaelii. "Where they are now. Are they even still in the waking realm? If so, do they think of me? Will they ever journey to Edraeth to find me? Will they come when I am gone? Will I miss their coming while I am away on this quest?"

"I'm sure you can ask your imaginary Oracle if we make it to Him alive."

"I've spent many nights asking the Oracle about them."

"And you'll spend many more, I'm sure. Now, if I may take my leave of you, miss. I have to think about the Road ahead."

"As you wish, good Hearthstone."

Kam rolled his eyes as he left her. *Good Hearthstone, hah!* He had walked almost half the length of the Verdant when he was met by Maughlin.

"You should sleep, Son."

"I can't, Uncle. I'm having doubts about the Aeries' Road. If the report of Maisor settlement there is correct, the Aeries may prove more treacherous than the Blades of Medras. Neither Road to the Sanctum is desirable. We must choose between facing our death in the open in the Aeries or finding it in a knife in our backs in the Blades."

"The Aeries will be easier to get through unseen," Maughlin replied. "Lucian thinks it the right road. We should continue on through the Eagloni ruins. Set your mind at ease, Son. Go and sleep."

The two walked back to the great stone hall in the center of the Verdant.

"Tomorrow we will restock our provisions and make for the Deltas," said Maughlin. "Arete' knows a few ferrymen who will speed us on. He will also send word to his brother Siyonte' the Golden in the north to give us aid. All will be well. You will see."

"I wish I held your certainty, Uncle."

"There," Maughlin motioned to a mass of great silk pillows. "Arete' has your bed prepared. We journey on the northern edge of the Lupinwood tomorrow. You will need fresh eyes and ears to lead us well. Collect them now in the gift of sleep."

"Good night, Maughlin."

"Good night, Son."

Kam did not know the weight of the day until he laid down. Sleep came like a thief and overtook him.

The beast thundered again, and Kam felt the heat of a thousand furnaces.

"I need your help!" Kam cried out in the darkness. "I can't see to strike! Please! My lady! Sing again!"

Thunderous bellows mingled with evil laughter echoed all around him. The heat increased, and Kam felt hot breath upon his face.

"Sing, lady, or we perish!"

Fire erupted before him. The sun itself could not have made for a more terrifying assault. It gave faint light, but not the light Kam was looking for. He heard a rustling at his back. In a moment, the woman was standing beside him. She held the glorious shield before them both. Both of them crouched behind it to be spared the blast. When it came, they were pushed back several feet. Kam put his left hand on the shield's grip to steady it. It was blazingly hot. He removed his hand in an instant.

Awestruck, he beheld the woman. She held the shield with both hands, unwavering. The look in her eyes was one of vengeance. She sang again:

> The night is long,
> Longer still before the dawn,
> But dawn must come,
> And all that hides must now be drawn...

Light rippled from her hands into the shield's grip. It spread to the edges and began to quench the flames on the other side. Her song continued:

> Drawn out to give account
> Of all the deeds done in the dark
> Of men and beast and demon-spawn
> To the One who keeps all time...

The shield now glowed with a golden fire. It wasn't clumsy or reckless like the fire that had just been hurled at them. The great shield glowed like heated crystal.

"Come, Champion!" she called. "We strike!"

At that, she leapt up and charged with her shield into the darkness. Kam's kopis was light in his hand. He kept his left hand on her right shoulder and followed closely behind. A roar of surprise sounded out in the murk.

"Now, Champion! Now!" the woman commanded.

Kam swung around her to face the beast. He had never seen the likes of it. It was as tall as the Rending Wall with four heads. The scales that were its armor glinted with mockery in the light of the shield. The heads of the beast looked like wolves, with the ears of a jackal and the jaws of a lion. The front claws of the beast were the talons of a great bird of prey. Its hind legs were those of a bear. The beast laughed at the sight of Kam with his father's kopis.

"So you would come to kill me, little one? Many have tried. You are smaller than most. I see you would take the road through the Aeries Gate."

For the first time, Kam realized that this was no dream. He was realm-walking, but there was no dome in this place to give him aid. A very real sense of danger gripped him as never before. The beast let out another howl followed by a great burst of fire. Kam dove back behind the shield that the lady held.

"This is no dream!" He cried out.

"You are not ready," she sobbed. "Leave me, or we both perish."

"I cannot!"

With that, he plunged back into the fray. Charging the beast, he rolled just under another fireburst. Jumping up, Kam redoubled his pace. He reached the beast's front left leg. Diving to avoid a great talon swipe, Kam looked up from beneath its belly. Knowing the kopis was not long enough to reach any vital organs, he went for a hamstring. The hide was too tough for a sideswipe. The beast was turning... Kam did his best to keep pace and stay in its rear guard, but the beast's steps were just too large. He plunged the kopis into one of its heels... It let out a horrendous wail.

The talon came for Kam quickly.

He was thrown through the air... The ground was an iron wall... The blackness was rushing upon him...

"*Kam! Kam!*" *Maughlin's voice rang out.*

"Kam! Up!" Maughlin was shaking him. "Wake up, Son! A dark day!"

Kam opened his eyes. He was back in the great stone hall in the Verdant.

"What is it, Uncle?"

Maughlin had tears in his eyes.

"Fidaelii was taken in the night."

13

Pursuit

"Taken!" Kam sat straight up. "How?"

Maughlin shook his head. "All we know is that they came in through the northern wall."

"It's impossible!" Kam answered. Seeing Arete' approach, he addressed the silver prince: "How on earth could anyone slip past your sentinels?"

"I am as dumbfounded as you, little Captain," said Arete'. "There is magic here in the Verdant that only Starsgol himself could confound. Whoever took your Acolyte, one thing is certain: they are fearsome foes. They slew my north wall sentinels in quick fashion and disguised themselves in such magic that no alarm was raised. If Fidaelii still lives, you will have to summon all the resources at your disposal to rescue her."

"Which way did the abductors flee?" Kam pressed. He stood up to dress himself for the day's business. Xander's kopis and dagger were quickly put on, and the pack was checked for necessary supplies.

"They fled the way they came in, to the northwest." Arete' answered. "I have sent scouts to track them. They have not returned. We found six sets of horse's prints."

"Is our Company ready, Maughlin?" Kam asked. "We need to leave right away."

"Kam, there is something else you should know," Arete' said. "The horses' prints weren't the only ones in the muddy track north of the Verdant. We also found signs of Lupine activity. Worse than that, there were reports yesterday of Pyropos activity in the Deltas. Your quest stands on the brink of darkness. If the Red Maisors are a part of your Acolyte going missing; you will need all the help you can get."

"I will gladly take any you can give," Kam replied, bowing low. Turning to Maughlin, Kam gave the order. "Assemble the Company! We leave at once."

In very little time, the company had indeed assembled at the northern wall of the Verdant. Before them stood Arete' with his personal guard of five brilliantly arrayed Maisorvantii. Kam surveyed the rescue party, and suddenly dread filled his heart.

"Where is Grimmalt?" Kam could barely hold the hysteria. He walked to Maughlin. "Where is the son of treachery? *You* urged me to bring him, and now we see what that choice has yielded! *He* has taken Fidaelii to Starsgol and their doom. I should have killed him in Rorgus."

"Let us be going," Maughlin urged. "If there be treachery among us, we will not find it here talking."

At the nod from Kam, Arete' gave the command: "Up! Argyrotu, up! Once more, we war for the Ancient Wisdom. We war to undo the evil visited upon us!"

The five Maisors hoisted Kam and his diminished Company onto their backs and leapt up into the air. Arete' launched close behind and soon took the lead of the company. They flew due north and soon met the edge of the Shifting Deltas. Upon seeing the water, Arete' signaled to turn northwest and make greater speed. Flying was terrifying to Kam, and he held onto the neck of the great silver Maisorvantii with all his might. The rush of the wind made his eyes water, and when the Maisors would turn, it took everything for Kam not to fall off. He tried to spy how everyone else was faring, but when he lifted his head, he was rebuked by the Maisor he was riding. The Maisor was trying to explain the particulars of flying. He kept saying something about "dragging" and "lifting", but Kam's mind was filled with thoughts of Fidaelii. The Maisor droned on for well over an hour until finally Kam noticed the silver beast's wings lifting to catch the air. They were slowing. Kam ventured a forward look;

the early morning scouts were approaching and signaled the ground below.

All of the Maisors landed. Jumping down from his carrier, Kam ran over to where Arete' and Maughlin were standing. They were pointing to a large patch of ground.

"Look!" Arete' shouted.

Before them appeared the prints in conference. Quite a bit of pacing. There looked to be a scuffle or two. Horse and rider and Lupine and Maisor tracks. Kam scoured the ground searching for traces of Fidaelii. He found some blood smeared on a low hanging branch. *Not human, too thick.*

"Any signs of Grimmalt?" Maughlin called to him.

"A Greefadth would have to make a mistake to leave traces," Kam called back, "normally when they're injured or disoriented. There are no traces of the traitor. No traces of the girl, either."

"She must have been left on a horse," Arete' said. "See, here! The tracks diverge. Most of the horses continue on northwest, toward the Daritundii. The Lupines follow. Then there looks to be one horse that follows the Maisorvantii prints into the thickness of the Deltas. What will you do, Kam?"

"I will follow to the Daritundii."

"Kam, remember what Skotos told us in Rorgus about the Daritundii Plains," warned Hathlos. "I would not seek Starsgol, even for the sake of the girl."

"The lone rider is a diversion," Kam answered.

"Can you be so sure?" asked Hathlos. "Perhaps we should hear what Lucian or Maughlin thinks..."

"I've heard enough from both Lucian and Maughlin!" Kam bellowed. "They are the reason we are on this Road hunting the traitor they argued for! Their wisdom has shown to be folly. If this quest is mine, then I will choose the Roads and be hung by the consequences. If you are coming with me, then come! Otherwise, find your deaths in the Deltas."

"I am sworn to your service, Hearthstone," Hathlos replied solemnly. "Hadros and I are with you, even to Starsgol's jaws in the Daritundii." Turning to Maughlin, he said, "Where will you go, friend?"

"Lucian and I will find a ferryman. The Aeries Road has always been my Road." Turning to Kam, Maughlin had sorrow in his voice. "I wish not to part with you, Kam, especially in this way. I think Fidaelii will be found in the Deltas."

"Grimmalt has no use for the Deltas, Uncle. His craft is better served by the Blades of the Streotas beyond the Daritundii. That is where we will find the Acolyte. Once I kill Starsgol, I will end Grimmalt as well. If I live beyond that, I will have many questions for the Oracle. Questions that he *will* answer."

"Very well," said Arete'. Addressing his lieutenant, the silver prince continued: "Thystote', travel with Maughlin and Lucian to the ferry docks, and leave your two guards to keep watch for their safety. After you have done that, take the scouts and return to the Verdant. Wait for me there. We will travel on to the Biting Fens and try to catch the main party unawares at the edge of the Daritundii by the Shifting Lake. Take the scouts! May strength go with you!"

"And with you!" Thystote' answered in a salute.

Maughlin approached Kam and embraced him.

"May our Roads meet in the Sanctum, Son."

Kam said nothing. Maughlin continued.

"Kam, if you are to succeed, your faith in the quest must be strengthened. You must see this as a worthwhile endeavor. You must see the world for what it is and value *all* of Skaaran as the Oracle does. Do *not* give in to the pull of those tides that would sweep you away into yourself. Look beyond. Look into the eyes of those whom your life could benefit. Find your resolve there. Never forget that I am for you, Son."

"Be careful, Uncle." Kam beat back sorrow. "If the Sanctum is real, you will find me there."

Maughlin walked to Thystote', turned one last time to face Kam, and gave a gentle smile. The old man raised his arm and was hoisted atop his host. Before Kam could form a goodbye, Thystote' and his four Maisors were in the air with Maughlin and Lucian, turning north toward the many ferry docks that peppered the southern shore of the Shifting Deltas. *Goodbye, Uncle. Your constant hope will be a new Remembering for me to carry on the Road.*

Kam turned to Arete'.

"Well, my lord, we must catch them without giving away our approach."

"My scouts gave report of seeing no cause for the tracks. They would spot the grey riders for a moment only, and then they would be gone."

"How can this be?"

"They must be realm-walking somehow. I've never heard tale of anyone being able to do it on horseback, much less an entire party on horseback. This is strong magic."

"How are we supposed to find them?" Kam hoped his desperation didn't show. Arete's answer offered little assurance.

"I don't know."

14

Captive

Fidaelii did her best to remember the old signal songs. Her hands were bound, her head covered with a sack that reeked. She was lying across a galloping horse and was held there by someone very strong. They had been riding for hours. Fighting nausea, Fidaelii closed her eyes and tried to remember what her abductor looked like. *Gaunt face. Grey cloak. Filed teeth. His eyes... they seemed so empty. And the insects! They were everywhere, crawling all over me!* She shuddered at the memory. The first few lines of a song fell into her mind. She sang.

> *"Spring forth! Spring forth,*
> *O blessed light, and overtake*
> *The night..."*

A Maisor cry ripped through the air.

"Shut that noise!" came a cruel hiss from a rider ahead. "Do you want us to be seen?"

A fist came down upon her back, and Fidaelii let out a cry. She was hoisted to a riding position in the front of the saddle. Fidaelii felt hot breath on her neck. The smell of it was rancid.

"Starsgol has some questions for you, my girl. Don't go makin' any problems, now. We know you need to get there in one piece, but the trampers don't." Laughter erupted all around her.

Trampers! Fidaelii heard many stories from Praius about them. *That would explain the insects...*

"Where are you taking me?" she asked the rider.

"Dunno," he replied. "My pay takes us to the ferry landings. That's all Brukkheom hired me for. He's the one you'll have to deal with soon enough."

There was no way for Fidaelii to track the time on the road, but she had never ridden a horse at the pace they were keeping. Its breathing was labored, and whenever it whinnied, the sound of it was more of a growl. The beast seemed to give no protestation to how hard it was being driven. The rider gave a cruel chuckle whenever his heels were dug into the beast's sides. It wasn't long before they were slowing to a canter and then to a trot before stopping altogether. *The ferry landings.*

"You're late." Fidaelii heard a voice that made her shudder. "I should dock you fifty fluerons."

"Killing the sentinels took longer than planned, great King," came the reply. "But we have the girl here. Why dicker about time? Here is your prize."

"Show her to me."

The sack was snatched from Fidaelii's head, and she peered into the darkness. The dawn was nowhere to be found. She wished for some light. In answer to her unspoken request, there was a hissing sound, followed by a click. A large sword of white-hot flame danced in the hands of a great, red Maisorvantii. Several more flaming swords were ignited all around her.

"Do you know who I am, little sprite?"

"No."

"I am Brukkheom, son of Brukkheon, king of all the Maisorvantii. My tribe is the Pyropos, greatest in war and treachery. Skaaran is mine by right, and it will be returned to me as a reward of the Oracle's overthrow. You are here to give aid to Starsgol. He says you know how to find the Oracle's Sanctum. Is this true?"

"No."

"You lie!"

"I've never left Edraeth in all of my life," Fidaelii said. "And if you think the Oracle's overthrow is possible, you are a fool. Those who would go to war with the Oracle will only be met with destruction."

"You can give that report to Starsgol, girl." Turning to his guard, Brukkheom pointed his sword down the road toward the Daritundii Plains. "Follow the riders and make sure the girl is placed into our lord's hands. Then return to me in the Aeries. I go to make ready our troops. For Starsgol!"

"For Starsgol!" They answered in salute.

Fidaelii watched Brukkheom give the leader of the grey riders a large bag. *Payment for his services.* The two moved north toward the thickness of the Deltas. Soon they were out of sight. She was jolted by the rider's crack of the reigns. Racing to a gallop once again, her captors set themselves to their work. Through the early morning gloom, amidst the fiendish glee of the riders and the cries of their driven horses, a song broke out from the Maisors above:

Starsgol reigns in strength and power,
Kind to those who give tribute.
In every dark and failing hour,
He makes the Brothers' voices mute.

He brings us war and brings us blood.
He brings us riches that are good.

The Ancient Wisdom is subdued
With acts of valor from our sword.
He has no answer for our brood;

Captive

The false one flees before our lord.

He brings us war, and glory, too.
We give him thanks; that is his due.

There is no use for peace with all.
The weak are conquered for their good.
The great will overtake the small
And rule in supreme brotherhood.

He brings us war, returns our land.
We'll rule Skaaran at his right hand.

The song continued on until the dawning. The faint light brought many horrors to Fidaelii. The horse she was on was blood red. The rider that held her tight was no living man. Before her flew Underland standards. The abductors kept to the road that skirted the Deltas with the edge of the Lupinwood on the left racing by. Fidaelii looked up to see the red Maisorvantii fly ahead then circle back to scout behind the riders. She felt the presence of concealing magic yet again. *Should I venture a verse?* It was hard to think in the midst of the Maisor's song and dark spells. She looked at her hands and twisted the rope slightly. *Loose! There may be a chance...* Suddenly, her horse reared back and rose up. Both Fidaelii and her captor were thrown several feet. Ignoring the pain from the fall, Fidaelii gathered her wits and stood up slowly.

All of the riders had been halted. There, no more than

fifty feet ahead of Fidaelii, stood the most terrifying and beautiful figure she had ever seen. His skin was that of polished obsidian. He wore robes of the richest scarlet and purple, and in his hand was a golden scythe. Fierce golden flames danced around his feet, which would occasionally leap as high as his shaved head. His skin bore the scars of lightning and fire and countless battles. He stood over the slain leader of the wicked troop and quickly brought the scythe down to finish the dying horse. Fidaelii watched his gaze become fixed on her.

"Fidaelii Charis," he called out. "Your deliverance has come."

Upon saying this, the warrior knelt to take up the fire at his feet. He stood again, and he threw the fire over his head. As it fell, he fell with it into the earth and was gone. Before Fidaelii could despair at his disappearance, golden fire sprung from the earth amid the riders and the warrior with it. He was upon them as a summer storm that comes in the heat of the day. There was little hope for the riders. They were clumsy in their defense, and his blazing scythe made quick work of two and their otherworldly horses. Only two now remained. The one nearest him began to change form. *What sorcery? A Greefadth!*

"Grimmalt!" Fidaelii cried out. "You traitor! Why have you conspired against the Oracle?"

Grimmalt gave no answer but ran past her to intercept the rider that held her captive for the length of their journey. He met the Underlander just in time and grappled his knife away. The scuffle continued only a moment more until Grimmalt overpowered the wicked one and ended the threat to Fidaelii. He turned to face the warrior.

"The Pyropos above!" Grimmalt warned. "Be on guard, Keires!"

"The red Maisors do not come," the warrior answered, scanning the sky. "They flee to give report to their king."

Grimmalt walked slowly to him. "My lord Iyoskothe, has my doom come?"

"I am come to keep the girl from reaching Starsgol," Iyoskothe answered. "I see no guile in your eyes, Grimmalt son of Grennam. You were willing to die for this girl?"

"Your brother Lucian believed her to be of great value to the quest. I could not wake the others in time. In the scuffle with the sentinels, I slew one of the riders and disguised myself."

"Fidaelii Charis," said Iyoskothe. "The mystery concerning your life will be revealed in time. For now, you are to go with Grimmalt and camp tonight just before the Biting Fens. When Kam and his party catches you, give report of all you have seen here and speak for Grimmalt's innocence. Once you are all together again, make haste to ascend the Streotas by way of the Shifting Falls and make for the Gap of Starsgol. The Aeries Road is closed to you now. That is the will of the Oracle for you in this day. Do you understand?"

"Yes, my lord." Fidaelii bowed her head.

"Grimmalt, son of Grennam," Iyoskothe said, turning to the Greefadth.

"Yes, my lord?"

"Stay with Fidaelii and watch over her until she is safe again in the hands of the Chosen One. They must walk the Harrows together. That is the will of the Oracle for you in this day. Do you understand?"

"Yes, my lord." Grimmalt acquiesced, bowing.

"I have been recalled to Medras," said Iyoskothe. "The Council of Thieves is at great unrest there. Your cousin Mendlakk is dealing with multiple plots from the younger Greefadths concerning his overthrow. When Kam comes, make haste for the mountain road. Do not delay! Our time is short. Stay hidden, and may the Oracle give you strength!"

At this, the great warrior shouldered his scythe. He turned from them and began to walk down the road toward the Daritundii. When he had made about fifty paces, he bent down to take up the flames around his feet. Throwing them over his head, he fell straight down into the earth and was gone.

"The Fens are only a half day's journey from here, Fidaelii," said Grimmalt. "We should get going."

Fidaelii did not move. The shock of the past hours came crashing down on her. She was truly alone. This Greefadth was a stranger to her.

If all the stories about him are true, he cannot be trusted...
...I'm going to die out here...

"Fidaelii," his voice was gentle. "I know you're overwhelmed..."

"Overwhelmed!" she cried, fighting tears. "My father Praius is dead! My captain Skotos... dead! I was taken while I slept to be a slave to Starsgol for reasons I don't know! The only thing I'm sure of is that I shouldn't be here with you. This is a mistake, Grimmalt. How can I trust you? Why should I believe anything you say?"

Grimmalt drew his dagger and walked to the girl. He placed it in her hand and knelt before her. The Greefadth then took her wrist and made her place the dagger at his neck.

"My life no longer belongs to me, Fidaelii," he assured. "I had to come to terms with that when I ran away from Medras after the Rending War. My exile in Rorgus taught me many things. Hard truths. Terrible reckonings. If you would feel more secure without me, take my life."

Fidaelii dropped the dagger.

"I was taught not to walk the Road of murder, thief. It is the Oracle's will that you lead me on. Speak not to me again unless I ask you."

Grimmalt nodded, then motioned in the direction that they were to go. He led her off the Daritundii trade road to the northwest. Soon they were in the underbrush on the edge of the Deltas and moving at a hurried pace.

Fidaelii kept her distance at first. After noticing that she was slowing their flight to the Biting Fens, she kept apace with Grimmalt on her left. They trudged on for hours. He would occasionally glance at her and beyond to check the flank. Fidaelii could see sorrow mingled with a desire to speak in his eyes. She thought of how skilled he was in battle, and how he leapt at the Underlander who was trying to backstab her. *He did risk his life by trying to save mine...*

"Grimmalt."

"Yes, young one?"

"How far to the Fens?"

"Another hour or two. We are very close now."

They walked in silence for the better part of an hour before either of them spoke again. It was she.

"Grimmalt."

"Yes, Fidaelii?"

"Why are you going to the Sanctum?"

He stopped, and she with him. The Greefadth heaved a sigh and faced her.

"I... I don't know. I suppose to reclaim a feeling that I lost a long time ago."

"What feeling is that?" Fidaelii asked.

Grimmalt turned again and renewed their flight. His pace was quicker than before.

"Usefulness!" he called over his shoulder.

Fidaelii ran to catch up. She didn't venture any more

questions. The girl half jogged to keep apace for at least another hour. The sun had peaked and was settling down in the afternoon sky when Grimmalt finally slowed. As soon as he did, Fidaelii felt her legs buckle beneath her. She collapsed.

"No. Not here," Grimmalt said as he picked her up into his arms. The old Greefadth carried her to a thicket. He placed her gently into the dense underbrush.

"You sleep now, little one. I'll not be far away. I'm going to get us dinner."

Fidaelii could hardly keep her eyes open long enough to watch him slip away. Sleep overtook her. It was dark when the smell of roasted meat woke her. She stretched and rose and walked over to Grimmalt. He was standing over two holes in the ground. There was a fire in one, and it yielded very little smoke. The Greefadth had arranged sticks over the fire where he was roasting a rabbit. The meat was wrapped in herbs. *Just as Praius used to cook it!* Fidaelii couldn't remember when she smelled anything quite as good in her life. The trauma of the day was washing away in this sweet reminder of home.

"Do you eat rabbit, young one?" Grimmalt asked.

"It's one of my favorite meats, especially the way you're cooking it!" Fidaelii smiled.

"Not too gamey, eh?" Grimmalt said.

Fidaelii shook her head.

As they enjoyed the meal together, Fidaelii sensed that

something was weighing heavily on Grimmalt's heart. She wanted more than anything to know what it was. Before she could think of the words to say, Grimmalt spoke.

"You should know that I put this Company in great peril, Fidaelii."

"Every part of the Wilds is perilous, Grimmalt."

"You don't understand, girl!" he said. "If we are to walk the Medras Road through the Blades and to the Gap of Starsgol, every person seen with me will have a death sentence on his head. I should go on alone and try to secure the Gap. Kam will be here soon. I've marked his scent as well as the bandits'. They come with three Maisor escorts for your safety. I must go."

Grimmalt stood to leave. Fidaelii stood to stop him.

"Don't go, Grimmalt! I know that you're afraid and ashamed. I will speak for your valor. Stay with me, please?"

"Kam Hearthstone will know no mercy when he arrives. He will see the race he hunted standing before him and will hear no sound reasoning. If I am to serve this Company, I must do it alone for a while. You will find me at the Gap of Starsgol, Fidaelii, if either of us live to see it. Hold me here no longer. Already the sound of Maisor wings tear at the air."

Fidaelii nodded. She fought the tears. In moments, Grimmalt was gone. *Thank you, strong Prince. Your kindness will not be forgotten.* She suddenly felt a strong hand on her shoulder. She was being turned around. A scratchy beard pressed against her forehead. The embrace was firm.

Kam Hearthstone.

15

The Wings of Eagles

Kam woke with a start. Surprising even himself, his first thoughts were for Fidaelii's safety. *Were the events of yesterday just a dream? Riding on the wings of the Argyrotu... Chasing the Underlanders that abducted the girl... Parting with Maughlin and Lucian at the crossroads into the Deltas... Finding Fidaelii at last and learning of Grimmalt's disappearance...* Kam rubbed his eyes and looked up. The sun was already well on the way to its midday height. He rubbed his eyes and looked around. The shelters were gathered and packed, except for his. He stood up quickly and stretched, and immediately began gathering his things to pack away.

"Why did no one wake me? The day is half done!" he complained gruffly.

"Good morn', Hearthstone!" Fidaelii exclaimed, approaching him. "Hathlos thought it best to let you sleep. He said you would need to regain your strength."

Kam shook his head in a daze. *No dream. Thank the gods the girl is safe.* He was stuffing the last corner of his shelter into his pack when Arete' and the two Maisorvantii scouts returned. Their landing was almost silent.

"What word of the Road ahead?" Kam asked him.

"Danger," Arete' answered. "Fraught with danger. The south side of the Shifting Lake holds a column of grey riders."

"We take the north side, then," Kam directed.

"The day will be spent traversing the Fens," said Arete'. "It will be very slow going. We could fly you there."

"There are only three of you," Kam said. "You would be slowed by carrying two, my lord. Stealth is to be held by continuing on foot. I don't want to raise any alarm with Starsgol this day if it can be helped."

"Very well, little captain. We will follow your lead." Turning to the rest of the Company, Arete' called out.

"Come! The Gap awaits!"

It was a day full of anxiety for Kam. The flight of the Argyrotu had brought them the distance of two day's ride on horse to the northwest, and the Maisors' presence was a comfort to him. Kam's thoughts turned to his father, and the many roads through the Streotas in the north that Xander walked in the Rending War. The magic that lay upon the mountains in the distance made the roads ever changing. There was no guarantee his little company would ever make the Gap. They were closer now to the Daritundii plains than ever before, and the rumors of Starsgol's return and prowling there came upon Kam again. He forced these out of his mind to refocus on his immediate objectives.

First, the Biting Fens. Then, we must make it around Shifting Lake to begin our ascent into the Streotas.

The Cyprus trees that skirted the Fens grew thick as a maze, and the morning dew was slow in burning off of the lower branches so that every garment in the party became thoroughly wetted. Though the sun made its course in its time, they could not mark it save for a few open thickets here and there that they dare not venture into. The thick air smelled clean and alive. Every breath, as anxious as it was, seemed like the first breath of the morning. There was a tension that hung in these woods of life and death. It was exhilarating and fearful all at once. Fidaelii's news of Brukkheom and the Pyropos from last night disturbed Kam. The Maisorvantii were the only tribes in all of Skaraan that were unconquered in the Rending War. In all of Kam's past travels, he never encountered any of the dragon peoples outside of their lands between the Stone and Skaaroth rivers.

Kam's grandfather Titus told him stories of the old days when he, as a boy, had gone with his grandfather to trade in the grand capital city of Reesliks in the south. Titus' favorite possession was an old weapon he brought back from the city. The weapon was passed down to Xander, who told Kam that it was the hilt of a fire sword. The weapon had been broken, and Titus tried for years to fix it with no success. Kam would study it for hours as a small boy, dreaming of the day he would finish his grandfather's work. "*One of the reasons they could not be conquered.*" Kam heard Xander's voice in his head. "*They rule the skies, the seas, and the land that they chose, and they chose the best land in all of Skaraan.* Why they would want anything to do with this forest was beyond Kam's understanding, so he sought to know more.

"Arete', why would the Pyropos want to hunt in this forest?" he asked in earnest.

"This was once all Maisorvantii land, Kam. All of Skaraan, from the great river that cuts the south, to the very center where your capital city of Skaaroth floats on a lake was ours. Skaaroth itself is built on the ruins of our first capital of Reesliks. Then came our civil war, and the great plague among us, long before your people came to this land. We made our way to the land you now know, burying our dead all along the way. The lesser tribes have prospered in these last hundred years, growing in number again, so that they must reach out for new resources. The hunting parties are small, with two or three in them at most, but still not to be trifled with."

"Fidaelii spoke of a fire sword," Kam said. "Can Brukkheom not breathe fire?"

"No," answered Arete'. "None of the common tribes of the Maisorvantii possess that ability. Only the three ruling tribes of the Maisorvantii peoples: the Argyrotu, the Chryseotu and the Damasotu hold both the Astori, the singing stars you heard at our feast in the Verdant, and the hearts of fire. The hearts of fire were given to us directly from the Oracle Himself. The Astori were entrusted to us by the last of the Eagloni Elders before the Great Hunt took them. The hearts of fire are our birthright. The other tribes must make their fire by... ...stranger methods."

"How did the plague come?" Kam asked.

"Long before any Son of Man set foot in Skaaran, Reesliks was the jewel of the earth. At that time, the Maisorvantii were ruled by the kings of the three noble tribes: the Damasotu, the Chryseotu, and the Argyrotu. Our lives were peaceful and prosperous until wicked rumors were spread that hearts of fire and nobility could be obtained through drinking Eagloni blood. We aren't sure where the rumors started, but we suspect it was among the Pyropos."

"Is that what caused the Great Hunt?" Kam asked. "By the gods!"

"Our fathers tried to dispel the rumors by calling on Iyoskothe and his Brothers for help from the Oracle, but Brukkheon, his son Brukkheom, and the rest of the

187

tribe's indignation only grew more hot. They thought we were trying to keep the secret of power to ourselves, so they hunted the Eagloni for years in their quest for power. They overthrew the ruling races of the Maisorvantii and exiled us to the Verdants. The plague came shortly after."

"From drinking the Eagloni blood?" Kam asked.

"That is the only explanation we have for it," Arete' answered. "The plague never visited our peoples. Only those who hunted the Eagloni. We keep the Verdants to honor the Eagloni and their ways."

The rest of the day was spent in very slow trudging. Kam kept running Arete's tale through his mind. The entire party spent all their energy devoted to stealth, feeling they were being watched. Traversing the Biting Fens proved to be slow going. More than once, there was a little outcry from one of the members who were nipped or stung by the native flora. After a very late meal, they came to the Shifting Lake with peat stacked up all around it.

"There is a magic upon it," said Arete'. "It is fed by the Shifting Falls, so named because you never know where they will go. The Falls' headwater is in Medras, capital city of the Greefadths. Because Medras moves, the Falls move. Because the Falls move, the Lake moves. That is why the Fens are so broad and the Deltas to the east so wide."

Kam turned around to see how Fidaelii was faring. She was smiling, talking with Hathlos and Hadros. *The bandits make for good company.* Arete's guards were just behind them, bringing up the rear. *We just may make the Gap with the help of these Maisors.* Kam's small troop had circled halfway around the lake on the northern side when an awful shriek was heard high above them.

"SQUALLORS!!" Hathlos cried out. "Care for the girl, Hadros! Find cover!"

Hadros stood transfixed. His eyes never left the sky. Kam followed his gaze, and despair took a deadly grip. Descending from the clouds were dozens of hellspawn. The name given to the beasts was a Greefadth one, because encountering one was like trying to live through a vengeful storm. Covered with black and brown scales, and breathing death with what looked like a hellish mixture of fire and lightning, Kam knew that the company's doom was nigh. He ran to Hadros and rammed the boy with his shoulder.

"Did you not hear your father, Hadros? Get the Acolyte to cover!" Kam looked to Arete', who was stretching his wings in the midst of a hail of lighting-fire from the Squallors.

"Up, Argyrotu!" commanded Arete'. "For the end of evil!"

The two guards rushed to the aid of their prince. Even as they did, Kam winced in the midst of the shower of death that fell all around him. *The Squallors have the heights. The Maisors have little chance.* Kam looked to Fidaelii. She was being hurried around the lake by Hadros. Kam and

189

Hathlos sprinted to catch them. With the noise of battle above, Kam would glance the skies to see Arete' slicing through the air to deal a deathblow as he pressed the party on. *The squallors are so many...* Kam hardly noticed that Fidaelii had stopped running.

"We have to help them!" she shouted. "Kam, we have to do something!"

"What can be done?" Kam asked. "Arete' goes to his doom for you, girl!"

"No!" Fidaelii cried out. Several of the squallors were swarming a Maisor guard. They were clinging to his body and wings and breathing deadly fire. The mortal mass plummeted into the lake. Steam rose from the spot they entered.

"Hathlos!" Kam said. "Your bow! Can you reach them to help?"

"Not yet." Hathlos answered. He walked to the girl. "Sing, Fidaelii. Sing now, and witness the lost glory of the Aeries!"

With that, Hathlos drew one of his sinister bolts, notched it, and squatted down. He began to flex the muscles in his arms and the whole of his old body appeared taut. With a mighty shout, he sprung into the air. As he did, two magnificent white wings erupted from his shoulders. Kam was so dumbstruck by this beauty that he forgot about the Squallors. Only Hadros' voice shook him to action:

"Kam! We must protect the Acolyte! Kam, please! Help me!"

The three found the brush quickly and watched in awe as Hathlos climbed for the heavens. Kam saw Fidaelii's eyes fill with hope.

"Eagloni!" Kam exclaimed in wonder. "The tales of their demise aren't true!"

"My father is the last," Hadros answered.

"He will need help with the Squallors!" Kam cried, "You must fly to his aid, however young you are!"

"Sir, I cannot!" Sadness took Hadros' voice. "Because I am not pure blooded Eagloni, my wings will not carry me off the ground. That is why we travel on foot, because of my father's love for me."

To Kam's horror, he saw no fewer than eight of the horrible demons break from the fight with the Maisorvantii to head off Hathlos. *Here ends the wondrous gift of the Elder Race...* As quickly as that thought possessed Kam's mind however, it was chased away by small, but strong, hope for the Eagloni. With deft strokes, and the surety of a master craftsman, Hathlos had maneuvered among the beasts and felled two by sure shots. It was like watching an old sculptor carve beauty from an ugly, ordinary rock. The Squallors were fighting the air, beating at it to catch and kill their prey. Directly opposed to their struggling, Hathlos appeared to be swimming in it, catching updrafts, downdrafts and cross currents as if he knew where they would be before they were there. With ease, Hathlos turned the creatures' might against them. He dove just as one of the Squallors unleashed a bolt of death from its mouth, accidentally killing one of its brethren. Enraged, the murderer set out to pursue the Eagloni. Diving after him, Kam saw Hathlos give into the pull of the ground, go into a freefall, and turn to face the beast as he did. The Eagloni skillfully notched an arrow and, before the demon could react, let it fly. As Hathlos twisted again, his wings burst forth from their wrapped position, caught an updraft, and carried him back into the fray. As he ascended, his mark fell to the ground as a stone, dead from the shot that found its way squarely into the right eye socket. As Hathlos was climbing, a hail of lightning blazed down all around him.

"Father!" Hadros cried. "He has given up the heights for a killing shot. It will be a miracle if he regains it!"

"I know of a miracle or two!" Fidaelii cried out, stepping from the brush. "May the Oracle add His voice to mine!"

With that, she lifted her hands and sang:

The night is long,
Longer still before the dawn.
But dawn must come,
And all that hides must now be drawn...
Drawn out to give account

Of all the deeds done in the dark,
Of men and beast and demon-spawn
To the One who keeps all time.
And spotless hearts alone will stand
In the day...
In the day.

As she sung, her voice grew stronger and stronger. Kam felt familiarity in the song, as if... *The dream!* By the fifth line, showers of sparks began descending upon them all, Squallors and Eagloni and Maisorvantii. The showers pained the beasts but seemed to give strength to Hathlos. As the demons were all gazing up to see how they may stop this new menace, Hathlos and the Maisors worked quickly. Four arrows were notched. Four found their mark. Arete' and his guard let loose their full fury, and the threat from above was banished. Hathlos was the first to land with the two Maisors not far behind. Kam, Hadros, and Fidaelii ran to meet them.

Arete' made his way to Hathlos.

"You honor the Elder Race with your valor, son of the Aeries!"

"That was marvelous, Father!" Hadros exclaimed, embracing his father, who by now was breathing quite heavily.

"The sky gave her aid to our cause," Hathlos said. "It seems Fidaelii is finding her voice."

"I've heard that melody in my dreams," Kam said. "It was so real. It was more real than my waking moments."

"You must tell me of these dreams!" Fidaelii begged.

"When we camp," Kam affirmed. "We need to make our way up and into the Streotas. Arete', will you..."

Kam was stopped by the sight of Arete's remaining guard collapsing. Rushing to him, the silver prince took him in his arms.

"The wounds, sire," groaned the injured Maisor. "They are mortal?"

"No," answered Arete'. "But your healing awaits in the Verdant. Kam Hearthstone, my Road with you ends here. I wish to go on to the Gap, but my heart burns for my people. May the Oracle send you light in the darkness."

"You have honored me with your counsel and your valor, Arete'," Kam said. "I will never forget your kindness. You have my thanks."

The Prince gathered his injured guard to himself and slowly climbed into the air. Arete' turned southeast toward the Verdant. Kam watched the shape of the Maisors grow smaller by the moment.

"By nightfall, the Grey Riders may make this side of the lake," Kam warned. "We should head for the Falls and begin our climb."

With that, the company gathered their supplies and headed into the foothills. They retraced the river that flowed down from the heights of the Streotas and into the misty lake. Kam knew that they would never catch Grimmalt before he made the Gap. He knew also that the passes beyond the Gap would be nearly impossible to navigate without Grimmalt's knowledge. *Those passes are a labyrinth to anyone unfamiliar with the Road, and many have perished trying to find their way through.* A wrong turn could take the company straight to Medras, and Kam had no desire to go anywhere near the Greefadth stronghold.

16

Unwelcome Reunion

Grimmalt looked over his shoulder to check his distance from the Shifting Lake. The sun was setting toward the plains below. *Hearthstone's company must be to the end of the foothills by now. They will make camp in an hour.* There would be no rest for Grimmalt. He knew the Gap of Starsgol was still a half-day's journey up, and beyond that, the Blades of the Streotas. His old home of Medras lay to the west, the Harrows of the Dead in the east. He had not walked these winding, steep paths in ten summers. Yet the feelings of home were stronger now, even though the tension of his return strained all things within him.

He climbed. The jagged, raw beauty of these heights called to him. There were not many green things to be found on the Streotas. The wind and the sun made certain of that. Any fertile rain clouds that approached the heights would shy away in despair and abandon hope of helping anything grow. Their elder brothers, as storms, would unleash their tumult upon the rocky slopes, however. In great numbers and sudden ambush, they would assemble in towering, black battle lines. Ruthlessly they would beat at the Streotas as if it were their commission. But these storms produced the rugged beauty Grimmalt thrived on. As a young one, Grimmalt would ask his father about the storms. He mused on such a memory now as he climbed, sometimes leaping over boulders, sometimes dashing over gravel. He could hear King Grennam's words in his head more clearly now than when his young ears first heard them:

"Does it surprise you, my Prince, that such a place as this is our home? The land is harsh; the weather unforgiving. But the heights...Ah, the heights are glorious, Grimmalt. What do the lowlanders know? Their view is very small. They are, by nature, shortsighted. But here, we see far. Let the Streotas teach you, Son. Climb up in their lap as often as you can and see. See the world as it is. See people in their need. Not just our people as they are your brother's charge. The second-born sons of our people, like you my son, are ambassadors...for our culture, our language, our customs. We have much to give the world, Grimmalt. And you must see that the world receives the gifts we are to give. To Grozshtef is given the weight of

the crown of Medras. To you is given the weight of glory of the Streotas themselves. There are riches here, my Son...Not only under the heights, but above them as well. Your spirit is bright and indomitable, Grimmalt! Never, never let it grow dark and cold."

Grimmalt sighed as he stared to the south.

How bright is my soul now, Father?

Shadows grew long upon the crags. Grimmalt caught sight of the Gap just ahead, a space wide enough for seven men to stand abreast between two steep mountains. The crossroads marked the entrance into the rooftops of the Streotas.

He found a nearby cleft in the side of the rock face to his left. Crawling inside, he began to refocus his thoughts for his task ahead. Medras had lost much of its prominence since the passing of his father and brother in the Rending War, and the wild things that haunted these heights had increased in number. Grimmalt did not fear death. He lived every day in its shadow. This was a matter of honor before him now. *I must play my part in this dangerous game. I must help the company reach the Sanctum. But first, this.*

Grimmalt gathered strength. *Swish, scratch, swish...*a familiar sound hit his ears. Instantly he understood it: *the tramping of Greefadth feet!* Silent to every living thing that was not a Greefadth, the race was stealthy and sure. But Greefadths have a tell-tale sign to their walk: the length of their lope. Grimmalt steadied himself, not desiring to be detected just yet.

§

Much farther down the mountain, the four left in Hearthstone's company stopped to make camp for the night. Hadros had found a small cave in which they all now sheltered. He had built a small fire near its mouth. Once they were all settled in their shelters, Kam spoke.

"Grimmalt will need help with the Gap. The dangers there are too many for one. The dead walk the Harrows. Squallors make their roosts in the Blades. Need I make mention of Greefadth patrols from Medras? And do not forget about the occasional stone gollum. We have no time for rest. We must make for the Gap *now*."

"A storm is coming," said Fidaelii. "Getting there before its arrival will be impossible at this point. But I agree that the prince will need help." At this she looked toward Hathlos.

"The only thing I owe Grimmalt is an Aeries bolt in his heart," replied the Eagloni. He walked to his son's fire. Gathering his thoughts in deep musings for a moment, he touched his strong chin and stared into the blaze. "I go only for the sake of the Oracle's Call, Fidaelii. Hadros," he said, touching his boy's shoulder, "stay close to Kam. Do all that he says, and you will live to see me again. Look after the Acolyte. Honor your mother's memory with valor."

Hadros nodded. Hathlos gathered his satchel, his quivers, and his bow. He packed a chunk of dried meat and stepped out of the cave into the cold breeze. He turned to face them, held his hand up in a gesture of parting, and in a moment he was gone. The thunder seething in the distance set an eerie mood for the rest of the night. Fidaelii walked over to the fire and sat down near Hadros. She appeared eager to settle her spirit with the giant's company.

"I've seen how wonderful your father can be," she said to Hadros. "Will you tell me now about your mother?"

The boy cracked a smile. He replied with misty eyes. "She died when I was born. All I have of her are my father's tales, but I will tell you one of them if you'd like." Seeing her nod, Hadros began a spirited story of his father and mother's enjoyment of Astori songs...

§

High above them, in the craggy cleft, Grimmalt watched and waited. As the Greefadth patrol neared, Grimmalt spied that it was the full count for a patrol. No fewer than eight strong warriors approached. They marched down the Medras Road from the Blades and through the Gap of Starsgol directly toward his hiding place. He gave a small smile when he saw their leader. It was his cousin Mendlakk.

The troop's scant leather dressings helped to serve the stealth in which they operated. The only metal to be seen was the thief-gains that Mendlakk had sown onto his fur to mark his rank. Thievery was lauded as sport in the Greefadth culture. Indeed, every king had to fabricate his own crown from thieving excursions to all the neighboring cultures. Greefadths stole not out of necessity or malicious intent, but as a rite of passage. No harm toward the owners was permitted except for the relief of their treasures. In the ancient times, all the other tribes in Skaaran would use the Greefadths' games as a means of testing the security of their lands and resources. Relations were, for the most part, cordial among the tribes. The ongoing Greefadth games became sport for everyone, everywhere—before the Rending War. The Elders of all the tribes had even began making allowance for it.

Grimmalt looked down at his chest, which was bereft of thief-gains. Having renounced the games for the sake of war, he longed for a day to come when the games would once again be played in Skaaran. So lost was he in this reverie that he didn't notice the movement. The very stone of the cleft where he sheltered shifted!

The motion wasn't lost on Mendlakk, however, and he cried out, "Stone Gollum! Make ready the forms!"

Crack! To Grimmalt's shock and dismay, the cleft

he was hidden in totally removed itself, ripping away from the mountainside. *What a lowlander I've become!* Grimmalt cursed. *I didn't even smell it!* The stone figure stood upright on two thick legs, dumping Grimmalt exactly at Mendlakk's feet. For the slightest second, Grimmalt's gaze met Mendlakk's. Grimmalt saw sheer disbelief in his cousin's wide, bright eyes. His reappearance was indeed an intrusion. The moment was short-lived, however. Grimmalt scuttled out of their way and prepared to do what he could to show his courage and allegiance. The Greefadth troop had little time to prepare for the Gollum's first assault.

Nearly three times the size of a Greefadth warrior, stone Gollums roamed the heights for little reason other than the destruction of life. Not a whit of reasoning could be found within them. Few lone Greefadths met with one and lived to tell the tale. Survival was to be obtained in numbers. Mendlakk's next order would be life or death for the troop.

Without hesitation, the two largest of the troop began to change. They flexed their backs into an ever-hardening mass. The two youngest, most agile Greefadths reached for their hammer picks and steadied themselves. Mendlakk and his companion grasped one of their large brethren, using him as a shield against the gollum's first blow.

"Steady, Orsould. We'll make quick work of him." Mendlakk said confidently.

"Be sure you do!" Orsould replied. "Too many years have passed for me to be useful much longer."

"Meshlakk, Orsoulth, now!" Mendlakk barked as yet another blow came to the back of his captain. The two young Greefadths sprang into action, running at full pace toward their company, who had by now faced them with the purpose of throwing them headlong at the creature. Two steps more found them in the air, pick hammers starving for stone flesh. The Gollum was ready for Meshlakk and caught the young Greefadth before he found his mark. Orsoulth was but a moment behind and landed deftly on the stone giant's shoulder opposite of his companion. He swung around to the moving vice that was beginning to crush his comrade.

Grimmalt saw the gollum's grip tightening around the young Greefadth's torso. The young one was trying to harden to buy life-saving seconds. Orsoulth went to work on the right shoulder joint in the beast's back, all the while negotiating safe spots from the left handed attacks. In all the commotion, Grimmalt noticed the Gollum favoring its right side. He double-checked the left knee and spied several cracks in the back of it. *This one's old. Only one thing to do.* Grimmalt formed the hardest right hand he could muster and went to work on the knee joint. The Gollum cried out in excruciating pain and wheeled around to face the new threat. Noticing the gollum so diverted, all the exertion of the troop went now to save Meshlakk, who was sweating profusely.

"Exploit the knee!" Mendlakk cried. "Oh, Iyoskothe, deliver us!"

As one, the troop rushed the creature, turning the joint to dust. The Gollum fell. Mendlakk went to Orsoulth's aid in severing the right shoulder. It took very little time to free Meshlakk. The troop finished quartering the giant and threw the parts into the fells below. When the noise of battle ceased they all approached the wounded Greefadth, whose breathing was shallow and labored.

"Oh, my Son, my Son!" Mendlakk lamented. "That I could take your place in the Blades with our fathers. I would give a thousand years' service to Iyoskothe!"

"You know that is not possible, Legatus," said a loud low tone behind them. "I do not bargain."

The troop turned to see the source of the voice.

"Iyoskothe!!" The words from Mendlakk's lips hung in the air for a seeming eternity.

The Lord of Death had stepped out, as it seemed, from another realm, from inside the mountains. He was almost as tall as the Gollum in their eyes, a mighty one. Iyoskothe's eyes burned with reddish fire. His robes of rich dark purple and scarlet flowed to the ground and found themselves emptying into fire which danced around unseen feet. His dark black skin bore the marks of generations of war yet looked more like grey ink than marring scars. His voice was the force of thunder. He bore no smile, indeed no emotion found its home with him. He was neither angry nor malevolent. He simply was and found complete peace in being so. He bore upon his back a golden sickle. It was thick and broad and long, mounted to what appeared to be a yew staff the size of a small tree. Living sinew held it there. The sickle was emitting a hum that made the fire dance.

"I come at the Oracle's bidding. I come for the Black Prince."

"Is my doom come?" Grimmalt asked for the second time.

"No, little Prince. I am bidden to walk with your company through the Blades to the Door of the Harrows and prepare the Chosen One for his meeting with my Lord the Oracle."

"Please, Keires!" cried Mendlakk, "Is there no remedy for my son? Can you not mend him?"

"I cannot give life, Steward of Medras," Iyoskothe replied flatly. "I have been created to take it as the Oracle bids. Your son has reached the end of days written down in the Oracle's book. His time on Skaaran is ended, but he has length of days yet unnumbered. He goes to live now beyond all life you know. He moves from changeling to changeless. You should rejoice for him. If you must weep, weep for yourself."

At these words, Mendlakk began to drown in great

sobs that shook his body. Orsould gave a solemn nod to his son, and the troop gathered Meshlakk upon their shoulders. He approached Mendlakk, embraced him, and attempted to steal sorrow from his friend. Mendlakk gazed over Orsould's shoulder into the eyes of Grimmalt with disbelief and disdain.

"If the Keires were not here, O Prince, Medras would be receiving two slain warriors this night! I know not what tapestry the Oracle weaves with you, but I pray justice comes to you swiftly!"

Grimmalt bowed his head away from his seething kin. Mendlakk's anger was justified. Grimmalt had robbed Medras of two kings in the Rending War, forcing Mendlakk and his line to serve as stewards over all Greefadths in Skaraan. His remorse was short lived as a great wind diverted his attention to the small pass where he first spied the troop. Hathlos had landed, bolt notched and ready to be raised. Iyoskothe had not turned, but his gaze remained fixed upon the grieving father. Hathlos surveyed the scene uneasily.

"Hail, last Son of the Aeries!" Iyoskothe sounded, now turning as he raised his right hand. "All is well. Our Master bids you peace."

Quickly sheathing his arrow and shouldering his bow, Hathlos kneeled dumbfounded. "Hail, Iyoskothe! Stories of you from our fathers now fall utterly short at the sight of you."

"Rise, friends." Iyoskothe replied to the Eagloni and the Greefadth. "I am not to be worshipped. I am no more than you, a life indebted to the Oracle's beauty and kindness. My brother is with your company. Is he well?"

"My Lord, Lucian has taken the Aeries Road with Maughlin across the Deltas," said Hathlos. "I do not know how they fare."

"Then we must make haste," Iyoskothe said. "For great danger awaits in the Aeires for them. Return to the company. I have secured the Gap. Grimmalt and I will journey on to Medras with the Greefadth troop. We will meet you back here in two days' time."

"My breath is yours to command, great Keires." With a sign of parting, Hathlos dove into the fells, his wings caressing the fierce drafts that lived on the face of the Streotas.

17

In the Hall of Kings

High above the Shifting Falls on the Medras Road as the sun was setting, Grimmalt trudged just before the Dread Lord Iyoskothe as a prince on the way to the gallows. The road of his youth, with all its nooks and crannies and playful overlooks, brought no comfort to him now. He had neither dreamed nor desired to ever return to this country. Indeed his only intention from Rorgus was to bring the Company to the Gap and then slink back down to the Lowlands. The sound of deft Greefadth feet ahead of him was almost too much to bear. The sound of Iyoskothe's voice behind him shook Grimmalt to his core.

"Have you walked the road, little Prince, since the War?"

"No, Keires. You know I haven't." Grimmalt replied, swallowing little pits of despair.

"Indeed," Iyoskothe countered. "My brother Lucian has often spoke of your life as a Lowlander with him in Rorgus in our conferences together. He told me your cooking is atrocious, but that resources in the East are limited."

"Keires, please," said Grimmalt, not wanting to speak of food. "Why must I return to Medras? Have I not done enough in my life to warrant my banishment? Have I not conspired? Have I not betrayed? Have I not lied? Murdered? Have I not done enough that my death should have come every day and swiftly for years now?"

"Your transgressions are both innumerable and vexatious, little Prince. They are a gross representation of everything wrong in Skaaran. You are walking with me as a living creature in this world, yet in my world you are already dead. This is why my Lord the Oracle has given me the command to walk the Medras Road now with you. He seeks to quicken you in my world. Broken things are meant to be mended, and He seeks to make a Mending War involving you and your Company. The Oracle makes war very differently than do the sons of Skaaran. These rocks, this home you know, is but a shadow of the home He desires to give you. Take heart, little Prince. The Oracle does not think little of your transgressions. They are grievous and vex Him exceedingly. They must be dealt with in perfect justice. All that will come in due time, but first we must stand in the Hall of Kings and give an account before all your people. Every evil done in your world and mine will give an account. That is perfect justice. And my Lord will render His judgments as He sees fit in keeping with the Ancient Wisdom."

"I know there is no hope for me, then," replied Grimmalt with stoic resignation.

"There is always hope," countered the Sage flatly. Calling ahead to Mendlakk, Iyoskothe voiced his wishes, "Legatus! We take the right fork! I do not wish to be seen in Medras-town. We take the hidden passage in the north wall that leads to the Hall of Kings."

"As you wish, great Keires!" came the reply.

"Repentance is neither quick nor easy, little Prince," Iyoskothe continued. "Until now, you have marked yours by hiding. That is never the way. Your greed and malice were public. Your repentance will be as they were: in the open, in the sight of all."

Grimmalt whirled around in rage. "*You!* You think I can hide from my father's and brother's ghosts?"

At this, the whole troop stopped to look back at them. Grimmalt nearly squirmed when he saw their hurt expressions. He felt so small. Iyoskothe raised a hand and motioned them on.

Grimmalt continued with breathless anxiety, "I tell you, their ghosts have a permanent seat at the table of my mind. I have yet to be free of them! I would give my soul to undo all I have done to my family, to Medras... to myself!"

Iyoskothe spoke no more to Grimmalt on the road. Upon reaching a familiar section of the ever-winding road, they spotted the hidden pass. With care, the ten mounted a huge, rounded boulder several paces away from the main road. Once over the gigantic rock, their silent feet found the concealed path, bound northwest.

As the troop continued their solemn march along the cold track, Grimmalt's mind was filled with memories of his plot to enlist Xander Hearthstone in his quest for the throne of Medras. Xander was all too glad to welcome a Greefadth spy, even if most in his command were disapproving of the traitor prince. Xander just wanted Medras to fall, while Grimmalt just wanted an end to the War. The death of the royal family blamed on the Innerlanders' chief warlord would bode well for him until everything began to unravel in the High Hall....

Grimmalt nearly ran into Orsoulth. The troop had arrived at the hidden door. Grimmalt held his breath. *The Hall of Kings!* To an Innerlander, it would appear to be one of the many rock faces, like the side of a Blade. To Grimmalt, it heralded feelings of home...and a stabbing dread. Mendlakk spoke three words in the Greefadth tongue, and two small, plain stone doors swung outward from the steep Blade. The opening was only wide enough for the six carrying Meshlakk to walk two abreast, so they lifted Meshlakk over their heads and shuffled closer together. Orsoulth followed as they bore Meshlakk's still body down into the slender, dark corridor. Grimmalt plodded after the eight with Iyoskothe at the rear. *What a homecoming.*

Iyoskothe passed through the doors and waved at them. They obeyed, sealing them all in. The light from the Sage's flames made a mockery of the sputtering torches that lined the passage on either side.

The ten followed the narrow way that wound downward to the High Hall. Even in his childhood, Grimmalt thought the name for the Hall of Kings odd because it was the lowest place in Medras. Grimmalt remembered all the other passages that branched off from the one he now walked. These passages were ideal for a young Greefadth's favorite game of *Cloak and Vanish*. It was in these small tunnels that a young prince could gain a meager understanding of his powers of stealth and train amongst his peers of the Greefadth court. Grimmalt excelled at *Cloak and Vanish*, even more so than his elder brother Grotzchef. Even in these games of his youth, envy would gnaw at him. Any seeds of contentment that tried to grow were squelched by desire for the throne. Grimmalt had always believed he was the one to rule Medras instead of his elder brother and felt justified in his actions at the time of the betrayal.

The passage widened. *The Hall!* Grimmalt's stomach

clenched. He almost turned to run. Every muscle screamed. If only he could slink back down the tunnel, out the doors, and all the way back to Rorgus. But he could not escape now. The Lord of Death blazed at his heels. A gold-embossed archway shimmered ahead. It marked the end of the tunnel and their entrance to the High Hall of Kings.

Grimmalt peered through the archway. No one else could be seen within the Hall. The whole room could be seen from the archway. It was very long. Two hundred paces it took to traverse its length but only forty paces to travel its width.

The troop entered. Grimmalt walked in after them as a stunned dog. The guilded throne sparkled nobly atop its smooth, sloping rise, the capstone of the Hall. It held Grimmalt's gaze for a moment. Between the archway and the throne, a long, polished banqueting table stretched itself almost the length of the Hall itself. Chairs with silver crests and jeweled benches lined it with enough seating for a hundred. One glorious tablecloth graced the wood with green, blue, and grey embroidery. On the near end of this table, the troop laid Meshlakk's body. A trickle of blood from his head stained the cloth. Iyoskothe glided in behind, foreboding as a thundercloud.

Great silvery walls of granite rose around them, encircling them in an embrace of stone. In the wall were detailed carvings. The images showed great Greefadth exploits. In one image, twenty warriors led by a crowned Greefadth carried a great square stone. *The Supplication Stone,* Grimmalt groaned inside. Over his years as a young one, he had studied these carvings depicting the theft of the Supplication Stone. In fact, the Stone loomed in this very room. It glimmered in the shadow of the throne. The Stone was an enormous piece of black marble crafted into a straight-edged square. It shone like glass. It had been brought to the hall generations ago as a thief-gain from the Maisorvantii in the south. One of the first and greatest kings of the Greefadths was its thief. *Our most majestic thief-gain.* Pride swelled in Grimmalt's heart but departed just as quickly as it came. *But no circumstance could be worse than mine for encountering the Stone.*

Grimmalt kept walking, still fixated on the throne. He touched each chair of the banquet table. Finally, he came to a standstill by the bottom of the throne slope. His eyes took in the throne's high, pointed back. Iyoskothe's flames glinted off of its gem-encrusted splendor. Its seat, bound to the throne frame by wrought-iron claws, was a perfectly flat slice of onyx. The seat itself and each gem were individual thief-gains, all stolen in their own conquests.

"Assemble the Elders! Call the Council of Thieves!" Iyoskothe roared.

The troop bent over Meshlakk. The young Greefadth heir to the Steward's throne was now breathing his last. Grimmalt caught Mendlakk's glare yet again as the

215

Steward of Medras watched his son perish. Mendlakk pulled away from them, brushed past Grimmalt, and tramped up to the thief-gain throne. Once he stood atop the smooth slope alongside the throne, Mendlakk reached for a thick cord that found its way through the ceiling of the High Hall. His eyes never left Grimmalt. He wrapped both hands tightly around the cord and wrenched downward three times. Three gigantic tones resonated in all of Medras from the heights all the way down to the Hall of Kings. Before the bell could cease tolling, the Steward Mendlakk had seated himself on the throne.

The tension was too much for Grimmalt. Every sweet memory of his father's reign in the halcyon days before the Rending War turned bitter in his mind. He wrung his hands. He could feel the sweat breaking upon his forehead. The Elders were not slack in answering the bell's toll. Though an eternity passed for Grimmalt, the hall soon filled with mighty warriors of the Greefadth race. There were males and females, and all were renowned. All came solemnly. Then they noticed Iyoskothe. Their stone expressions disappeared.

At once Grimmalt saw that everyone struggled to remain calm. The Lord of Death from their stories stood before them in their High Hall. The sight of Iyoskothe was at once both terrifying and mystifying. Some could not believe, even when they saw the subject of their bedtime stories now come to life before them. A pack of younger Greefadths could be heard quietly scoffing at Iyoskothe. The word "ghost" was whispered about. Older ones, though, either smiled in wonderment or shuddered with fear.

Each in turn spotted Meshlakk, the son of their Steward, mangled and bleeding on their banquet table. Gasps and sobs broke out. Growls and even a roar echoed in the chamber. A cacophony grew.

Finally, not one of them could believe the sight of the Black Prince. A few Greefadths exploded with curses. A chaotic din of shock, mourning, and fury crashed through the hall from their mouths. *Grimmalt the supplanter stands within their most revered chamber.* Glares cut toward him. Many spit in disgust if they were not already yelling with everyone else. Their reactions brought yet a deeper wave of dread upon Grimmalt. He longed for the end of his life with every breath. *All of them curse me in their hearts.*

"The bell has tolled, the Thieves assembled!" Mendlakk cried out, his voice dark. "Let the Prince now stand upon the Stone!" His mood was oppressive, and his voice carried above the ranting council members. Everyone hushed. The somber faces returned. Each member took a seat at the banquet table as did the rest of the troop. All stared with wet eyes at Meshlakk's body before turning their chairs to face the throne.

Grimmalt carved out a slow gait to the Supplication Stone. He lifted a foot high and planted it on its slippery surface. His Greefadth foot suctioned to it, and he brought the rest of himself up. Grimmalt was now upon the Stone of his fathers. He stood on display before them all. The pits of his treachery opened wide their maws in his soul. *I have wronged all here, young and old.* He grimaced at his burden, and longed for release. Mendlakk sought out Iyoskothe's eyes for direction. The Sage nodded to the Steward to continue. "Bring forth the charges that stand against Grimmalt," barked Mendlakk.

At this, Orsould walked up to the throne and knelt to find a small door built into the side of its base. Taking a key braided into his fur, he unlocked the door. He removed a small golden chest that was covered in dust and held it up to the Steward. Mendlakk opened it and removed a scroll. He sighed the longest sigh Grimmalt had ever heard. Then Mendlakk shut the chest with such force that its echo resounded in the hall. Orsould took the scroll. He moved down to stand between the Steward on the throne and Prince standing trial. The Greefadth Captain unraveled the scroll. He began to read:

"*The charges against Grimmalt, son of Grennam, son of Gremmult stand for all the heavens and Skaaran to bear witness. Let no creature, living or dead fail to heed these words –*

For deserting your father's post as Lord High Ambassador;
For swearing allegiance to the Sons of Men;

For enlisting in the Innerlanders' Army;
For aiding Xander Hearthstone in the War of Rending;
For leading the first incursion on Medras in the history
of Skaaran;
For uncovering the sacred secret passages to the High Hall;
For the murder of your brother Grotschef;
For the murder of your father Grennam:
The charge of highest treason is brought against you
The sentence levied against you is death.

Death. After reading the charges, Orsould gave the scroll back to Mendlakk and took his place among the Council. Mendlakk's gaze never left Grimmalt. The glare was enough to mete out the judgment in the charges. For many moments, it was the only exchange in the hall. Mendlakk finally spoke to the hunched figure atop the Stone.

"What say you in reply to these charges, *my lord*?" When Grimmalt only dropped his gaze, Mendlakk spit, "What say you, murderer?"

"I am guilty of them all," Grimmalt looked back up and stared into Mendlakk's face. "May Greefadth justice be satisfied."

Mendlakk's glare only intensified. "How many innocent lives were lost in the invasion? How many children fell to the Innerlander's profane blades and arrows?" he cursed. "There is no way that your death alone will satisfy Greefadth justice!"

Grimmalt did not answer and could not even raise his eyes from the Supplication Stone. *What could* that *mean?*

Iyoskothe rumbled an answer. "Indeed." He moved to stand beside Grimmalt. Even though Grimmalt stood on the Stone, Iyoskothe still towered over him.

"There is nothing that will bring those innocents acknowledged in the charges back to your world. My Lord the Oracle recognizes your charges and counts them all as weighty against the Prince..." Grimmalt heard the Sage pause for a moment. "Grimmalt's sentence is thus from the mouth of the Oracle Himself:

"Grimmalt, Grennam's son, is to walk the Underland Road and collect a thief-gain crown for me. He will then return to Medras and deal with its Council in perfect justice."

At this, a large portion of the Greefadth Council erupted in laughter and murmuring. Complaints from the younger members sounded from many corners of the room. The older ones, however, were silent. They maintained their reverence. Iyoskothe noted the reaction. He leapt into the midst of the Thieves' Council, flames roaring up onto the banquet table next to the body of Meshlakk. Tearing his scythe off of his back and clutching it in his right hand, his left became a firebrand. With the brightness and heat of a star, Iyoskothe lit the scythe and brought it down upon the table with great force. The blade dug into the polished table right above Meshlakk's head. The fire around Iyoskothe's feet roared up to his knees before settling again. He wrenched his scythe out of the wood. Splinters flew and showered the table with singed flecks. Everyone was silent.

"This is the Oracle's judgment," Iyoskothe said. "Speak now in protestation if you wish."

"The judgment is clean," said Mendlakk from his throne, emotionless. "The Prince faces unfathomable tortures on the Underland Road. He will not survive the journey, and the Underlanders will make better work of him than any devices we possess here in Medras."

At this, a din of complaints grated on their ears.

"Murderers deserve death!!"

"Kill the Black Prince!"

"Rid us of Grimmalt now!"

The Council of Thieves held a tension that was suffocating to Grimmalt.

"The judgment is clean!" Mendlakk roared, once again bringing quiet. "Any Greefadth who dares to speak against the Oracle or the great Keires Iyoskothe will be met with my blade! A new Order may one day rise in Medras, but I will not be alive to see it. We will not go the way of the Innerlanders while I live!" His statements echoed over the ears of all in the room. Then the Steward turned again to

Iyoskothe. He bowed. "Our trust is that you will return news to us concerning the Oracle's justice meted out in this matter, great Keires."

"News will come," Iyoskothe answered.

"Very well!" replied Mendlakk. Grimmalt cringed. Then Mendlakk set his jaw. "Let the Prince sleep in our finest dungeon tonight!"

Grimmalt nearly fainted off the Supplication Stone. In his next waking moment, he found his arm grabbed by Iyoskothe. He was carried down from the Stone and pulled out of the Hall.

18

Many Talons, Many Claws

Maughlin paced the ferry dock. He glanced at Lucian, who was resting under a fat cypress. It was the second day after he and Kam had parted ways, and Maughlin felt as though the Argyrotu had brought them too far inland. This was the eighth ferry dock that yielded no ferry, and Maughlin was growing impatient.

"Calm yourself, friend," Lucian said. "The Deltas will wait for us. If you're that anxious to cross, you can ask Thystote' to fly us over them when he returns."

"I do not wish to announce our presence to the Pyropos," said Maughlin. "The red Maisors would be all too happy to be rid of you, Lucian... Where is the Silver Captain? How long does it take to find a ferryman?"

"Your ferryman comes."

Maughlin wheeled around to see Thystote' coming through the bracken. He was forcefully escorting a young boy of about thirteen years. His two guards were just behind him.

"This little one says he's been looking for a Lucian Pharmakeos. I told him I would eat him if you failed to vouch for him, Keires."

"Lucian!" cried the boy. "Don't let him eat me!"

Maughlin helped Lucian to his feet. The old physician smiled.

"Sokii, I've told you that Maisorvantii don't eat people. My friend Thystote' has been having fun at your expense."

Thystote' released Sokii, and the three Maisors roared a terrifying laugh.

"What I want to know is how you traversed the length of the Lupinwood without being eaten by Lupines," said Thystote'.

"Sokii can remain hidden as much as he likes," Lucian said, "one of the benefits of his giftings as a Brother."

"This little one is a Keires?" asked Thystote'. "I beg your forgiveness, my Lord!"

"It's all right," answered Sokii. "Happens all the time. I'm not meant to have the prominence of my elder Brothers."

"Be at ease, Thystote'," said Lucian. "If a ferryman indeed is coming, I will thank you and your guardsmen for your generosity in our watch-care. You may take your leave and return to the Verdant. We will travel on from here."

"Are you sure you no longer require our services, Keires?" asked Thystote'. "We will go on to the Aeries Gate and our deaths if need be."

"There will be a time when that may be necessary," answered Lucian, "but not this day. Maughlin and I still think our Road is best served with stealth. If the lone rider carries Fidaelii, we will be enough to reclaim her. Thank you again for your pains. Be at peace."

"As you wish, Lord Lucian," said Thystote'. "Strength go with you."

Turning to his guards, he gave the order: "Up Argyrotu! Up! To the Verdant!"

Maughlin watched them until they were out of sight, then walked over to Lucian and placed a hand on his shoulder.

"They are gone, my friend," he said.

"Good," said Lucian. "We have much to discuss before the ferryman gets here. Sokii, I wish to hear all about your Road here."

"The Road from Skaaroth to Rorgus was relatively uneventful. The weather remained fair, but when I made it Rorgus, Captain Tulpos had dozens of questions..." said Sokii. "questions about the High Council, questions about the Arbiter's school, questions about why I was going into the Wilds. He asked when new Elders were coming from

Skaaroth to Rorgus to replace you and Grimmalt. I told him, 'What do I know? I'm just the chief stable steward for the High Council. I'm not privy to their meetings.'"

"How did he receive this news?" asked Lucian.

"With skepticism," said Sokii. "I have long suspected Tulpos to be in league with Starsgol. His attitude in our conversation and the tone of his questions only feed my suspicions."

"Can you be so sure?" asked Maughlin.

"Fairly sure," said Sokii. "Whenever Tulpos comes to Skaaroth on Pilgrimage, he spends a great deal of time in The Eagle's Talon. It's a public house where those sympathetic to Starsgol's rule gather to sing the new songs of the High Council. It's there that the Sons of Men plot the Oracle's overthrow."

"Could it be that the Captain goes to merely know the goings-on in the establishment?" Lucian inquired. "Perhaps he goes there to be better informed as an Arbiter..."

"Highly unlikely," Sokii replied. "Many an evening my charges and I have helped the knights home after riotous times in the Talon. Tulpos is one of *them*, I'm sure of it. He will no doubt send report to Starsgol on every traveler that has passed through Rorgus in the last week."

This news greatly unsettled Maughlin. *If Sokii speaks the truth, our time is shorter than I thought.*

"We cross the Deltas and find the girl," Maughlin said.

"We make for the Aeries Gate and the Sanctum beyond. Starsgol must not stop Kam from retrieving the Vessel."

Just then, behind them a voice called out: "Ho there, sojourners!" The voice was low pitched and strong. Turning round again to face the approaching ferry, Maughlin answered.

"Ho ee ferryman! Do you go the length of the Deltas?"

"When sojourners carry enough fluerons," chuckled the ferryman. "Most have not of late, so I take them northwest to the Biting Fens."

"We are not interested in the northwest, friend," stated Sokii smiling. "Our Road takes us northeast."

"There is nothing northeast but peril, friend," replied the ferryman, now docking the boat. "My price is two hundred fluerons to cross all Deltas. What business have you at the Aeries Gate?"

"A reunion of sorts," answered Lucian. "Two hundred fluerons is an egregious amount, young man."

"These are egregious times, ancient one," smirked the ferryman. "I don't see many passengers." Raising his hands and wiggling his fingers for effect, he continued. "Mostly because the Maisors *eat them*."

"Save your terrors for little children, fool! Maisors don't eat people." Maughlin said, throwing a small satchel at the ferryman. "Here are eighty fluerons as a deposit. Get us and the horses across the Deltas, and you can expect eighty more."

"As you wish," replied the ferryman. "Only no one must know about me cutting my prices! I'll lose my reputation as being a *hard man*."

Maughlin rolled his eyes as he gestured for Sokii and Lucian to board first. They did so, and before long the ferry was underway. As the ferryman poled the boat through the first delta, he spoke of his hut on one of the cypress islands in the distance. He then began talking of cooking and trapping. Sokii feigned interest, but Maughlin became annoyed. Something did not settle with him. The ferryman's vocal tone seemed anxious and forced. It was more than just about the danger of the nearby Pyropos. More than once, Maughlin could glimpse the ferryman looking around and craning his neck as if listening to a whisper. As the ferry ride drug on, Maughlin became gradually more and more disturbed. He was about to ask what the ferryman was hearing when he noticed they were heading straight for a considerably large island in the middle of the second delta. Sokii noticed it as well.

"Don't we need to go around?" Sokii asked as he pointed to it.

"Quiet, boy!" the ferryman hissed. "There are three Maisorvantii directly overhead! Maybe the coming darkness will aid our escape if you can keep your mouth shut!"

The three passengers all looked up simultaneously. Their guide had spoken true. The dusk had not quite fallen into night among the cypress trees, and the silhouettes were menacing. The wings of the Maisorvantii were majestic to behold, and they cut through the air like the sharpest swords dancing. The setting sun reflected off of the scales on their golden breasts like a thousand mirrors. The beams flirted with the water's ripples. The most serious laughter could be heard coming from their maws. Maughlin was relieved that they were caught up in reverie and not scanning the surface of the delta. The island the ferryman was making all haste to reach was particularly sparse in cover. Hiding the boat would be impossible. The Maisors seemed to be engaged in some game of sport. Just as the ferry reached the island, one of them dove to the delta's surface. Reaching it, he scooped some water into his mouth, ascended once again to the others, and promptly gave a great blast of steam in the face of one of his brethren. The unblasted Maisor gave such a laugh that it caused the one who was blasted to catch his joy, and another thunderclap of laughter was had by all. This rollicking continued for well over an hour all around the island where the travelers took refuge. As night fell, the noise of the Maisorvantii seemed to move off to the northeast. An occasional firebolt could be seen in the distance. It was always accompanied by more laughter.

"Two hundred fifty fluerons," spoke the ferryman at last. "And not a quintle less. I'm too old to do this anymore. This is my last journey to the Gate." As they all led their horses onto the ferry, his complaining continued.

"It is getting worse, you know. There was a time when the Deltas were full of ferrymen! I had to work twelve-hour days poling the length and breadth of these swamps just to scratch out a living before the Maisorvantii moved in. I never thought I would long for those days again." He poled out to deeper water. Coming around the island and turning to the northeast, he questioned his passengers' resolve. "Are you all absolutely sure you wish to make for the Gate? I could turn round and take you some place better, my dears."

"We must make the Gate and beyond, or die," Maughlin stated firmly.

"That you may," the ferryman breathed, scanning the moonlit sky. "That you just may."

No sleep came to man or beast that fretful night. Movement was slowed because of the Maisor encounter, and the ferryman hugged little islands that offered cover from the skies. The moon lit up the Deltas almost as much as had her brother the sun. This did nothing to assuage anxiety. As the night crept on, Lucian began to hum quietly. Maughlin thought him slightly mad. He recognized the tune as one from his childhood. It was a counting-six song about darkness, with very few words. Maughlin began to sing it softly:

Oh the Master, Oh the Master
Oh the Master of the darkness

Oh the Master, Oh the Master
Is the Master of the light.
Even the darkness shines
Even the darkness shines
Even the darkness shines
As a light to You
As a light to You.

As Maughlin and Lucian were humming and singing on the prow of the boat, Sokii—who was in the stern with the ferryman—noticed the ferryman twitching. By the time Maughlin began to repeat the children's ditty, the ferryman's face began contorting. At the end of the repeated verse, the ferryman gave such a cry that no living thing could mistake it for anything less than torture.

"Shut up! No! No singing on my boat! None, none!" he raged. "There are two Masters, yes, my dears! Two! Masters! And one will rule the other! Yes, yes! Yes, my dears, yes! You will see! Yes, and soon! For one is greater than the other! Yes, yes, my loves!" At this he grounded the ferry on the little island they were hugging. "Now, be good lads, and NO MORE SINGING! No! No more! Get off! Everyone off! I don't care about your fluerons now! We will see how you get along without me!"

On and on he went, for a dozen minutes or more at the top of his voice. Even after they exited the ferry onto the tiny island, still he shouted. He had poled out to the middle of the delta, shouting curses at them all the way when fire lit up the surface of the lake. The Maisorvantii had returned. They had not set the boat on fire, but rather the swamp around it. As they landed deftly on the boat, the ferryman had not changed his cursing one bit. So fixated was he in the words of the children's song that he did not seem to notice them. Pointing instead at the party on the little island and shrieking curses, he was barely affected when the largest golden Maisor picked him up with his mighty clawed hands and effortlessly tore the man in half. As he did, the party on the shore watched in horror as what looked like a million insects fled from the carcass of the ferryman. The mass exodus flew away or drowned in the delta. The largest Maisor threw the legs of the ferryman into the water and carried the torso with him as he leapt into the sky, wings opening. The other two Maisorvantii followed suit. When they were all in the air, they set fire to the ferry-boat and swooped down to stand before the party. The largest, most golden one spoke.

"What brings a stable boy and two old men to the Shifting Deltas on this cold night? Are you also Trampers like this filth?" he growled as he flung the carcass to the ground.

"Majesty," Maughlin replied steadily, "We were merely singing a children's song about the darkness when that Underland toad manifested himself. We were completely oblivious to our guide's true identity."

"We shall see." The golden Maisor narrowed his blood red eyes. "Sing me this song if you value breath!"

As the three sang, Lucian's clouded eyes exuded a playful light. Seeing it, the golden one recognized Lucian, knelt and motioned to his companions. The other two followed his example. Lucian motioned for the song to stop and for the dragon people to rise. He raised his hands in honor to them.

"Hail. Siyonte', Lord of the Red Harbor! One hundred years have passed since last we feasted. My brother Iyoskothe sends his salutations and longs for word from Roibunto. Are your people prospering?"

"Keires, please forgive my insolence," the golden one replied. "I mistook you for a Tramper. The Underlanders have been masking their movements in the bodies of men who brave the Outerlands for ten summers now. Had I known the Brothers were once again walking among us, I would have..."

"It is forgiven," replied Lucian, clasping his arm. "We seek the Oracle's Sanctum beyond the Harrows. How is the Way through the Aeries?"

"Perilous," came the reply. "Very perilous indeed. The lords of my peoples vie for the Aeries. Brukkheom and the Pyropos have settled in great numbers there. The land is rich in resources. You will find them impassible. Is there no other way? Perhaps the Gap of Starsgol..."

"There is no time, Majesty." Maughlin interrupted,

bowing. "There are loved ones who are, as we speak, making their way to the Harrows by way of the Gap. We must meet them at the Oracle's Sanctum with all speed if we are able."

"My brother Iyoskothe will meet us at the Aeries Gate after he has taken Kam's company to the Door of the Dead," said Lucian. "At least, that is his intent. That will afford us some safety, surely."

"*Some* safety, yes..." Siyonte' mused, "but not complete safety. There are tribes of my brothers who do not know you or your Oracle, the Pyropos who know you and hate you. You know this, yes?"

"Yes," replied Lucian. "Whatever aid you may lend will not be forgotten in the chronicle of this age, Siyonte'. Can you take us to the Aeries Gate?"

"The night is young yet, Keires, and the land by the Gate fraught with danger. You should rest here and now. We will wake you at dawn and take you to meet your Brother. Please, I beg of you, rest."

Lucian nodded his head in agreement, and the party slept in the bright moonlight, out in the open.

As Maughlin nodded off to sleep, he could hear Lucian humming like a child.

19

To the Door of the Dead

Far away in the west, Kam led his company ever upward. Now on their second day of travel since Hathlos' word of Grimmalt's capture, they were immersed in the Blades. There was magic upon this part of the Streotas, and as the sun rose over the peaks ahead of them, Kam could see its effects clearly. Sometimes wavering, sometimes violently shaking, the heights ahead seemed to be in constant flux. The company's current road climbed up the side of what appeared to be one of the highest peaks in the area. As Kam tried to focus on the Road, Fidaelii spoke.

"Your weapons are beautiful," Fidaelii commented. Making note of the intricate guilding and jewelled settings, her next words came naturally. "I have never seen a dagger like that."

"Nor will you again," Kam countered. "It was my father's: a reward from the High Council in Skaaroth for his valor in the Rending War. Like your cloak, it is ostentatious and absurd. Highly functional, mind you, even in its current state. I bore it when I was High Arbiter at Rorgus. I bore it when..." Kam began to break. "When my son..."

"I didn't know you had a son." Fidaelii ventured gently. "I have never seen him in Edraeth. Does he stay on the farm and help you?"

"He died fourteen years ago," Kam answered. "He was but ten years old... he was... his mother's greatest joy." Gathering his wits once again, he held up the dagger. "It represents the high opinions men hold for themselves while in an authority position. My father led the Innerlander armies in the War of Rending. He walked these roads. I am sure of it."

"We could use his knowledge of the path ahead," Fidaelii said, Kam's head hanging. Noticing it, she continued. "You are your father's son, Hearthstone. Your valor saved us at the river before Rorgus. It will be enough to take us to the Oracle."

"Will it?" he laughed. "Have you ever been beyond the Gap of Starsgol, girl? I haven't. I only dared venture into the Streotas one other time in my life. That was far to the east, into the desolation of the Aeries. Never would I dream to dare walk the Blades or the Harrows alone. We are in the nest of the Greefadths, girl, make no mistake about that. They are the most silent race in all of Skaaran. One of their knives could be in your back as quickly as your next breath, and you would be none the wiser. They are treacherous in all of their ways! And directly opposed to the Blades are the Harrows. None that have entered there have come again to give report. It's the road of the dead."

"But we have Kam Hearthstone and Hathlos the Eagloni with us," Fidaelii said. "That surely accounts for some measure of safety!"

As Kam turned to answer Fidaelii, there came a great trembling of the ground beneath their feet. Everyone clung to each other and to the side of the Blade. Fidaelii let go of a great shriek as she fell against Hadros. The small giant deftly caught her before she fell further and set her once again on the path. When the tremor ceased, Kam spoke.

"The Road is ever changing! How are we to make the Gap?"

"This disturbance is new," replied Hathlos. "The Blades have always been fluid in shifting but never this violently. The shifting nature of the Blades is directly tied to the Council of Thieves in Medras. When they are in one accord, the shifting is subtle. Natural. This is a bad omen. The Steward Mendlakk may be in danger of a revolt, especially in light of the Oracle's judgment concerning Grimmalt. We must hurry on the Oracle! We are only a half-day's hard walk from the Gap now. We must not fail!"

Kam looked at the puzzled expressions of the others in his company. He shook his head but urged them on. The tremors continued the rest of the day. The creatures that would normally threaten travelers on the Road were occasionally seen fleeing their habitations. It was late afternoon when the Gap of Starsgol came into view. Amidst the tremors, the company made their way from cleft to crag, ever mindful to stay as hidden as they possibly could. They found a particularly large stand of fallen rocks and sheltered among them. Several hours passed before anything was said. The dusk was beginning to paint the Blades a deep purple when Kam spied light on the Medras road to the northwest.

"There!" he pointed. "Iyoskothe comes with Grimmalt."

To their great relief, they saw the Prince. To their horror, they beheld the mighty Keires. Kam even shuddered at the sight of Iyoskothe. When Lucian took Kam into Rorgus' keep for the Brothers' council, the fiery one was intimidating. In person, Iyoskothe embodied nothing short of despair treading fire. Fidaelii offered encouragement.

"Let us go to them. Don't be afraid, Iyoskothe loves and serves the Oracle."

With great trepidation, the bandits followed behind Kam, who was at Fidaelii's side. Hathlos guarded their rear, just as they had traveled for the past two days. They all approached the Gap as one, making their way into the great crossroads.

For centuries, the Gap of Starsgol stood as the meeting of all roads in the Streotas. Travelers to the heights used it to mark meetings and plans. Legend spoke of this place as the landing of Starsgol himself from another realm. Hallowed and feared by the Outerlanders and Innerlanders alike, the Gap held a magic that could not be contained or utilized. Some cultures believed there was a Hall of mystic doors somewhere near the Gap, and that if one could find the Hall, countless dimensions and the pleasures they held could be apprehended. None have ever found the mystic Hall or its doors. Tales persist, especially among the Vulkeeri, who value new realms and journeys above all other things. Many of these desert nomads have left their bones in the Blades of the Streotas searching for the mystic Hall. These legends filled Kam's memory as they approached the crossroads of his grandfather's tales.

"Hail, Keires!" Fidaelii called. "It's a great relief to see you once again!"

"Hail, Daughter of the Song!" Iyoskothe returned. "It is good that we are here together. Our meeting must be brief. I journey on through the bowels of the Streotas southeast to the Aeries Gate. Already the Night threatens. Maughlin's Road is among the Pyropos. The red Maisors will not take kindly to intrusions. We must make all haste."

"Very well, my Lord," Fidaelii said. "Will you at least lead us to the door of the Harrows?"

"I will." Iyoskothe answered. Turning to address the rest of the company, he continued. "When Starsgol was thrown into Skaaran, he landed here in the Streotas. Still clawing to return to the blessed realm, he made great marks upon the heights: *the Harrows*. You all have been told legends of this place around your dinner tables or while in your beds. I assure you, *nothing* in any of your stories compares to the actual steps on this Road. Nothing *can* prepare you. Even if this were a return visit, you still would not be ready. There is residue that remains from Starsgol's great crash here upon the Sons of Magic and Men."

Turning to Fidaelii, the Iyoskothe's eyes were piercing. "In the midst of the madness, *you* must hear a song. The Song is ever singing. It never ceases, never diminishes. The din of despair is deafening, but *you* must *hear* beyond it. This is the reason for your call to the Sanctum. This final stretch of Road. If you fail, all is lost. This company will fall into darkness and all of Skaaran with it. Here begins the purpose of your birth. All of the time spent with Praius in your training in Edraeth was for this moment until the end of your days. Are you ready?"

Kam looked at the small girl, who was trembling greatly. She could not speak. He stepped forward to her side. "Do not fear, young one. I will live to protect you."

"And who will protect *you*, Kam Hearthstone?" asked Iyoskothe. "Who will spare *you* in the Harrows? Do you know what they hold for you?"

"I fear neither man nor beast nor demon-spawn." Kam answered, toeing up to the Sage. "I have killed every race in this land. I will kill again."

"Neither man nor beast nor demon-spawn awaits you in the Harrows, Hearthstone," Iyoskothe replied. "Enough talking. No one will rest tonight. You make for the Sanctum. Fidaelii will take you there, or you will all die."

At this, Iyoskothe Mortibundis turned and left the crossroads. The fiery keires led them northeast for more than an hour. Fidaelii was right behind him. Kam and Hadros followed her with Hathlos and Grimmalt bringing up the rear. The night had taken them when Iyoskothe stopped. Turning to his left, he placed two strong hands upon the side of a Blade. The outline of a blazing door appeared and burned a hole in the side of the mountain. Looking for one last time at Fidaelii, Iyoskothe gave a final word of parting:

"Here is the secret door of the Harrows, Acolyte. May the Oracle give you ears to hear the Song in a way unknown to most of the Sons of Men. I go to my Brothers at the Aeries Gate."

Lifting his hands in blessing, he spoke to the company: "May we meet in the morning in the Garden of the Sanctum."

Looking at Kam, he spoke one word:

"Remember."

Still staring at Kam, Iyoskothe reached for the fire around his feet. Pulling it up like a garment, he threw it over his head. As the fire fell back to the earth, Iyoskothe fell with it, into the mountain.

He was gone.

Fidaelii looked at the others, terror in her eyes. Kam stepped forward and embraced her. She was choking back tears. He spoke softly.

"There is no time for fear, Fidaelii. The Song and the Oracle await. Walk."

Fidaelii nodded and took a deep breath. She wiped her face with her sleeve. She reached in her pack, took out her cloak and tied it around her neck. Wrinkled but brilliant, it unfurled like a standard. Kam watched her set determination into her shoulders. She turned to the company.

"Come," she said, fire blazing in her eyes.

With that, Fidaelii stepped through the door.

20

Fire at the Gate

The smell of stagnating water filled Maughlin's nostrils as he awoke. He surveyed the delta as he stretched. Midway through his scan, he saw Siyonte' speaking with Lucian on the bank of the little island. Something was amiss.

"Where are the horses?" he asked Sokii.

"Our hosts have taken them to the Aeries Gate," came the reply. Sokii held out some bread and cheese. "Here, sir. Have something to eat."

Maughlin took the food readily. As he ate, his stomach reminded him of how little he had taken the day before. He coughed with a mouth full of dry bread. Sokii handed him a water satchel. After a long drink, he approached one of the smaller Maisorvantii.

"Good morning, my Lord," he spoke with a slight bow. "Thank you for your watch-care last night. When can we expect to make for the Gate?"

The younger Maisor spoke nothing, but instead looked to his prince and nodded. Maughlin mirrored the Maisor's look and nod and made his way over to the bank where Lucian and Siyonte' stood. He began to repeat his query to the larger Maisorvantii.

"Good mor..."

"We leave now!" Siyonte' called out. "Junyote', you take the lad. Miyoste', take good care of this one. I will bring Lucian!"

Sokii hardly had time to secure his pack and Maughlin the water satchel before they were snatched up under the arms of the great Maisorvantii. The ascent had a few bumpy moments, but in no time they were over the trees. Once there, each Maisor wrapped a great arm around his cargo's torso and another around their knees. Carried like fleshy lances, Maughlin glanced over at Sokii, who had his arms stretched fully out. Sokii ventured one giant yawp of joy before being shushed by his carrier. The speed at which they were traveling caused such a wind that Maughlin's eyes teared up. Every wing thrust was so powerful yet almost completely silent. The Shifting Deltas raced by below. Their drooping cypresses and myriads of islands appeared as if someone had taken a great cloth and made a smudge of them. After an hour, the Maisors slowed their flight and began a descent. Greyish-brown land rushed up to meet them. Maughlin looked at his host's wings. They cupped to catch the wind and glistened in the morning sun. As each Maisorvantii landed, Maughlin and his company were placed down with the greatest care. They were on the north edge of a small forest of fir trees.

"You will find your horses tied up in a small clearing just behind you there," Siyonte' said, pointing. Turning left, he raised his claw to the west. "The Aeries Gate is two leagues away. You cannot miss it. The Eagloni made it to welcome all the Sons of Magic to their domain." He continued in sadness: "Never once did I give my hand to hunting them. I opposed it at every turn. They were a magnificent race. Skaaran is all the more beggarly without them."

"Ever have you been a picture of grace and mercy, my Lord," Lucian answered. "Tell us now, for you have walked them lately: which road through the Aeries is the most safe?"

"Truth, Keires," Siyonte' replied, "I tell you one Road has just as many teeth as another. Because you are hard pressed for time, you should take the High Road if Iyoskothe indeed goes with you. It is the widest and best for horses since you ride. Take care though. It is also the most watched and traveled. But if you are not captured, you will make the Blades in two days' time. Every other Road, though safer, will bring you there in no sooner than four."

"It seems as though our choice is made then!" said Sokii with glee.

"You are reckless, boy," said Maughlin giving him a shove. "But there is no other way it seems. I wish the Aeries were once again full of Eagloni instead of this Pyropos threat. Come. Let us pray we find Iyoskothe at the Gate." Turning to Siyonte', he and Sokii knelt. "Majesty, we thank you for your kindness. Let the chronicles show that true nobility still exists within the Second-born Race of Skaaran."

"And let them show that valor still moves in the hearts of the Sons of Men!" Siyonte' answered. Clasping his arm, the Maisor continued: "The Oracle's hand be upon you, little Maughlin, until you see Him face to face in the Day."

After all raised a hand in a sign of parting, the Maisorvantii erupted into the sky and were gone. The three travelers made their way through the fir trees and into the promised clearing where their horses were tied. Mounting his horse, Maughlin breathed the clean mid-morning air in deeply. The coolness was invigorating and spoke hope to his mind.

The three set out with renewed determination. Their deliverance from the tramper the night before was a good omen. As they left the forest, Maughlin surveyed the Eastern Streotas. They were less imposing than their Western brothers, more gentle in their rises and falls. Indeed they looked more like they were shaped on a great potter's wheel. A rolling horizon sprawled out before him. *How pleasant it would be to make one's dwelling here,* he mused. *Little wonder the Maisors are fighting over it.*

The sun had just passed its zenith when the Gate came into view. Sokii let out a gasp. Rising several hundred feet, the Aeries Gate was covered with legions of banners. Most of the banners were now tattered or singed, but some remained unharmed. Even those were faded by the elements across the years.

Under the banners were scores of intricate reliefs. The reliefs told the stories of the Eagloni and their desire for harmony with all the Sons of Magic. No doors stood on the Gate. It was a magnificent open archway, welcoming all sojourners to the Aeries. As they rode through, Maughlin noticed tears in Lucian's eyes. Maughlin was about to speak, then thought better of it. Sensing his question, Lucian offered an explanation for his sorrow.

"I don't know which tragedy gives me greater pain," he wept, "the Rending War or the Great Hunt. In all of our Councils, we Brothers have searched and searched for the reason behind the Hunt. All such searches have proven futile. Iyoskothe believes some of the dragon peoples are bent on retaking all of Skaaran. He believes they began with the Eagloni and that their terrors will spread to all the Sons of Magic and Men. The Maisorvantii are as unpredictable as the weather of this land. Who can know their mind? Who can plumb the depths of their hearts?

When Maisors such as Siyonte' stand before you, it is easy to make assumptions about the race. Such assumptions are deadly."

"The High Council in Skaaroth believes the Maisorvantii race to be failing," Sokii offered. "The Sons of Men believe they are diminished enough from the plague that they can be conquered."

Now on the other side of the Gate, Maughlin stopped them. "The High Council are fools. None have ventured beyond the Rending Wall in twenty summers. What do they know of the Wilds? Why, the three Maisors we met yesterday would make such short work of..."

Maughlin couldn't finish his thought due to a great wind descending upon them. Ten great red Maisorvantii surrounded them: terrible and beautiful to behold.

Pyropos! Maughlin thought. *Our doom is nigh.*

Dismounting quickly, Maughlin moved to help Lucian down. Sokii was already off of his horse and rushed to Maughlin. Drawing his sword, Maughlin shouted at the largest Maisor.

"Majesty, we are servants of the Oracle! We travel to His Sanctum by way of the High Road. Do you dare hinder us now? We have one of the Brothers with us! We ask for passage!"

"Passage?" the red one leered. "PASSAGE! The High Road is *our* Road. These lands *our* lands! I am Bruukheom, High Marshall of the Pyropos and rightful ruler of all the

Maisorvantii in Skaaran. We know not your Oracle, nor do we grant you passage. There is no hope for you."

"You are a spoiled child who fights with other spoiled children for the scraps of a dungheap," said Lucian. "Your self-importance will be consumed by the Oracle's return to these lands."

"You're bold for a cripple!" Brukkheom answered. "I know a thing or two about being consumed. Come here, little mouse. I have gifts for you."

At this, he drew a short pole with a spout from his belt. Pressing a knob on it, the spout sparked to life. A white-hot long flame spewed forth. The other Maisors in turn armed themselves with similar weapons that sparked and hissed all around Maughlin's company. Lucian stepped forward. He raised his hands and began to sing.

"I walked once with Y..."

The Maisor's flame was cruel as it cut right through Lucian. So intense was it that the Sage's body began to burn on the ground as he fell dead at Maughlin's feet.

"No!" Maughlin heard Sokii cry out behind him. "Do you know what you have done? The Brothers were a gift to this land! They taught us the Ancient Wisdom!"

"And now you see where the Ancient Wisdom takes you," Bruukheom replied caustically. "Who will be the next to join him?"

"*You* will be the next," a deep voice boomed from behind them. The whole Maisor troop turned at once to face the Aeries Gate. Directly under it, the ground was on fire. The voice was coming from it. *"Bruukheom son of Bruukheon, ever long has the cup of the Oracle's wrath been filling for you. Your father drank his cup full at the end of his days. Now I bring your cup to you. Are you ready to drink it?"*

"Bring the cup here!" Bruukheom bellowed. "I fear no devilry conjured up by you!"

"Whether you fear or not matters little," the voice answered plainly. "You *will* drink now. You will drink *deeply*."

With those words, Iyoskothe sprung from the mountain for his prey. Humming sickle in one hand, otherworldly fire in the other, he gave the Maisor troop pause.

"Kill him!" Bruukheom ordered. "Now you will taste Maisor fire, demon!"

Flaming weapons revealed, the Maisor troop rushed Iyoskothe as one. Iyoskothe had just moments to touch his burning hand to the great scythe. It combusted with a great noise and began to glow as if it had just been pulled from the forge.

"Fire?" Iyoskothe challenged. "FIRE?" he boomed as he cut down two of the Maisor troop like harvest wheat. "Fool!" Iyoskothe called to Bruukheom as another Maisor melted beneath the thresher. "I am the Vengeance of the Oracle Himself gifted to the evil of Skaaran!"

The sickle fell yet again, cleaving another of the troop in

twain. Leaping from the slain Maisor, Iyoskothe was swift to close the space between himself and the Maisorvantii lord. Bruukheom swung the flame sword at Iyoskothe's head, but the Sage caught it with his bare hand. Shoving the shaft of his sickle under the chin of the Maisor, Iyoskothe lifted Bruukheom off the ground. With a gaze that would pierce a star, Iyoskothe whispered:

"*I* tread the *ancient* fire."

With a mighty thrust, the Keires flung Bruukheom into the air like a child's plaything. Launching himself before the Maisor lord could spread his wings to flee, Iyoskothe brought his sickle over his head and back down again squarely into the crown of Bruukheom's head. The slain Maisor's body plummeted to the ground under the weight of the blow. Falling with it was the Keires, who landed in a great blast of the flames surrounding his feet.

Seeing their captain so dispatched, the five remaining dragonlings dropped their weapons in despair. The Pyropos took to their knees and bowed their heads in reverence and fear. Still in his furious state, Iyoskothe approached them.

"I press you now as heralds into the Oracle's service!" Iyoskothe bellowed. "Travel the length and breadth of the desolation of the Aeries and publish the tidings that Iyoskothe Mortibundos treads in the open lands of Skaaran once again! Bear witness, all of you, the end of all those opposed to my comings or goings! I make for the Sanctum. Let no living thing prohibit me! Now, go."

The five Maisors retrieved their weapons and fled in every direction. As Iyoskothe diminished his glory, he walked over to Maughlin and Sokii. They were kneeling over the charred body of Lucian, weeping.

"Do not despair, little ones," Iyoskothe commanded. "He will live on in the chronicles of the Oracle."

With those words, Iyoskothe knelt to lift Lucian's body to himself. As he embraced the fallen Keires, the Sage's body began to quiver and hum. Maughlin watched in wonder as the body began to dissolve into very fine dust and blow away in the western wind. Iyoskothe stood and faced Maughlin and Sokii.

"Get on your horses," Iyoskothe commanded. "You have a full day and night to ride through the desolation. We make for the High Road!"

21

The Harrows

Kam peered through the mystic door into the other realm. A heavy mist crawled out from the Harrows and clawed at his feet. Inside, the twilight loomed. The sting of Iyoskothe's parting words was fresh in his ears. Stepping through the burning door into the Harrows, Kam called for the Acolyte.

"Fidaelii! I will walk at the head of the company. You will be safest behind me." He drew his kopis and walked past the girl as she protested.

"Did you not hear the dread lord Iyoskothe's command? I am to listen for the Song! You would do well to heed his words!"

"You would do well to heed mine, girl! None of us

know what to expect in this place. I was the one "called" by the Oracle. *I* will lead us."

Kam took position at the head of the company. He no sooner began trudging than heard a voice cry out from down the Road.

"Murderer! Look what you have done!"

A young Greefadth mother came limping to meet him, bearing a young child in her arms. Both the mother and the child were sorely wounded. The Daughter of Magic approached Kam as he walked and took pace beside him, screeching in his ear unceasingly and holding her new slain child up to his eyes. Kam turned around and questioned the Acolyte.

"Do you see her?"

She nodded, mouth agape.

"Hear her?"

"She needs help!" Fidaelii answered.

"Who needs help?" Kam heard Hathlos ask from behind.

"No one! All is well, Hathlos!" Kam called back. He looked again at Fidaelii. "They cannot see or hear. Strange..."

"Kam, she is hurt!" Fidaelii insisted. "We must give her aid!"

"There is no aid for her, girl." Kam answered, as the Greefadth mother raged on. "I have made certain of that. Come, we need to keep moving. Just... ignore her."

At that, Kam turned again with the rabid mother at his neck as he walked. With every bend in the road, another wounded Son or Daughter of Magic would appear with cruel shouts of accusation. After a mile or so, a great Greefadth warrior stood in the middle of the Road to challenge Kam. Kam rushed to do battle, but when Hearthstone tried to shove the Greefadth, he just shoved the air.

"Stop! Kam, just stop!" Fidaelii cried out. "There is no fighting them."

Still the jeering and taunting went on and on. Dozens of misty figures surrounded the company with their insults and threats. *They must all think me mad,* Kam mused. *See how they look at me! Hathlos and his boy will want to put an end to me...* He noticed the Eagloni's perplexed look. *I have to gather my wits....*

"I need a moment with Fidaelii." Kam muttered under his breath.

"What, Hearthstone?" asked Hadros.

"A moment!" Kam shouted back, startling everyone. "I need a moment! With the girl!"

Grabbing her by the arm, Kam led Fidaelii a stone's throw from the rest of the company. Still surrounded by the ever-pressing mob of Greefadth slain, Kam looked directly into Fidaelii's eyes.

"I need you to tell me everything you know. What is happening, girl? What are you sensing?"

"Please, sir," Fidaelii answered, "I... I don't know."

Becoming impatient, Kam further pressed: "How is it that you can see and hear them?"

"I... I..." she stuttered, "I can't explain it. I don't know why I can see your ghosts or hear them! All I do know is that we cannot stay in this place. If you want to escape, you need to allow me to try to hear the Song!" Grabbing his arm, she became desperate. "Please. Kam. Please send Hadros up to the front with me so that I can try to do what Iyoskothe has commanded! I am begging you, sir. Please take this devil's din away from me. Please walk as far from me as possible. I need to listen for the Song!"

Looking back at the gawking company, Kam realized for the first time that he and the girl had been shouting at each other.

"Very well," he resigned, removing her hands from his arm. He turned and began to walk back through the midst of the company. Meeting Hathlos at the rear and never looking up from the road, he made the Acolyte's request known to the Eagloni. Hathlos took Hadros and moved forward to take position just behind Fidaelii and the Keires. For the longest time, the company stood unmoving. Disgusted, Kam shouted toward the front.

"Well, what are we waiting for? Let us be going!"

Kam noticed Grimmalt turn to speak to him. *I do not need another Greefadth rebuke!* As soon as he opened his mouth to voice his thought, Kam spied a look of horror in Grimmalt's widened eyes. The Greefadth Prince was just staring over Kam's right shoulder. He knew what Grimmalt was seeing. He voiced his guess.

"Your father and brother?"

Grimmalt could just nod, tears now streaming down his face. Kam heard the Prince clear his throat and venture a question. "Can you... Can you see them?"

Turning, Kam looked for them.

"No," he answered. "I have enough specters of my own to deal with at the moment." Looking again ahead, Kam noticed the company was finally on the move. Dealing harshly with Grimmalt, Kam grasped a big clump of fur on the shoulder of the Son of Magic and shoved him up the Road. Turning to toe up to Hearthstone, Grimmalt breathed a threat:

"Lay another hand on me, Son of Xander, and I will walk with three ghosts this night!"

Pressing his kopis against Grimmalt's neck, Kam answered, "I can ensure your walk with more than three if it would please you!"

An Aeries bolt glanced off the rock wall mere inches from the both of them, and they heard Hathlos' sobering tone in the distance.

"We all have demons to face here, lads! The Acolyte moves for the Song! If we make for the Sanctum, let us do so with speed. I fear this twilight will not last long... the Night comes with doom upon doom."

Cautiously, Grimmalt turned his back upon Kam and loped to catch the other three. Within moments, Kam had caught them as well. Joining him were the myriads of Sons and Daughters of Magic, all broken. Here a Maisorvantii maid reached for him in a desperate gesture. There a Vulkeeri Elder sat stoicly as he passed and glared at him. And all along the way, the Greefadth mother was joined by dozens of other shouters as she ranted and railed at him. Kam kept his eyes down, longing to return to Laurl and his grandfather's farm on the outskirts of Edraeth. He reached into his satchel and scratched around.

He felt for the ribbon. He felt the locks.

Trudging for hours, he held her hair up to his face. Following the party, all that was left for him to do was to think of her. Dwelling on her smile. Meditating on the way her eyes would dance when she was up to mischief. He strained his ears through the rushing river of ghostly voices to hear her hum as she worked about the house. He began to walk faster.

Flanking Grimmalt now, he thought about his wedding day with Laurl in the waist-high wheat. So engrossed was he in the memory that he did not notice the Sons and Daughters of Magic abandoning their pursuit of him. He remembered the sadness in her eyes when he told her of his intent to join the Garrison in Skaaroth. *It would only be a year's training...* Kam had caught up with Hadros as his memories drove him forward. *The letters. The letters*

she would write me... Always sent with a dried river lily...
He had reached Hathlos. *One of the sweetest letters... Right before I was to go to Rorgus... She was with child...* He clasped the locks that Laurl had gifted him tightly as he walked swiftly next to Fidaelii. Kam looked all around. His army of ghosts was gone.

"Do you hear it?" Fidaelii asked with tears in her eyes. "Please tell me you do! I have yet to hear anything more glorious."

"I hear nothing," Kam answered, relieved. "How much further to the Sanctum?"

"Can you not see?" Fidaelii replied. "Look! Just ahead!"

Kam strained his eyes up the next rise. He saw the silhouettes of fruit trees rising in the distance just above the mist. His feet began to tread on something that he never dreamed he would see again: grass. His ears were greeted with birdsong. The whole company quickened their pace. They almost dared to run. As Kam started up the rise, a small figure began to emerge from the brume. His gait was eerily familiar, and Kam was cut to the quick.

"No..." he breathed, almost as a prayer. *No.* He stopped and shut his eyes. As he felt all of the company pass him by, he stood all the more resolute. He dared not venture a gaze toward the garden again. Indeed, he wished nothing more than to turn and abandon the quest altogether. *No...*

I think I should die. Now it is time. Now must be the end.
He sheathed his sword.

Kam reached for Xander's dagger. He freed it from its belt-casing.

Kam pressed the short blade to his breast. He was about to plunge it in when he felt a small hand on his wrist.

"Kam," Fidaelii whispered, "we are so close. Please don't do this. No good thing could come of this. Think of your wife."

Kam's grip was unrelenting. He shook his head. Slowly, his eyes opened to the sight of the boy standing inches away, gazing up at him. In utter shock, Kam fell backward and scrambled to get away. Now fixated with the apparition walking toward him, Kam saw the gaping hole in the lad's chest. His shirt was stained with dried blood from the old wound.

"Stay back!" Kam choked. "Don't come any closer!" He looked to the skies. "If there is an Oracle, may he deliver me from this curse!"

Kam watched in despair as the boy approached and sat down next to him on the roadside. Remorse drenched Kam's mind as the boy smiled and reached out for him. *I cannot stay here...*

I cannot...

"Father," the boy beamed, "Father, I have missed you so! Oh, it's so good to be with you again."

Kam wept and wept. Great heaving sobs seized his body as his eyes were locked up in the prison of the lad's gaze.

"Titus," he convulsed, "I... I never meant to..."

Kam sat there with his son and said nothing more for what seemed an age. He slipped in and out of time. His mind returned to the madness of fourteen years ago when he roamed the Wilds like an animal. Visions of rivers and fields flashed before him, running from forest to sea-bank to glade, not caring of life or death for months on end. He closed his eyes once more as the heaviest of aches seized his very being. Every sense of comfort and stability was slain in that moment.

He once again felt the tiny hand, this time on his shoulder.

"Kam," Fidaelii encouraged, "the Oracle awaits. I have seen him. He waits for you just beyond the grove. Please, sir. There is no time."

Kam shut his eyes tightly and nodded. Bracing himself against a rock, he rose unsteadily. Taking one last look at his son, he sheathed his father's dagger. He looked down at his chest and the cut that left a little trail of blood. Kam didn't know how he climbed the hill toward the Oracle's garden. As the smell of fruit breached his nostrils, Kam turned to look once more upon Laurl's greatest joy. The lad was gone.

22

The Sanctum

Reaching the garden, Kam was in a daze. Every voice from the hours of traversing the Harrows still fought his sanity. They were all there, every ghost. When Titus wished to speak, his voice would crowd out all the others. The company had found suitable places to rest scattered throughout the lush landscape, but this was no haven for the Lord High Arbiter. He shot doleful eyes toward the Acolyte, and Fidaelii motioned to a small opening among thickly grown grapevines. She gave a solemn nod as he passed by, and Kam could see a gentle smile trying to bend her lips. Passing into more mist through the grapevines, Kam's spirit matched the hanging of his head.

At last...

The reckoning comes at last.

The vineyard seemed to part to Kam's left and right symmetrically. In the open space there were several benches around a great plain wooden table. Seated on a far bench was a man dressed plainly. The man looked to be no more than forty years old. *He looks like a vagrant!* Kam derided to himself: *Not much has changed since I first saw him in Rorgus' keep. Why, I've seen hundreds like him in the streets of Skaaroth. This is no Oracle. We shall see what this "mighty one" knows...*

"Many welcomes, Kam StoneHeart, Son of Xander, Son of Titus!" the man called, standing to his feet. As he made his way around the great table to the place where Kam was standing, he continued his address. "Long have I awaited this day. You come to prove them all wrong, eh?"

Kam spoke not a word but rather spent a moment measuring the man. If the supposed Oracle was taller than him, Kam could not mark the difference. Matted hair fell to his shoulders where dingy clothes hung over a half-fed frame. The man was slightly paled from lack of sun. His hands were filthy from working earth. His shoulders hunched slightly from years of bending over vines. Walking past Kam to inspect the vineyard, the Oracle spoke again.

"Does our meeting disappoint you, Kam?"

"To be honest, my Lord, I had no expectation of ever seeing you," Kam answered. "So I have no feelings concerning our meeting at all."

Taking a pruning shear from his belt, the Oracle snipped a few clusters of grapes and turned to face Kam once more.

"There is no room for pretense or formality here, StoneHeart. You will not find any answers in playing games with class and station. You no more think me your lord than I think you my subject. Let us speak plainly with one another."

"Very well," Kam replied through stiffening lips. "If you *are* the Oracle, why do you not even call me by my proper name? One would think you knew it! My father was your chief warlord in the Rending..."

"Your father never once served me," the Oracle interrupted, examining a cluster of grapes. "I sent word through the Brothers to the High Council of Skaaroth that war with the Sons of Magic was strictly forbidden. Do not sully my name by laying that War at my feet. The purity prescribed in the Ancient Wisdom has nothing to do with harmony by subjugation. That is Starsgol's perversion."

"And yet you blessed the Rending War!" retorted Kam. "You gave aid to the Sons of Men to drive out the Sons of Magic from their midst!"

"Enough!" the Oracle roared. "You know nothing of the War save that which has been told to you. Your counsel is darkened, Kam StoneHeart." Taking a deep breath, the Oracle continued: "Surely you have not come here to speak to me about your father and his folly. Why have you come?"

"Why do *you* ask *me*?" Kam mocked. "*You* were the one who called me! What is it that *you* desire? What do you suppose *I* could do for *you* in all of Skaaran that you could not possibly do for yourself?"

"Nothing," said the Oracle. "There is nothing in Skaaran that I cannot do. I have called you to help lead the Sons of Men and Magic in discovering truths about themselves. The Song will teach all in Skaaran that they are indeed dependents: both upon the Ancient Wisdom and upon each other. A great crucible lies before you, Kam StoneHeart. As you step into it, there are some aspects of yourself that will be saved for the future. That which you perceive as your true self will be lost. The sweetest end of the crucible is that the man you have longed to be will be found."

"Save your riddles, vagabond," Kam lashed out. "I have no need of truths, or crucibles, or Sons of Magic or Men. Speak plainly to me if you can."

"The task I have set before you will come to light soon enough," replied the Oracle. "But first, there is something that entered your mind all those days ago when you met with Praius in Edraeth. In the Day's Grace that you were given, Maughlin Ravenhill counseled you concerning Rememberings. You told your wife you were coming to me to seek answers. Why do you now deny it? Now that you are here and have braved many perils. Ask, Son of Xander," said the Oracle. "Ask what you wish. Ask now, or leave."

"Why is my son dead?" Kam blurted. "Why does he walk the Harrows ever wounded? Where is your kindness and beauty made manifest in the face of such sorrow?"

"You know why your son no longer walks in the changing world," the Oracle replied solemnly. "You mistook him for a Greefadth while patrolling the Lupinwood outside of Rorgus. You plunged your father's blade into the bush where he was watching..."

"I don't need to be reminded of what I did!" Kam raged. "Why does he now walk the Harrows without rest?"

"He does not walk the Harrows," the Oracle answered. "I spoke to him this morning. He is changeless."

The Oracle smiled. His thoughts were far away. "Titus makes the greatest games..."

"You lie!" Kam exploded. "*I* snuffed out his light, and quickly!" *Just as I extinguished so many others.* "Where were *you*? Why did you not prevent him from following me?"

"Why would I prevent a child from living every moment to be with the father he so loved? You were everything he wanted to be."

"And the ensuing madness?" Kam volleyed. "Where were you in the Wilds? For more than four years I... I.... I don't remember... ...but they gave me up for *dead*! My wife received Titus' body, and I was not there! *You* were not there! What *can* you do? *Anything?* What *good* have you done since you have come to this land?"

After hearing no response, Kam pressed the issue. "Well?"

The Oracle left the vines and approached Kam. "What is it you need, StoneHeart?"

"Stop calling me that!" Kam shoved the man away.

"My name is Kam Hearthstone. It is the mightiest name among the Sons of Men in Skaaran! My father was Xander Hearthstone. His name struck terror in all the Sons of Magic. You would do well to mark the name, *fool.* You would also do well to fear it. It has been the bane of every tribe, men or magic, drawing breath in Skaaran. When the High Council in Skaaroth seeks an end, there is only *one* name to which they turn."

"On that," countered the Oracle—retracing his steps to face Kam, "we fully agree. Long have the Sons of Men sought their own answers. Long have they relied upon the strength of their own arm. Long have they whispered against the Ancient Wisdom. Long have they given only lip service to the Brothers that I gave as a gift."

"We care nothing for your 'gifts,' Kam muttered under his breath.

"Here, I bear a gift for you, *mighty* Oracle."

Stepping directly before Kam, the Oracle had bedrock in his voice:

"You must now do all that is in your heart, Kam."

Nodding, Kam gnashed his teeth. As swift as the rising of the summer storm, Xander's dagger sprung from its sheath. Kam looked down at his hand gripping the ornate handle that protruded from the Oracle's chest. A great stream of blood flowed from the groove of it, and soon his hand was soaked.

Kam felt the weight of Laurl's sorrow lift from him momentarily. He took one last burning look into the Oracle's wide eyes and shoved the dirty vagrant's corpse to the ground. As the familiar thud of a slain body against the earth sounded in his ears, Kam noticed everything around him fading into darkness. The benches, the great table, the grapevines, the Oracle's body—everything— was now swirling into a great void. Kam felt himself caught up in it. He could hardly mark the entrance into the vineyard to make his way back to the garden before the Night engulfed him.

All was lost.

23

Stone and Flame

The darkness screamed for light, but no light answered. No trees. No sounds. No wind.

Nothing to remind Kam of the natural world's comfort showed itself.

The sound of his breath whispered, muffled. The very atmosphere steadily constricted, fighting life. Everything once known now assumed an alien form. When he realized he was alone, fear threatened. Due to circumstances of his or another's choosing, he had been alone before. His solitude was normally a haven. Yet, nothing from his past experience could serve as a platform to comprehend this realm.

The Oracle spoke of a crucible, of finding "truths", and of saving, losing, and finding. Nothing thrived here except confusion! Wisdom did not exist in this place. How could he expect to find anything when he struggled even to find his bearing?

Kam sensed he wavered upon solid ground but dared not take a step for fear of tumbling into a pit or plummeting off some precipice. Clenching his eyes tightly, he longed desperately for one spark, one glimmer of hopeful light.

Just one!

He burst them open. His breath rushed out.

Nothing.

Shutting his eyes once more, he delved inward. Kam yearned to hear a sound, but his ears were deafened. More than his next heartbeat, he craved the melody of any song he'd heard on his journey to the Sanctum. *Better yet, that Song from my dream!*

Not a verse could be found.

Kam sought to quiet his mind. He reflected on the last time he felt the weight of this darkness.

This is senseless.

He felt as if he were underwater. Even his breathing came sharper now, and shorter.

If that devilry of a vision had not so disturbed me, I would have never even sought out the Edraeth Council...

Kam tried to retrace every step that led him away from his beloved...

The argument with Laurl...

The conversation with Praius...
The warning from Skotos... the threat from Starsgol...
The foolishness of Edreath's council...
The burden of bringing Fidaelii...
The...

In a burst of woe, all that came rushing to his mind were the memories of Titus and the others he met in the Harrows. Now joined in the void, his fervent longing was for the silence that first met his ears upon the initial descent. His son's words in the Harrows burrowed into Kam's psyche with every passing moment: *"It's so good to be with you again, Father...*

There was no escape, for there was no Road. For the first time in his life, the mighty Hearthstone was rendered absolutely helpless. There was no way to mark time. There was no way to mark if time even existed in this place! Kam felt for his sword, but it was not there. He searched the right side of his belt for Xander's dagger.

Ugh! It is still in that vagrant's corpse...

Kam craned his neck almost as hard as he strained his eyes. He looked as far as he could in every direction. Every point of the invisible horizon brought on more discouragement.

He screamed.

As he did so, he felt the air from his lungs rush back at him. The sound of his voice was so weak that he began to tremble. He looked for his feet but could not see them to mark the ground to run. There was a sickness of death in this realm, an overwhelming oppression of hopelessness that Kam had never known. It was stifling his spirit. As Kam began to shrivel there in the emptiness, one last thought crossed his mind.

Isolation.

Am I still standing or becoming part of this void?

As soon as he pondered this, Kam felt the faintest breeze. He gasped, trying to chase it with his mouth. He mustered his strength. He longed for the breeze to return. Then came another, this one a bit richer. He choked in a gulp of it. He tried to look for the source of the breezes. Far away in the distance, Kam imagined he saw a pinprick of light.

I am going mad. This darkness has seduced me... there is magic at work here.

Another breeze.

Another gulp of air to escape the oppression.

If it was an evil seduction, Kam did not care. He desired the light to grow more than he desired the next breeze. As if listening, the light responded.

Now growing to look like a distant star in the midst of the crushing night, the light seemed to be drawing nearer. Kam's hope was stirred. With every new zephyr he was gaining strength, very little by very little. Without being able to mark time, Kam could have been many years in that place.

He cared little.

His heart cried out for the light to move closer. The Arbiter longed for rescue.

As soon as the light illuminated an actual horizon, Kam could see that it was emanating from a figure.

A man, transfigured to effulgence. He blazed brighter than the sun. He looked like a firstborn star, his strides deliberate, his gaze obliterating.

Kam's terror of the dark was now consumed by his terror of this light. His vision of the light from the lady's shield made terribly real. The zephyrs had fled, and Kam once again felt as he was drowning. He wanted to run, yet his legs had resigned to perishing.

As the man approached, he held out his hands. The whole of Kam's body shook as he beheld Xander's dagger there, still protruding out.

This was the Oracle, and His beauty was terrible to behold. In the Oracle's left hand was what appeared to be the same light from Kam's vision all those nights ago. As he looked more closely, inside the light was a beating heart. Kam watched as the Oracle gave a flick of his wrist, and set it on fire.

The Oracle then took his right hand and cradled the blood groove of Xander's dagger, collecting blood for a moment. When the mighty One had enough in His hand, he quickly clenched His fist and produced a fiery quill. Never releasing Kam from His gaze, the Oracle deftly wrote all over the fiery pulsing object in His left hand. After He finished, the Oracle flicked the blood quill away.

Moving to stand face to face with His murderer, the Oracle thrust His right hand into Kam's chest. Pulling it out with a vengeance, He retrieved a polished onyx stone the size of a man's fist. Before Kam could cry out in pain, the Oracle immediately thrust his left hand with its blazing contents into Hearthstone's chest. After he pulled His left hand out again, the Oracle issued a command:

"Hear," he smiled.

"Hear and sing."

The contents of his dreams with the lady's song were a poor sampling of the reality Kam now found himself flying through. Melody and countermelody. Rhythm and polyrhythm. Descant and round and harmony moved colors innumerable through his being.

At once, he knew the Song.

Kam loved and was thankful for it. The air was never so sweet. He heard the voice of every creature singing their verse. Every fiery host of heaven sung in their orbit.

Every wave.

Every wind.

Every light.

Even the darkness lent its voice to the cry of the cosmos.

Every question answered.

Every purpose clear.

And for the first time in his life, Kam sang. Not only

was he full of boldness, he was full of joy. He did not wish to leave this place. After what seemed like an age, the Oracle approached him.

As He did, Kam fell down before Him and wept.

"Forgive me, Oracle," Kam sobbed. "I had no knowledge of all of... this."

"I forgave you before I issued your call," the Oracle answered. Helping Kam to his feet, he gestured. "Come. There is someone who longs to see you. Speak to him only and touch him not. Not yet. There will be all the time in the cosmos for that later."

The Oracle led Kam to the outskirts of what he could only guess was the blessed realm. Still the Song rang out unceasing. Over the joyous din of it, the Oracle called out.

"Titus! Come, Son! Your father has a question for you."

"Coming, great Lord!" rang a voice more alive than any Kam had heard in the Harrows. The merry lad was clothed in brilliant regalia from his head to his feet. No wound could be found on the boy. He came and stood just a few feet from the Oracle and his father. Seeing Kam with the Oracle, Titus beamed.

"Father! You made the Sanctum! We have all been cheering you on."

Kam wept.

"Titus. Son, I never meant to harm you. After the Rending War, the Greefadths were threatening, and..."

"Are you still living in that day?" the boy chuckled. "Honestly, Father, I have yet to think twice of it."

Giving the Oracle a wink, he continued: "I know who loves me!"

"Son, I..." Kam groped for words. "How could you ever for-"

"Father, I do not live in a prison here," Titus assured. "The Oracle tends to tear those down. You see my clothes? My dwelling and the food are no less glorious. We feast all day long to the Oracle's beauty and the Ancient Wisdom's goodness. We sing the Song that never ends! Nothing here is touched by Skaaran's brokenness. You will see for yourself soon enough!"

Taking a few steps closer, the boy leaned in to whisper: "You speak of forgiveness. You have been living in it. I have never stopped loving you."

Tears streamed down Kam's face. He looked at the Oracle, whose joy exceeded that of the boy.

"Come," the effulgent One commanded. "We must return to the others. They will be wondering why we are so long in our dealings. There is much work to be done yet in my Mending War!"

As they walked away from Titus, Kam glanced over his shoulder at the boy, who was still beaming.

The lad raised a hand in parting and was last heard to say: "Just a few blinks, Father! Just a few blinks until we are all together again. Give all my love to mother!"

As sad as Kam was to leave the blessed realm, the Song spurred him on. It was the consummation of every desire he never knew he had. The realm of color and sound began to dim, and Kam once again found himself in the open lawn of the vineyard among the great table with its many benches.

They had landed back in the Oracle's Sanctum in Skaaran. As Kam's head continued to swim with the sights and sounds of his latest journey, the Oracle placed Xander's dagger in his hand.

"Summon the others here," urged the Oracle. "We must draw up our battle plans."

Kam nodded and ran down the misty path to the Orchard.

24

Another Verse, Another Voice

As Kam Hearthstone made his way through the mist, the heralds of morning greeted him. Birdsong erupted from almost every branch of tree and bush. Sunlight had come to the garden. The muted colors of the night before had melted away. The whole orchard seemed to dance in the morning breeze. Even the grass was stretching every blade to take hold of the light. To Kam's surprise, Maughlin was there and was rousing everyone that had slept under an enormous apple tree. Kam voiced his delight.

"Good morning, Uncle! I didn't think to see you here. How is it you were able to travel so swiftly?"

"So swiftly?" Maughlin laughed. "My boy, it took us

three days' journey from the Aeries Gate, and that was with the dread Lord Iyoskothe's aid!"

Kam must have had a bewildered look on his face as Fidaelii approached him and joined Maughlin's mirth. The Acolyte tried to give Kam some grounding.

"This is the morning of the eighth day since you entered the Sanctum," Fidaelii explained. "We wondered if you were even still alive!"

"I have not lived until this day," Kam answered. "Come, the Oracle has summoned us all. We must see what He has in store for..."

Kam could not finish, for it was at this point that he turned around again to face the viney path that led to the Sanctum. What he saw then filled him with such awe that his mind was instantly captivated. Instead of a small, dirty path among grapevines, there stood high ornate golden walls. Upon the walls grew hanging gardens. Myriads of gilded pots with flowers and vegetables and fruit of every kind pouring forth from them clung to the walls. The view made for an intimidating presence. Down the sides of the walls at every point, water trickled and danced in such a way that it made the glint of the gold more beautiful. Around the base of the walls ran a narrow drainage trench lined with white stones. The pure water filled the trench and flowed around the building to empty into a stream on the eastern side of the Sanctum. A golden footbridge spanned the small trench just before the entrance. There was no roof on the structure. Noticing Kam's frozen state, Fidaelii let out a giggle.

"Good Hearthstone!" she teased. "You act like this is the first time you have ever seen the Sanctum! Where do you think you have been these many days?"

"I..." Kam stuttered, "There were... ...and the grapevines..."

"The Oracle awaits!" Iyoskothe boomed to everyone.

With a jolt, the entire gathered company made their way across the footbridge. Kam led the way with Fidaelii and Maughlin right behind. Following them, Grimmalt made careful strides. Hathlos and Hadros were joined by Sokii and Iyoskothe at the last.

As Kam passed through the thick golden walls of the Sanctum, another wonder was to be seen. The vineyard remained, but instead of spreading out as far as the eye could see to the right and the left, it graced the walls and climbed to their tops. Massive clusters of rich red grapes sprung forth all over, offering treats to whoever would gather them. In the middle of the Sanctum was a golden banqueting table, the likes of which Kam had never seen. Stretching half the length and the width of the golden hall it was. It bore roasted pigs and hens, cooked vegetables from all over Skaaran, smoked fish and casks of wine and mead. Wheels of cheese and sides of beef and mutton lay before the Company, flanked with all manner of sweets: sugared fruits and custards. As they approached the table,

Kam saw the Oracle stand up from where he was seated at the head of the feast and spread his arms wide.

"Welcome! Welcome, friends! We have much to discuss. Yes, much!" he exclaimed. "But first, first you must break your fast. You must feast as you never have before. There will be many Roads to walk, but now you must feast. No words! Not yet! Feast with me."

Indeed no words could be spoken. The smells and the tastes at that meal would inspire stories for years to come. And always in the midst of the feast was the Song. Harmonic tones would ring throughout the Sanctum in such a way to drive the feast on. Kam would often say later (to anyone that would listen) that he ate far more than he ever should have and yet was only ever perfectly satisfied. The feast lasted for hours. Only after three courses or so did companions begin to speak. Any anxiety was instantly quelled by the meal. When the last of them pushed back from the banqueting table, Kam noticed the Oracle make a dismissive gesture toward the food with His hands. Immediately obeying, the food and all the utensils vanished. Only the drinks remained. The Oracle took His cup and drank a long draught. Placing it down, with a merry smile he spoke.

"Now, sweet friends, let us see what the next verse of the Song will be! Maughlin Ravenhill! Come and stand before me."

Kam watched his beloved neighbor stand and pause for

a moment. Maughlin looked directly at him. Maughlin made his way to where the Oracle was sitting. He knelt before the Oracle. In a few moments, he was flanked by Iyoskothe and Sokii. Chuckling, the Oracle stood up and placed his hand upon the old man's shoulder.

"For more than five hundred summers you have been a faithful friend to me, lonely Son of the East. When I first found you as a boy lost in the Aeries all those years ago, you had my heart. Never once have your loyalties wavered, even in the midst of great loss. There is a rest prepared for you. Do you desire it now?"

"My Lord," Maughlin answered through tears, "It is all I have ever wanted."

Kam watched in awe as the Oracle addressed the other two.

"Are you in agreement with your Brother, Sokii?"

"My Lord," smiled the lad, "I grow weary watching over the inner workings of the High Council. They fear you not. There are some with waning allegiance to the Ancient Wisdom that may yet be won back, but my time in Skaaroth is at an end."

"Very well," spoke Iyoskothe out of turn. "If this is the will of the Brothers, I will not hinder it. My heart is that Skaaran still needs us."

The mighty warrior paused to gather his thoughts. He soon continued.

"But if Maughlin Ravenhill desires rest, who am I to

forbid him? Let us return, then. The next verse in the Song must be given to another voice in the great Mending War to come."

"It is agreed, then," the Oracle pounded the table. "Rise, Maughlin Ravenhill. Say farewell to your Brothers and to those you have helped bring together."

Kam watched Maughlin stand with the help of Iyoskothe and Sokii. He embraced each one of the Sages, and as he did their presence flickered slightly. After a few moments each one seemed to be absorbed into his body. With each passing Sage, Maughlin appeared to grow stronger. Kam saw him face the Oracle once again.

"My Lord," Maughlin asked, "would it not have been better for Iyoskothe to stay? He was invaluable to me on the last Road through the Aeries. I cannot imagine the Outerland campaign without his aid."

"Indeed?" the Oracle replied. "That would mean you staying here with me in the Sanctum until I return in splendor to the Sons of Men and Magic. Would you not rather depart to the blessed realm?"

"I made a promise to the boy's father," Maughlin answered. Kam caught the old man glancing at Fidaelii. "I would think that extends to his offspring."

Kam looked at the girl. He saw the same puzzled look in her face as he was sure was in his. He saw Maughlin walk over to place an arm around the Acolyte. Maughlin began his explanation.

"Your mother came to me after members of the Garrison at Rorgus bore your brother's body home. They gave report that your father fled in grief and madness. They searched for him for quite some time with no success. After burying your brother, Laurl Meriis waited several months for your father, but he never returned. She came to me with the news of your impending arrival. I counseled her to seek out Praius for counsel. It was she who gave you up to him as an Acolyte. I am sure it was one of the hardest decisions of her life."

"I am the daughter of Kam Hearthstone and Laurl Meriis?" Fidaelii asked.

Nodding his head, Maughlin continued: "It was she who named you. Even in the midst of great sorrow, she held great hope. Hope for your father's well-being. Hope for you to know the Ancient Wisdom. Hope for all of Skaaran to be healed once more. Laurl and I were of the same mind concerning the Rending War. She holds the Sons of Magic in high esteem."

Walking over to where they were, Kam spoke his disbelief. "How can these things be? Laurl never once tried to prohibit me from going into the Wilds with the news of expecting a child!"

"She discovered she was with child after Titus' body was brought to the yew grove," answered Maughlin. "She did not know until after you were engulfed in the

287

madness of grief and lost in the Outerlands. She gave you up for dead."

Maughlin directed his next question to the child.

"Fidaelii, how are you feeling about this news?"

"I have been an orphan my whole life," she replied. "I have accepted my station as privileged servant to Praius and the Oracle with gladness. I... I don't know how to feel about this news. In some ways, I am glad to know from whence I come. In many ways, I am saddened at the news of the Brothers' departure from this land and their ties to you, Maughlin. Must you really go? My life before held so much purpose! I can't just throw that away now that I have learned I am no different from any other maid in Edraeth. If you leave, what is to become of me?"

Kam looked into the welling eyes of his daughter.

Daughter.

He then heard the Oracle speak.

"Maughlin, what is your desire for the child?"

"What is *your* desire, my Lord?" came the reply.

"With her knowledge of so many verses, it would be a shame not to have her voice sing them," the Oracle said, walking to meet the three where they stood.

Kam saw his daughter's eyes grow wide. Fidaelii clamped her hands over her mouth to stifle a squeal. As soon as the excitement took hold, though, he saw doubt creep upon her face. It made its way to her mouth.

"But, Lord," she said, "I don't have five hundred years'

worth of Roads in my feet. I am utterly unqualified in any task you may set before me! If it is in your mind to gift me to Skaaran as a Keires, it would be your greatest mistake."

"Oh, but you are old for a Keires!" Maughlin chuckled. "I was but ten years old when the Oracle gifted me to our world."

"Is it true?" Fidealii was struck with disbelief as she turned to the Oracle.

"It is true," He replied. "You *are* old, but you have had the benefit of sitting under a Brother. Maughlin did not even have that. Does this knowledge help assuage your doubt?"

"Somewhat..." she sighed. "I am resigned to Your commands, Mighty One. I know not your battle plans, but if I may play my part as an arrow, it will please me."

"Not as much as it will please me!" replied the Oracle. "You are well loved and well received, Fidaelii Charis. Your feelings of inadequacy are correct: you are inadequate. All my friends are poor and broken. That is how our love drinks so deeply. You will take the Song to all the Sons of Men and Magic who will hear it and learn to sing it. Your father and your mother will journey with you as well as any trustworthy friends you desire to take. That is my will for you in this day, Fidaelii. If you can accept it, I will gift you to this land as the last Keires to walk the Roads. What say you?"

Taking a deep breath, Fidaelii replied, "I live for your

love, my Lord. Whatever you command, I will breathe to do."

"And I live to give you love!" the Oracle bellowed. "Be then gifted to every inhabitant of Skaaran!"

Taking the girl in His great arms, the Oracle embraced her as a father would his daughter. A great light engulfed them. Turning her around to face the company, He looked at them one by one.

"Now," said the Oracle. "We must return to this subject of the need of Iyoskothe's set of skills for the Road ahead."

The Oracle walked back to his place at the head of the table. He lifted his voice in song.

Giver of gifts, both great and small:
Every gift given is given for all.
All we need do is but dream of and ask;
You equip those you have called for the task.

A great, round shield appeared on the table before the Oracle. When he hefted it onto his arm, a great flash of the dream seized Kam's mind.

The lady! ...Fidaelii?

Another flash of the vision.

The shield!

All at once, Kam recognized the unending Song in the Sanctum as the one in his dream. He watched the Oracle pick up a pitcher of wine. The Oracle carried the shield and the pitcher to where Kam was sitting. He knelt before Kam with the shield and the pitcher.

"Kam Hearthstone," said the Oracle. "This shield is what the Sons of Men call the Vessel of Power. There is nothing extraordinary about it, however. The power in it comes from my Father, the Ancient Wisdom. This Vessel serves different purposes, depending on how it is used..." At this, the Oracle paused. He was lost in a memory.

"When I first gifted Maughlin to Skaaran all those years ago, the boy needed a guardian. This is why Iyoskothe came. Iyoskothe was the first and strongest of his Brothers. He loved Maughlin Ravenhill fiercely. Fidaelii needs no less. If she is to travel the length and breadth of Skaaran, she will need you to protect her. I wish to give you the means. Now, take off your shoes."

Kam hesitated for a moment, but when he saw the stern look in the Oracle's eyes, he obeyed.

The Oracle flipped the shield upside down so it became a basin. He lifted Kam's feet and placed them in it. Taking the pitcher, the Oracle poured the wine on Kam's feet and washed them.

The wine was unusually warm. *Odd,* Kam thought. *It's getting warmer as he's pouring... ...by my word! It's blazing hot! Can that be... ...fire!*

Kam's thoughts were not those of madness. The wine *had* caught fire. The Oracle was now pouring liquid fire into the Vessel. Kam could feel it traveling from his feet into his very bones. By the time the fire reached his mind, Kam felt the strength of it in his muscles, strength as such he'd never felt before.

"Rise, Son of Xander," said the Oracle.

Kam stepped out of the Vessel's fiery bath. He fully expected the flames to diminish. They did not. They danced around his feet. *Just like Iyoskothe!*

"Yes, my Son," said the Oracle. "Just like Iyoskothe. But you will not walk openly in power as he did. Your power will manifest itself only in the presence of threatening evil. The flames will serve as a warning both for you and your adversary that you walk in my will. Now, let me see your father's weapons."

Kam drew Xander's kopis and dagger. He handed them to the Oracle.

"You know that these will never do," the Oracle said. "These were for the Rending of Skaaran. They must be unmade and repurposed."

He placed the kopis on the ground and laid the dagger on top of it. Seeing them arranged to his liking, the Oracle once again took up the pitcher of wine and poured liquid fire upon the weapons. Kam marveled as the wood in them was burned up. The metal of the blades melted together. He watched the Oracle blow upon the glowing mass of liquid metal. It glowed white-hot.

"Now, farmer," said the Oracle. "For your thresher..."

Kam beheld the impossible as the Oracle used his bare

hands to pick up the glowing mass. His hands blazed with fiery light. He worked the metal into a curve. As he did, the Oracle's eyes gave a faint glimmer of the transfiguration that Kam saw in the void where he was given his fiery heart. The Oracle seemed to be pleased with the shape of the tool and walked to the stream that bordered the great golden wall of His Sanctum. The hot metal let out a hiss and a great cloud of steam as the Oracle dipped it in for its cooling.

"Come here, Kam," the Oracle called. "Bring a bucket of water."

Kam obeyed and met the Oracle at a large, rounded rock. The Oracle nodded for Kam to wet the rock. Kam did so, and the Oracle set to sharpening the blade.

"There's an axe to be found in the orchard by the benches on the eastern side," said the Oracle. "Go find any sapling you like and cut it for your staff. I'll have this done when you return."

Kam left the Sanctum and crossed over the ornate footbridge that spanned the stream. *This stream is wild! It seems to travel wherever it pleases...* For all of his life, Kam would never forget the vivid beauty of that place. Everything seemed to dance around him. When he entered the orchard, the wonder that there was no dead and rotting fruit on the ground struck his heart. The place was so well tended as if there were no sleeping moments for the gardener. Every leaf was in its place. Every blade of grass was left to grow long and lie thick in a lush carpet of the deepest green. A gentle, sweet-smelling breeze was constantly being woven through the park. The birds that made their dwelling there sometimes sounded out in breathtaking harmony. In the next moment, they were telling jokes to each other and laughing in their way. He must have lost track of time in the orchard for when Kam heard the Oracle's voice behind him, he was embarrassed that he hadn't even looked for the axe.

"Kam!" said the Oracle, now holding the sharpened scythe. "Are you having difficulty choosing your staff?"

"I'm having difficulty doing anything but being wrapped up in this place, sir," said Kam.

"Be easy, Son," the Oracle let out a hearty laugh. "That is as it should be." His voice then set a more serious tone. "But while Starsgol yet roams the changing world, we must war with evil. His downfall is set in time, and you must play your part in it."

The Oracle walked to an oak sapling. "Here is the kind of tree your grandfather planted next to your dwelling. Does it please you?"

"Your wisdom pleases me, my Lord," Kam answered. "I will gladly take any gift you give."

"I will gladly give it!" the Oracle said. He pulled the sapling out by the roots.

Such strength! Kam thought.

The Oracle then used the scythe to trim the roots and

branches off the sapling. He made a cut in one end of the staff for the blade of the scythe to be held. Placing the blade and the staff together, he breathed on the joint. The sapling came alive and wrapped around the metal to hold it fast. The Oracle made his way back to the footbridge, looked at Kam, and smiled.

"Well, Kam, don't you want your gift?"

"I... I'm sorry, Lord," Kam shook himself out of his daze. "Of course."

Kam ran to the footbridge and took the scythe from the Oracle. When he did, the flames and heat returned to his feet and ran up to his hands. The flames continued on until the staff and scythe were dancing in them.

"This fire is my heart for you, Kam Hearthstone," said the Oracle. "Never doubt it. Carry my heart for all who would love me. Carry my justice for all who would oppress their brothers. Be a defender of the innocent, of the oppressed, of the maligned. Be my words for love and mercy. Show no mercy to the unmerciful. Show light to the ones who have known only darkness. Come now, the others still wait. There are many Roads your little company must now walk."

The Oracle turned and walked back into the Sanctum. Kam followed.

25

Many Roads, Many Plans

The Oracle's pace back into the Sanctum was almost a skip. Kam was overwhelmed by the energy that he exuded. *It's like he's a young child!* Kam thought. *He's so driven.* Kam saw the others take note at their return. They all stood up to await the Oracle's next words.

"Fidaelii Charis!" the Oracle said. "Come here and stand beside me, Daughter!"

She ran to him, and they embraced with great joy. He spun her around to Kam. Kam scooped her up into his arms and held his daughter for what seemed an age. Feelings of love deeper than he'd ever known rushed over him. *Oh, my girl!* Kam reluctantly placed her back on the ground. She walked to the Oracle.

"Are you ready, my new Sage?" the Oracle asked her.

Fidaelii nodded. Kam beheld a wild look in her eyes.

The Oracle then walked to the place where the great shield lay. Picking it up, he emptied the wine on to the ground. He took it to the little stream by the golden wall where he worked on Kam's scythe. The Oracle washed it out thoroughly and dried it with his clothes as he walked back to Fidaelii.

"Every shield maiden needs a shield," he said, looking it over one last time. "May this Vessel serve you as well as it once served me in Starsgol's expulsion of the Blessed Realm. May it continue to repel the deceit he revels in. May it cause you to walk in my strength!"

He handed it to her, and it almost swallowed her. Kam thought his daughter would never be able to lift the thing. To his surprise she hefted it easily.

Turning Fidaelii around to face the company, the Oracle looked at them one by one. Sizing up their needs, he addressed each one in turn.

Facing the Black Prince of Medras, the Oracle began His address:

"Grimmalt, Grennam's son."

"Yes, my Lord," Grimmalt answered as he came before the Oracle and knelt.

"I have spared you from death at this time. You will walk the Underland Road in its length and breadth. You will not walk it alone. I send with you a light in the darkness!"

At this, the Oracle whispered something in Fidaelii's ear. She let out a tremendous giggle, and the giggle materialized into a sprite. The sprite was as tall as a snapdragon flower, and she was bluish-white in hue. Her wings were a brilliant silver, which she stretched as she flew all around the company. She landed at last on Fidaelii's shoulder and promptly sat down, legs dangling.

"My Lord," Grimmalt winced. "Is there not another Keires you can send with me? A... a troll perhaps, or maybe a nightshade? No offense to the girl, but a sprite seems a poor choice to..."

"Your most powerful enemy on the Underland Road will be the rut of drudgery." The Oracle answered plainly. "All Roads down there seem the same. This sprite will help keep things...." He paused to smile at Fidaelii "... interesting."

"What is the small one's name?" Grimmalt asked.

Fidaelii thought for a moment.

"Antic!" Fidaelii laughed. "Antic Annick! She will like that!"

Upon hearing her name, the sprite appeared to become self-aware. As if waking from a long dream, Antic stretched and stood up. She leapt into the air and flew directly to Grimmalt's hairy shoulder and plopped down, assuming the position she once held with Fidaelii.

At this the Oracle roared with laughter to the point that it spread throughout the whole of the company.

Even Grimmalt's initial reservations about the sprite were conquered. He stood and took his place again with the company to await further commands.

"Hathlos, last son of the Aeries!" the Oracle beckoned. As the Eagloni came and knelt before Him, the Oracle continued: "There are other children of the air in the lands to the north of here. You must seek them out and tell them of our plight against Starsgol. You must teach them to hear and sing the Song. That is my will for you in this day. Can you accept it?"

"My Lord," Hathlos hesitated. "What will become of my son?"

"Your son Hadros must walk the Road of his choosing," the Oracle replied. "I offer you a tribe again, Eagloni, if you are so bold as to find it."

At this, Hathlos turned to look at Hadros. The gigantic boy walked to Hathlos and knelt beside him. Placing a massive arm around his father, Hadros embraced him.

"Father, we have walked so many roads together. You have taught me so much, yet for all your teachings I could never take away the sorrow you bear. Now you have this gift laid at your feet. You must take it. I will find my way well enough. Who knows? Maybe I will walk with Kam Hearthstone a few days more."

Hathlos gazed at Kam. Kam gave him a slow nod. Hathlos turned again to look into the eyes of the Oracle.

"I will go," he said.

"Good!" the Oracle gave answer. He gave a tug at Fidaelii's back and pulled a great form from her. Shaping it quickly, he gently solidified it and breathed life into it: another Eagloni. Dressed in stunning silver armor, she was gifted with a magnificent bow and quiver full of silver bolts. Her brown wings were not as large as Hathlos' white ones but were nonetheless glorious in their own right.

"What shall I call her?" Hathlos asked.

Fidaelii thought a moment.

"Fyurii. Fyurii Hupomeno!" Fidaelii answered as the Keires sprung to life.

Hathlos and his son stood and took their place beside Grimmalt. Fyurii joined them and gave a knowing glance at Antic, who was dangling her legs on Grimmalt's shoulder all the while.

"My Lord," Maughlin spoke as he moved forward from the company. "There is still the matter of the Pyropos and the rebellious tribes of the Maisorvantii."

"Yes..." said the Oracle. Fidaelii whispered into his ear. The Oracle gave a laugh. He pulled once again from the girl's back. A form greater than Fyurii came forth. The Oracle shaped it into a great Maisor maid. She was Damatu, one from the brilliant diamond-armored tribe in the North. He breathed life into the Daughter of Magic. Turning again to Fidaelii, he asked:

"Her name?"

"She's a marvel!" Fidaelii answered. "This is difficult."

After the girl gave no answer for several minutes, Maughlin spoke.

"What about the Maisor word for marvel?"

"Yes!" Fidaelii answered. "What is it?"

"Merivelya," said the Oracle.

"Mer-i-veel-ya..." Fidaelii sounded it out.

At the sound of her name, Merivelya seemed to wake from a sweet dream. Seeing the company all around her, her eyes grew wide. She then noticed the Oracle. A beautiful smile spread itself into eyes full of excitement. She knelt before the Oracle. Her voice was deep and rich as she spoke.

"Hail, great Giver of Life! What is it that you require of me in this day?"

"I desire you to walk with your Sister Fidaelii across the Daritundii to the gate of Koftus," answered the Oracle. "Once she is safely there, seek out your people in the Northern Verdant and await my word."

Merivelya bowed low.

"My life is yours, great Son of the High King," she said. Standing again, she took her place with Fidaelii, Kam, and Hadros.

The Oracle walked slowly to Fidaelii. Placing His hands upon her head, the Oracle pronounced a blessing:

May the Song ever lead you;
May your ears be ever open;

May your hands be ever healing;
May your feet be ever swift to help;
May your mouth be ever singing;
May your eyes be ever seeing;
May your heart be ever loving.

"Gather provision for your Roads," the Oracle encouraged the company. "Do not try to employ modesty concerning your need. Be *voracious*. Take *more* than you think you may need. There is no lack in this place. I will send you all off from the Orchard at the sun's peaking this day. Go quickly now and prepare wisely!"

The next hours were spent in obedience to the Oracle's command, and when the sun was at its peak, the company found themselves assembled in their prospective groupings to depart. To Hathlos and Fyurii, the Oracle spoke first:

"Make your flight due north from here. Take care, there are fell things in the realm beyond the Streotas. Look for great green fields and the peaks beyond. When you come to the S o M there, give report of our need. Sing the songs of reclamation. Sing the songs of home. I am ever with you, lending my voice. Go in strength and courage."

At this, He gave a sign of blessing. Hathlos and Fyurii received it and returned a sign of thanks and parting.

Hathlos gave Hadros one last long embrace and kissed him on each of his massive hands. After these things were said and done, the two Eagloni climbed for the heavens and turned to the north. The company watched them climb ever higher until they disappeared into the clouds. The Oracle then turned to Grimmalt and Antic:

"Perils unnumbered await you in the Underlands. As you make your way through the Eleven Kingdoms, fashion for me a crown worthy of the ruler of the dark lands. Make note of the size of their armies as well as their readiness for war. Use discernment as well, for not all of the Underland Kingdoms are entirely hostile to the Ancient Wisdom. Above all, listen. Starsgol's influence lies heaviest there as he moves unprohibited throughout the Road. I am with you through the drudgery. I am with you in the darkness. Go in joy and mischief."

Giving the same sign of blessing, the Oracle motioned to a path close to a cistern in a corner of the Orchard. Grimmalt walked to it and turned one last time to give a sign of parting before he and Antic were on their way.

The Oracle then spoke His final commands to Fidaelii and Kam: "You must go back through the Gap and down by way of the Shifting Falls. The swiftest way home to Edraeth and Laurl is the Daritundii Plains just north of Kofthus in the Rending Wall. Kofthus is where you will leave Hadros. There is a merchant there named Pulnos. Look for him in the market. He is a date seller there, very fat. Take a few days to regain your strength once you arrive home, but do not delay. Starsgol raises revolt, and may yet roam the Daritundii. He would seek to make another Rending War in Skaaran. You must prevent this at all costs. I am with you in the strange lands. I am with you in your troubles. Hear, and sing."

Kam's eyes filled with tears as he looked at Maughlin.

"Come now, Nephew," Maughlin said. "My chapter is written in the chronicles. I've finished the work that the Oracle has given me. Now *you* must write another verse with your family. I no longer fear for your drifting, Kam. You have found your anchor at last. Let Laurl and Fidaelii sing the songs to teach you."

Kam wanted to speak so many words at once but could not. He could only nod. He found himself being wrapped up in the arms of the man who was more of a father to him than Xander ever was. Kam wished Maughlin could return to Edraeth with him but also wanted this place to be Maughlin's home forever.

Kam looked to the Oracle.

With a great smile on His lips, the Oracle gave His final sign of blessing to the four about to set out on the Road for the Gap. They returned a sign of thanks and set out on the road home. As they made their way down the knoll and into the Blades once again, Kam gave one last glance over his shoulder to see the Oracle making His way back into the Sanctum with Maughlin. A great mist was overtaking the Orchard, and Kam began to wonder if the whole thing was just a dream. Turning again to walk beside his newfound daughter, a tear began to creep into Kam's eye. Placing his arm around her brilliant blue cloak, he ventured an apology.

"I am sorry for all those things I said on the Road to Rorgus, Fidaelii. I'm sorry for every-"

"It is forgiven, good Hearthstone," she winked.

26

Back from the Dead

The three days navigating the descent from the Sanctum through the Blades proved challenging. The Blades of the Streotas were still in great flux, and more than once Kam had to ask Merivelya to take to the skies to scout the road ahead. The Maisor maid was more than happy to acquiesce, yet Kam felt a twinge of apprehension for the chance of giving their position away to unseen dangers. He saw the Blades with fresh eyes: they were barren, yet filled with beauty. Kam had not breathed cleaner air in all his travels. The vistas that the Streotas offered were great gifts.

Now on their third day of travel, the sound of the Falls drew near. To his left toward the south, Kam could spy the great Shifting Lake, now shimmering in the early morning light. The Daritundii Plains lay beyond. Kam stared in wonder at great flocks of birds below them in the distance. He stopped the company for a moment to rest.

"Kam," Fidaelii said. "Do you think Starsgol still waits for you in the Daritundii?"

"There is no way of knowing for sure," Kam said. "Skotos believed the reports. Isn't that where your captors were taking you?"

"Yes," Fidaelii said.

"There's nothing for it but to cross once we make it down to the Lake," Kam said. "We should try to cross the river here closer to the source. That way we won't have to traverse the Fens again."

"I... I don't swim well," said Hadros.

"We shall see what it takes when we get there," Kam said. "Let's be going. We should reach it in just a few hours."

The company did indeed reach the river in the time Kam had allotted. When Kam saw it, he was relieved that the broad swath it cut was only a few feet deep. Once having crossed it, the three of them began their descent under the capable watch-care of Merivelya. She would glide down to an outcropping and call out directions for the safest descent path. Kam was relieved at the lack of Squallors and other fell beasts on their journey back. *It's odd,* he thought. *It's almost... too easy.*

The day was spent on the descent. When they finally reached the foothills and made camp, Kam was exhausted.

I can only imagine how tired Fidaelii must be. She's carried that shield the whole way.

He must have been staring at it in the midst of these thoughts, for the girl spoke.

"It's all right, Papa," Fidaelii said. "It really is quite light." She hefted it on her arm. "See?"

Kam shook his head and smiled.

Papa.

I'll have to get used to that again...

Firewood was gathered from the scant offerings that could be found in the area. Hadros was glad to build the fire and cook the evening meal. Not much was said all evening, and sleep was not difficult to find for anyone in the company. They all took a watch, and when the next day's light came, they were up with it and packing away their shelters.

"One hour's walk and we'll be in the open of the Daritundii Plains," said Kam. "You should all ready your-selves for whatever we may find. We will have to spend at least one night in the plains. Pray we don't have to spend two."

"Could we not move eastward to skirt the northern reaches of the Lupinwood?" asked Hadros.

"That will add a day to our journey home," Kam said. "I will not spend one day in the Wilds I do not have to. We make for Kofthus with all speed. Come on, let's be going."

The hour's walk out of the foothills raced by, and Kam marked the land sloping into the Plains.

The Daritundii were not an open, flat expanse. The Plains were known for their gently rolling green pastures. Here and there they were pocketed by long, brown grasses and varieties of sedge, but overall the Daritundii was a relatively fertile space. Kam kept his company mostly in the vales and off the hills of the Daritundii. In this way they were successful in remaining hidden the entirety of the first day of travel across the Plains. Merivelya thought it good to continue on through half the night. Against his better judgment, Kam consented. So consumed with thoughts of Laurl and home was he that he drove the company once again to exhaustion. As the opportunity to stop for the night presented itself, no fire was made. No shelters were raised. No luxury was thought of. The travelers' rest was short lived: the light of dawn came quickly after such a hard day.

Kam renewed his hope. *One day of travel to Kofthus,* he thought. *It will not be long until I see my Leigh aga-*

A low-pitched horn sounded a doleful cry in the distance. *Underlanders!*

"Stand ready!" Kam ordered. "Merivelya! How many?"

The Maisor-Sage took but a moment to mount the wind. She climbed for the heavens and quickly called down:

"Two columns! Almost a dozen, I think. They have a

captive with them! Someone wounded... ...thrown over the leader's horse!"

Twelve grey riders!

Kam quieted his mind.

"How far?" he shouted.

"No more than two leagues!" she called back.

They'll be upon us in less than an hour.

Merivelya landed next to him in a whisper of wind.

"Should I look for a ruin nearby that could serve as a redoubt?" she asked.

"No," Kam answered. "They may overtake us while you are away, and I will most certainly need your strength in this fight. Could you discern who their captive was? Did it appear to be a Son of Man?"

"Yes," said Merivelya. "His armor, though sullied, still shone in the sunlight."

Maybe a scout from Kofthus... Kam mused. *There has to be a way to divide the column.*

"Hadros," Kam said, pointing to the southwest. "Do you see that hill there?"

"Yes."

"Take your position on it, and taunt the riders."

"*Taunt* the riders, sir?" Hadros asked in a doubtful tone.

"Go now, boy!" Kam said. "You're not the fastest runner. Get going!"

Kam watched Hadros make for the hill. Turning to Merivelya, he said:

"I want you to harass the column that bears not the wounded captive. Can you do this?"

"Gladly!" she said.

"What do I do, Papa?" Fidaelii asked.

"Stay with me, my darling," Kam said. He pointed to a hill just to the north of Hadros' position. "We'll take position on that hill that flanks Hadros."

"I'll go to the boy once I've done my work," said Merivelya.

"That was to be my next order, beauteous one," said Kam. "We take a greater risk by dividing ourselves, but we also force them to choose to divide as well. Merivelya, if they do not divide, carry Hadros to us. Choose wisely but boldly. If they don't split, come to us quickly."

Merivelya wasted no time mounting the winds.

"May the Oracle's strength go with you!" she called down to them.

"And with you!" Kam called back.

Kam took Fidaelii's arm and ran toward the hill to watch the drama unfold. By the time they made their ascent, Merivelya had almost reached the riders. *They're so much closer than I thought. They drive like madmen. I don't know how the horses survive such treatment!* Kam saw the leader now call the riders' attention to the Maisor maid. A cry of terror and more horns sounded from their midst.

A few arrows were loosed at the ever-nearing threat from above to no avail. Curses flew through the air next for the failed attempt.

Merivelya's iridescence was terrible to behold. The sun flashing in her diamond skin gave her the appearance of a comet as she circled for the first of many killing runs. Her roar detonated through the valley. She came about along the southern flank of the column and made for the riders bringing up the rear. These were the ones that sent up the hail of fruitless arrows. The fire from her mouth was blinding white in color as if she had drunk deeply the heart of a star. Three riders were thrown into the air in a glowing mass. Two more brought their horses to heel before the ground that now stood alight.

"See, Papa!" cried Fidaelii. "Their number is almost cut in half!"

"We will have work yet to do, Daughter," Kam said. "Ready your songs."

The columns were now just a half-a-league from Hadros to the south. They turned northeast and made their way for his hill. Merivelya made another circle and finished the two straggling riders. The Captain of the hellish troop lowered his spear in the direction of Kam and Fidaelii. He then shouted an order, and four of the riders peeled away to make for Hadros. The other two followed their Captain toward Kam and Fidaelii. *Come on,*

Merivelya, get to the boy! Kam had little time to think of anything else.

The riders were upon them.

Kam reached for his scythe. To his great surprise, the weapon nearly leapt into his hand. A great wind blew across the Daritundii, and the flames given to him in the Sanctum presented in force. Seeing these, the evil ones reigned in their horses. Fidaelii took up the Vessel and held it in front of her. Father and daughter stood side-by-side against the evil.

The Underland Captain threw his captive on the ground before him. Kam recognized the markings on his armor.

"Skotos!" Fidaelii cried out. "Oh, my Captain! What have they done to you?"

Skotos did not answer. He did not move. Kam couldn't tell whether he lived or was slain.

"Come now, Starsgol!" Kam cried out. "We have the Vessel. This is not your hour for triumph. Let us end it."

"Indeed," said the dark Captain. "My lord Starsgol has spoken of the Vessel of Power for some time. If he had known you would have delivered it to him here, he would have never gone through the pains of joining your company."

"What?" Kam said.

Skotos rose slowly. What Kam saw in his eyes would haunt him for years to come. *The eyes of the beast!*

"The threat of the Oracle's greatest enemy is enough to cloud the vision of even the wisest of the Sons of Men," Skotos said. "Deceiving the fools on the Council of Edraeth was the easiest part of the plan. The hard part would be getting back to the Sanctum through the Harrows. It was fortunate that the Pit in Rorgus was built over Communing Stones."

"You overheard the Sages' Council where you rested in Rorgus!" Kam said.

"When I heard the girl brought no ghosts, I knew I had to steal her and take her to the door of the dead. The Lupines were easy enough to control. I didn't expect Iyoskothe to cross the Daritundii so quickly. As soon as I sensed his presence, I urged Brukkheom into the Deltas to wait for Lucian and Maughlin. I was going to follow them through the High Road of the Aeries until Brukkheom's pride became his undoing."

"I trusted you!" Fidaelii cried out. "You were my advocate on the Road to Rorgus. You were my Captain!"

"And I still can be, sweet girl," Skotos said. "This doesn't have to end in bloodshed. You can be a footstool for the Oracle, or a queen in my hands. Skaaran isn't the only land I rule. I can take you all manner of places. Think of the sights, Fidaelii! Think of all the people you can help with my assistance. I know your heart is for the healing of Skaaran, and the world! I can help you. I just need to examine the Vessel..."

"Deceiver!" Fidaelii said. "You can only speak perversion and lies! You twist words for your own purposes. I'll die before the Vessel falls into your hands."

"So be it," Skotos growled. He dashed for Fidaelii, his hand reaching for the Vessel. Kam brought down his scythe just as Skotos' hand touched the great shield –

There was a great flash of light; then, all was darkness.

"Papa!" Fidaelii's voice cried out in the darkness. "Papa! Help me! I need your help!"

"Where are you?" Kam cried back. "I can't see anything! Do you have light with you?"

From the voice in the distance a Song rang out, and a light shone forth. The Song danced with Kam's being like the very elements themselves. Storming, burning, and crashing with one another in a structured tempo and melody, the verses were contained in perfect order. Intonations both ancient and cosmic sang and percussed, dashed and frolicked. Mystery lived in it, like the trackless oceans and starry infinitudes, the rushing rivers and steadfast rocks: all the wild things surmounting mortal comprehension or control. It was very far away, but Kam found it useful to get his bearings. He began to run toward the light, but just as he made some progress, the Song stopped and the darkness returned.

"Sing again!" Kam called out through the darkness, which seemed even darker now.

"Sing again!" Kam shouted. "I need the light to help you! Sing out! Send the light again!"

Now the Song rang out, and Kam began to run in the direction of the light. When Fidaelii had to take breaths, the light would dim, but then it would resurge in brilliance when she started again. As Kam ran, the patch of light ahead grew nearer and nearer.

"Fidaelii!" Kam called. "I'm coming darling girl! Stand fast, Daughter!"

Kam saw Fidaelii ahead, just as he remembered her. She bore the enormous golden shield. She was singing the sweet Song. Kam ran harder. He gripped the fiery scythe more tightly. As he did, he heard the roars of a dread beast and Kam felt the heat of a thousand furnaces.

He reached her at last. The sweetest relief was in her eyes.

"Papa's here, Fidaelii," Kam said. "Don't be afraid."

Fire erupted before them. The sun itself could not have made for a more terrifying assault. Fidaelii held the glorious shield before them both. Both of them crouched behind it to be spared the blast. When it came, they were pushed back several feet. Kam put his left hand on the shield's grip to steady it. It was blazingly hot. He slowly removed his hand. Awestruck, he beheld his daughter. She held the shield with both hands, unwavering. The look in her eyes was one of vengeance.

"Don't be afraid, Papa," Fidaelii smiled, looking at him with the flames of death clawing at them. "The Song is here."

She lifted her voice:

The night is long,
Longer still before the dawn.
But dawn must come,
And all that hides must now be drawn...

Light rippled from her hands into the shield's grip. It spread to the edges and began to quench the flames on the other side. Her song continued:

Drawn out to give account
Of all the deeds done in the dark
Of men and beast and demon-spawn
To the One who keeps all time...

The shield now glowed with a golden fire. It wasn't clumsy or reckless like the fire that had just been hurled at them. The great shield glowed like heated crystal.

"Come, Papa!" she called. "We strike!"

At that, she leapt up and charged with her shield into the darkness. Kam's scythe was light in his hand. He kept his left hand on her right shoulder and followed closely behind. A roar of surprise sounded out in the murk.

"Now, Papa! Now!" Fidaelii urged.

Kam swung around her to face the beast. He had never seen the likes of it. It was as tall as the Rending Wall with four heads. The scales that were its armor glinted with mockery in the light of the shield. The heads of the beast looked like wolves but with the ears of a jackal and the jaws of a lion.

The front claws of the beast were the talons of a great bird of prey. Its hind legs were those of a bear. Its voice was full of cruel mockery.

"So you would come to kill me, little one? Many have tried. You are smaller than most. You trust those trinkets the Oracle made for you? They will be your doom."

For the slightest moment, doubt seized Kam's mind. Could he trust the weapons that were given to him? The beast let out another howl that was followed by a great burst of fire. Kam dove back behind the Vessel and looked into his daughter's eyes.

"You are ready," she said softly. "Go. Your call awaits, Son of Xander. The Oracle is with you. Do not doubt."

In the midst of raining hell, Kam kissed Fidaelii on the cheek.

"I love you, Fidaelii."

"End this, Papa."

With that, he plunged back into the fray. Charging the beast, he rolled just under another fire burst. Jumping up, Kam redoubled his pace. He reached the beast's front left leg. Diving to avoid a great talon's swipe, Kam looked up from beneath its belly. Kam summoned fire to his left hand with his mind. It came so effortlessly. The beast was turning...

Kam knew it was trying to find an opening to employ its size.

"The flames!" he heard Fidaelii cry. "The flames! At your feet!"

He reached for them and threw them over his head. He fell into the earth as a great bear's paw tried to grind him to dust. He wished to be at the beast's rear flank. Before another thought could come to him, he was springing from the ground in an explosion of flame. There was the rear flank, looming before him.

Kam gave two great threshing swaths through the beast's heels. There was a great cry of pain and fear. The beast's back legs buckled. It scrambled to turn as they did. Its maws snapped at Fidaelii and Kam in desperation. The two of them ran toward each other to present a united front once again.

"Run!" Fidaelii cried. "Get behind the Vessel. Hurry!"

Kam dove just in time to avoid another blast.

"I'm going to sing a blinding song," Fidaelii said. "You should go for one of the heads."

Kam nodded.

The Keires lifted her voice:

You are light,
And in you there is no shadow.
In you there is no shadow
Of turning at all:
Your light is our life
In you there is no shadow;
In you there is no shadow
Of turning at all.

At this, the Vessel began to vibrate and hum. With the hum came a great expulsion of focused light. Fidaelii directed the beam into the eyes of the floundering beast. It raised its heads in attempts to avoid the great beam of light coming from the Vessel. Kam watched one head's eyes squinting. The head strained forward in order to stop the light. Kam sprung from behind the Vessel, scythe raised. He brought the white-hot tool down upon the straining neck of the beast. It came off cleanly. The other heads wailed in agony.

"Enough!" The other three heads cried in unison. "Walk no longer in my realm!"

Kam felt himself being hurled through the darkness

27

The Beginning

"Kam!" It was Hadros. "Kam Hearthstone!"
The Waking Realm...

Kam rubbed his head. There was no fire in his hands.

Fidaelii! He sat up. "Hadros. Where is my girl? Does she live?"

"She is well," said Merivelya. The glistening Maisor stood behind the gigantic boy. "She is eating breakfast. You left me seven trampers to deal with, Hearthstone."

Kam stood up and made sure his scythe was nearby.

"Where is Skotos?"

"He disappeared with you," Merivelya said. "He has not returned."

"You vanished!" said Hadros. "Where did you go?"

"I... I don't know," Kam said. "No familiar settings

presented themselves. Fidaelii and I battled Starsgol himself! I feel like a fool to have had Starsgol in my company from Edraeth...from the very beginning! The illusion of Skotos was so real... he seemed so true to the quest... Starsgol was using us the whole time to try to steal the Vessel for himself." Kam's first question arrested his mind. "Where is Fidaelii?"

"There," said Merivelya. The Maisor pointed behind Kam. He stood up slowly and started walking toward his daughter.

"The trampers!" Merivelya called to him.

Kam stopped and turned around.

"You should know the corpses were marked in Shadow Guard regalia," she continued. "It could be that Stargol used Skotos' body to raise up an elite army for himself. Underlanders have infiltrated the capital city."

"I will consider it," Kam said. "For now, my Laurl awaits. She will no doubt wish to know her family still lives." He turned again to walk to Fidaelii. Calling over his shoulder, Kam said, "We are not even a half-day's journey to Kofthus. Pack camp. Hadros! Help her, lad. We leave at once!"

Kam saw Fidaelii look up from the campfire. She spotted him. He broke into a run. She leapt up and ran for him. He met her with a great embrace.

"I'm so pleased with you," he whispered. "I know the Oracle is pleased as well."

Fidaelii laughed and cried in her papa's arms. He was just about to let her go when she scolded him.

"Mama's waiting," Fidaelii said. "She's been waiting too long."

Kam nodded.

"Let's go," he said.

The few hours spent on the Road to Kofthus passed as a dream. Kam spent half the time trying to decipher the battle with Starsgol and the other half settling into the truth that nothing for his family would ever be the same. As the great city came into view, Kam stopped everyone to bid farewell to Marivelya. Fidaelii shed a few tears, but the Maisor maid gave her comfort.

"We're a part of each other, young one," said Marivelya. "We can talk anytime you'd like. Surely you've watched Praius in conference with his Brothers?"

"Yes," said Fidaelii.

"You are the Keires now," replied the Maisor. "And we are your Sisters: Antic, Fyurii and myself. Set your affairs in order, then send for us. I'm sure Antic and Fyurii will want to hear from you and give report soon. I am a servant to the Oracle's will. I will seek out my people, the Damatu, in the Northern Verdant."

"Go in the Oracle's strength!" Fidaelii said, embracing the great Daughter of Magic.

"Go in His love!" Marivelya said, being careful not

to crush Fidaelii. She gave a sign of parting to Kam and Hadros and climbed for the northern winds.

Kam led the children through the mighty gates of the northernmost outpost of Kofthus and headed straight for the market to seek out Pulnos, the fat date seller. He wasn't hard to find.

Before they left the gigantic boy in the hands of the merchant, Fidaelii pulled Hadros aside and gave a few words of encouragement to him.

"We will not be long in Edraeth, Hadros. Remain here with Pulnos for a week or two. Look for us by the time of the new moon."

"Farewell, Keires," Hadros whispered, making sure the merchant did not overhear. "I look forward to the next Road walked with you." Turning to Kam, he said, "Kam Hearthstone, I am thankful I could offer my life for your safety in the river that day."

"I am glad to have had your company, brave Hadros," Kam replied. "I will be glad to have it again soon. Fidaelii speaks truth. We will not be gone long. Stay out of trouble until we return." Hadros gave a nod and a sign of parting.

Departing from Koftus, Kam and Fidaelii could barely keep from running all the way to Edraeth. They paced themselves, however, and in two days' time spied the buildings of the town rising like protrusions on the spine of some great, brown beast. As they came into the village, Fidaelii's now dingy, blue cloak fluttered in the breeze and caught every eye. The cry went up that the sojourners had returned, but they heeded it not.

Many people came out to greet them and welcome them home.

Fidaelii and Kam cared little.

There was only one voice they longed to hear, one face they lived to see.

Passing through the town and its people proved to be yeoman's work. All the citizens of Edraeth crowded around them. When at last the two of them reached the road to Hearthstone land, the foot race began. Around the final bend, they spied grandfather Titus' trees framing the humble cottage where *she* would be waiting.

Fidaelii reached the door first and boldly turned the latch. Flinging it open wide, she almost fell into the great room as Kam bounded in behind her. There was Laurl, sitting by the fire in her chair, drinking mulled cider.

"Laurl Meriis!" Fidaelii scolded with a twinkle in her eye, "Your daughter would have a word with you!"

Kam watched through great sobs of joy as his wife shrieked, dropped her cup and leapt out of her chair to wrap her arms around their girl. He grabbed them both and hefted them in the air with such force that it squeezed every inch of air from their lungs. All of his wife's time spent with Praius made sense to him now, and he cared not for the whispers from his friends and strange looks about Edraeth.

DEPENDENTS

Kam was never to be the same.

He was home.

www.ingramcontent.com/pod-product-compliance
Lightning Source LLC
Chambersburg PA
CBHW060356260626
47160CB00006B/2329